BLOODSHOT

BOOKS WRITTEN BY FRED VAN LENTE

PROSE NOVELS

Ten Dead Comedians

The Con Artist

Never Sleep

Bloodshot

GRAPHIC NOVELS

Cowboys & Aliens

Weird Detective

Murder Kingdom

COMIC SERIES

The Silencers

MODOK's 11

The Incredible Hercules
(with Greg Pak)

Marvel Zombies

The Amazing Spider-Man

Wolverine: First Class

Taskmaster

Captain America: The First Avenger

Archer & Armstrong

Generation Zero

Ivar, Timewalker

Conan the Avenger

Jennifer Blood

GRAPHIC NONFICTION

Action Philosophers!

The Comic Book History of Comics

Action Presidents!

The Comic Book Story of Basketball

The Comic Book History of Animation

Gamemasters: The Comic Book History of Roleplaying Games

A VALIANT UNIVERSE NOVEL

BLOODSHOT

FRED VAN LENTE

BLACKSTONE PUBLISHING

Published in 2025 by Blackstone Publishing
Cover and book design by Sarah Riedlinger
Cover illustration by Mico Suayan

Printed in the United States of America

First edition: 2025
ISBN 979-8-212-70830-2
Fiction / Science Fiction / Action & Adventure

Version 1

Blackstone Publishing
31 Mistletoe Rd.
Ashland, OR 97520

www.BlackstonePublishing.com

PART ONE

ONE

I awake.

Her face is the first thing I see.

"Hey, are you okay?"

Wispy blonde hair swept over the side of her head past her left ear, right side shaved. Green eyes, long lashes. Small silver nose stud, left nostril. Robin's-egg-blue hoodie. Looming above her are ashy pine trees, naked, stripped of green and bark, pale-white ghost trees like skeletal fingers pointing accusingly at the sky.

"How many fingers am I holding up?" she asks, still filling up my vision, like she and the trees and the sky are the only things in the world.

"You're . . . you're not holding any fingers up," I say. My voice is that of a stranger, totally unknown to me.

A monster steps into view behind her. He's some kind of crab thing, with spiny legs where each ear should be. He has a computer interface blinking in the center of his chest, wires curving out and going to his back. As monsters go, he's pretty short.

"Is he dead?" Crab-Face asks.

She rolls her eyes without looking back at him. "You just heard him talk, dummy."

The crab monster removes its head to reveal a brown-haired kid with glasses underneath, four or five years younger than the girl, but with the same green eyes. "Don't call me a dummy, dummy. Look at his skin. He looks like a zombie's ghost."

I raise my hands in front of my face. The fingers sticking out of my fingerless biker gloves are indeed chalk white and deader looking than the dead trees creaking overhead. My breath catches in my throat.

"Oh my gosh, look at his eyes!" The boy staggers back. "He's got red eyes! Zombie ghost *vampire*!"

"You know, Clark, you don't have to say out loud literally every single thing that pops into your head, right? You're gonna freak him out." She stands up and reaches out her hand to help me up. "Ignore my brother. It's what I do. I'm Kalea."

I get up. It's harder than I thought it would be. The ground is extremely uneven. When I'm on my feet, I look around and see why. The ghost trees on the edges of the clearing got off lucky. All around me are smashed trees, some charred and blackened, some reduced to gray, powdery, ashen versions of their former selves. Some are still steaming; some are still smoking. It's hard not to notice that the flattened trees all radiate out from me, where I'd been lying. I'm literally at the center of this.

"Yo, man!" Clark snaps his fingers inside the plastic claw covering his hand. "My sister just told you her name, now you're supposed to tell her your name. That's how we usually do things in, you know, non*undead* society."

"Clark!" Kalea snaps at him, but then looks back at me and says, more gently, "What . . . is your name?"

It's a perfectly normal question. One everyone above the age of two should know the answer to. But it beats me. I look down at myself, as if there are answers there. I am wearing dark-green cargo pants, spotted here and there with ash. I put my hands in my many pockets. They're all empty. I touch my chest. I'm wearing a black T-shirt with no logo.

My chest tightens with panic. My brain buzzes with questions for which it has no answers. I feel dizzy all of a sudden, like I woke up on the top of a tall cliff, and in the act of waking, I'm going to stumble over the edge accidentally.

Is this what it feels like to be born? To have everything come at you, all at once, with no preparation or warning? Is that why all babies come out crying?

It's hard to keep my feet under me. I stagger, but she's there, and she grabs onto me. I'm ashamed. I try to look anywhere but her eyes, but she moves her face with mine until I don't have a choice.

"It's okay. Hey! Look at me. It's gonna be okay. Let's get you back to the road where we can call for help."

"C'mon, Kalea, what about our movie?" Clark whines.

"Jeez, Clark, can't you see he's in trouble? Forget the movie. Just grab our stuff and we'll come back to shoot tomorrow." She squeezes my hand in hers and leads me stumbling across the fallen trees.

"I've got Scouts tomorrow," Clark mutters but turns, grabs a bucket full of little men—action figures?—and a collapsed tripod off the ground, and follows us.

The devastation of the clearing doesn't last long. Within minutes we're surrounded by trees, bushes, the trickle of a brook, the rustling of squirrels chasing each other overhead, blue jays squawking out the boundaries of their territory.

"I've been coming into these woods all my life," Kalea is saying, "and I've never seen a section flattened like that. That wasn't there last week. You see what did that?"

I shake my head. There's just nothing there. "I don't know anything that happened before you woke me up."

"Ooh, boy. You don't look that hurt, and you seem to be walking fine, but I guess we should call an ambulance. Service out here stinks, but once we get to the road, I'll call nine-one-one. Okay?"

Not knowing what else to do, I nod.

I could let go of her hand, but I don't.

We emerge from the woods into an empty parking area with a trio of picnic tables in the side grass. The sun is dipping low and red near the tree line. The sight is stunning to me, whose entire life story has only lasted ten minutes.

Where Kalea is is fifty-eight degrees Fahrenheit, or, if you prefer, fourteen degrees Celsius. Where Kalea is is forty-two minutes past nineteen hundred hours, Eastern Daylight Time. Where Kalea is is forty-one degrees twenty-six minutes north, eighty-one degrees eighteen minutes west.

These impressions come to me in a voice that is not a voice, that is in my head without entering through my ears first. I look to Clark to see if he heard it too, but he's just staring at his feet and grousing about all the famous directors, like Ethan Cohen and Lilly Wachowski, who have supportive siblings who don't try to ruin their careers single-handedly. "You know, I was absolutely planning on thanking you in my Oscars speech, but now? I'm not so sure."

I turn back to Kalea, and she has a cell phone to her ear, and that's when outside data starts flowing inside my head again:

Kalea is calling the numbers nine, one, and one. The request is being routed through a cellular base station approximately eight miles to the southwest, or, if you prefer, 12.87 kilometers.

Request picked up by County Dispatch. Connecting . . .

"Nine-one-one, what is your emergency?" says an actual voice in my head this time, a woman's voice. *The dispatcher's name is Joelle Newsome. This is the tenth hour of her double shift.* I can hear the weariness in her tone.

"Hi, uh, yeah, my name is Kalea Derby? And we found a kid, uh, a boy, like, maybe sixteen? Lying out in a smashed-up part of the Greenwood Glen. He doesn't know his name or how he got there, and while he doesn't look like he has any injuries, his skin is really chalky and his eyes are super red. Who knows how long he's been out there?"

"Is he conscious? Can he walk?"

"Yeah, he's conscious. He can walk. But we are out in the middle of nowhere, and I don't have a car, and neither does he—"

"I am sending an ambulance. Please confirm your location."

"We're in the Greenwood Glen parking lot, between, uh, Bell and River Road."

"The ambulance should arrive in about twenty minutes. Keep him sitting up and talking until then."

"Okay, got it, thanks." She ends the call and turns to me. "Ambulance should be here—"

"In twenty minutes," I say without thinking. "And I should stay sitting up and talking until then."

"Yeah." She blinks with a puzzled smile. "You heard that?"

I nod. I choose not to say anything about machine telepathy. She's returned the phone to her pocket, but it won't stop talking to me.

Kalea's favorite contacts are her brother, Clark; her mother, Carrie; and Rosie's Pizzeria. Mason Miller is in Favorites too, but she hasn't called him in over a year. Here are videos of Clark blowing up, melting, dismembering, and otherwise tormenting various action figures in various monster costumes. Here's a photo of her blowing out candles on her sixteenth birthday. Here's her at the rec center pool with the other lifeguards. Their names, from left to right, are Mason, Liliana, Ruby, and—

That's enough. Kalea's phone is an oversharer. I close my eyes and silently tell it to stop deluging me with info. The data stream immediately goes dark.

"Oh no!" Kalea cries when she sees my strained expression. "You're not feeling—worse, are you?"

"Maybe his guts are all gnarly and messed up inside," Clark says, but trails off as Kalea shoots him a nasty look.

"No." I shake my head. "Just a lot going on all at once."

She laughs and claps me on the shoulder. "Yeah, I bet. Well, help's on its way. It's almost over."

I nod in agreement, even though I don't believe her.

TWO

I sense the ambulance before I see it rounding a bend up the road. Each piece of electronic equipment inside the vehicle pulses or hums with a distinctive frequency, like sections of an orchestra. The defibrillator practically trembles with anticipation: It can't wait to shock a dead heart back to life. The radio is a gossip, crackling with reports of other people's misery. The air-powered respirator sits holding its breath.

Both EMTs get out of the ambulance after parking it across three spaces. They are a man and a woman, both with very close-trimmed hair. They roll a gurney out of the back and ask me to get up on it.

"We're going to strap you in for the ride to the hospital," the woman says, patting the pillow.

"Strap him in?" Kalea frowns. "Really?"

"Standard procedure," the man says, "in case he has internal injuries."

"It's okay," I say, and get in. They tie straps around my ankles and wrists.

I say goodbye to Kalea the same way I said hello: with her leaning in puzzled concern over my prone body. "Okay, then. I hope, uh, everything turns out all right. I'd give you my email for you to let me know how it goes, but you don't have a phone."

"Don't worry, I'll find you," I say.

Kalea frowns in surprise, and I hastily add, "To thank you, I mean." Of course I can't tell her that her own phone has already cheerfully told me without prompting her cell number, email address, street address, and locker number at school (126). It even flashes me a satellite photo of her house before I tell it to cut it out.

"Good luck, Mystery Man." Clark waves as the EMTs roll me into the back of the ambulance. "We won't forget you, even though I bet you're gonna forget us."

The male EMT sits by my side while the female EMT gets behind the wheel. As the ambulance drives away, I crane my head up and see through the back windows Kalea and Clark still standing in the middle of the street, watching me go as the vehicle turns a bend, and then they disappear behind black birches. I have a sudden pang of separation anxiety, and Kalea's green eyes float in my memory briefly before fading. They are the first two people I've ever met, or at least that I can remember meeting, and it feels profoundly sad to see them go.

The driver speaks into a military-style satellite phone with much better encryption than Kalea's. It will only talk to me in pops and hisses. I'm pretty sure that if I had the time, I could persuade it to open up, but I don't have the time.

"Package secured and en route to pickup point," she says into the phone, then clicks off without waiting for a response.

They are not taking me to a hospital.

I look at the EMT sitting next to me, looking down at me with his cold eyes. I can see a dark dab of blood on the collar of the uniform jacket that's too big for him. *Rodriguez* is etched on the name tag of this blonde-haired, blue-eyed man.

I may not have any memories, but apparently I have instincts.

My instincts say things are about to get messy.

A few kilometers later, I sense sophisticated laser-targeting weapons moving rapidly above me. The encrypted chatter spikes, pinging off satellites high in the sky. Advanced flying machines, gyros or hovers, approach, slowing, preparing to land.

I meet Not-Rodriguez's gaze with my own.

"Who am I?" I ask.

I'm a little surprised when he chuckles. "You wouldn't believe me if I told you."

I can hear the gyros now, barely—they're definitely gyros—whining above the thrum of the ambulance's tires. They're overtaking the ambulance to land in front of it; even now, it's slowing down.

"I believe you," I say.

I snap out of all four restraints at the same time effortlessly.

Not-Rodriguez loses the smile. "*Tango!*" he barks at the driver. He reaches inside his jacket. Everything slows down, as if I'm watching a film of this after the fact, in a small cubicle, studying the footage for strengths and weaknesses, as opposed to experiencing it in real time.

My muddy boot is on Not-Rodriguez's throat and pinning him back against the cabin before he can draw the pistol out of his jacket. By the time he does, my fingers are already wrapping around it. It's a Beretta 92FS semiautomatic, standard US military sidearm for decades.

I can't spell my own name, but I guess I have an encyclopedic recall for guns. Go me.

Not-Rodriguez manages to shoot the floor, but I yank the Beretta out of his hand. The finger that's in the trigger guard snaps like uncooked spaghetti. I didn't mean to do that, but I don't have time to feel bad about it either.

He tries grabbing my throat, pressing against my leg. I smash the pistol into the side of his head, and he goes limp. I drop-kick him to the floor and roll off of the gurney, but when I'm on my feet, I'm looking at a .50-caliber Desert Eagle pointed at me by the driver. The hand cannon kicks with three roars in her hand, I'm punched twice in my chest and once in my arm, and back I go through the doors in the rear of the ambulance and bouncing, tumbling across the hard gravel of a back road.

Finally, I'm able to stick a foot out and stop my backward momentum. Before me is a big factory or warehouse, long abandoned to graffiti taggers and stone throwers. The sky is alive with giant bugs with three spinning vertical propellers for wings, and they shoot blinding lights down on me.

"Bloodshot," booms a bullhorn overhead, "there's nowhere to run. This doesn't have to be hard. Surrender now and let us get you some help."

These guys murdered at least one, probably two, ambulance drivers to snatch me up. Trusting them to help me is not on the table.

I've managed to hold on to the Beretta. I grip it tighter and sprint toward the giant brick hulk in front of me. The voice from the loudspeaker begins to say a swear word but is cut off by the sudden high whine of an M134 NATO Minigun spinning to life from its open side compartment. The big barrel spits bullets at me, but I manage to outrun the gunner's arm and dive through the giant yawning cavity of the loading dock before I get hit.

That time, I mean. The female not-EMT already shot me three times. My chest and arm sting, and I look down at my wounds and nearly cry out at what I see:

The blood spilling out of the smoking holes in my T-shirt changes its mind midstream and starts crawling back up into my body through those same holes. The wounds then pucker like lipless mouths and close, sealing up altogether as if my injury were just a bad dream from which I've already woken up.

A chill runs down my spine that I'm sure I won't heal so easily from.

"Who am I?" may not be the right question to ask myself.

"*What* am I?" could be the more important one.

The gyros shine their floodlights through what's left of the windows in this dump, everywhere except where I am. There are four individual floods, so I guess there must be at least four birds in the air around the warehouse, but the creepy thing is they don't make any more noise than the wind through the trees. They're so quiet the thuds and grunts of the men landing on the roof three stories above me are louder than the aircraft they're jumping from.

Once again, I don't have thoughts; I have impulses. My body knows better than my brain about, well, everything, apparently, and it's screaming at me to move. They're expecting me to hide. The bugs circle the warehouse perimeter with their lights, thinking they've boxed me inside. The men with guns (I don't see the guns, but come on, they're there) are rappelling down one by one, gathering on the roof in a show of force to come down and flush me out. They're expecting to overwhelm me with numbers.

I see a rusty ladder that has not totally rotted away from the wall leading up to the catwalk overhead. I take a running start, leap halfway up to grab the rungs, and scamper the rest of the way like I'm half-spider. I put a foot up on the railing of the catwalk and leap straight up through the skylight above.

I explode out onto the roof in a hail of frosted glass. There are six of them already on the roof, with two more coming down from cables dangling from the gyros overhead. They're wearing full-body armor and face-plated helmets so I can't see their expressions when I show up.

But I can see myself in the reflections of their visors, and I look pretty darn scary to me.

I land right on the first guy, putting both feet in the middle of his chest, sending him flying back into the other skylight. With a crash and a scream, he disappears from my view.

I give the second guy a spinning kick to the face, shattering his visor. He leaves his feet and isn't done spinning all the way around in midair before I whirl and empty two rounds from the Beretta into the body armor of the third guy, launching him through the hole I just made in the closer skylight.

The fourth and fifth guys manage to point their rifles and fire at me just as the second guy lands on his face to my left side. They're aiming at where I used to be, though. I drop my pistol and dive and grab on to the long, scoped semiautomatic rifle strapped to that second guy's back. A Ruger SFAR—I can tell even in the harsh light of the floods. I roll and rip the Ruger free of the strap, and when I land in a crouch, I spray the fourth and fifth guys with automatic fire. I catch the fourth guy in the kneepads, and he drops with a curse just as the fifth guy weaves away.

Suddenly the world goes white, and I hear a bang right after. There's the scrape of a boot behind me, and I turn, not knowing where the blow will come from. It comes from the back, the piercing sting of a knife blade nearly missing my shoulder blade.

The sixth guy brings the knife back for another strike, but unfortunately for him my eyes heal from flash-bang grenades as fast as the rest of me heals from bullets: retinas contracting correctly, optic nerves flushing away the overdose of light. I block his wrist plunging down with the knife with my Ruger, then shatter his helmet visor with its butt.

The knife flies out of his hand, and I grab it by its hilt and throw it into the hand of the fifth guy as he's taking aim at me again. He drops his weapon with a cry.

That knife was probably a marine Ka-Bar, but I'd have to see it longer to really be sure.

The sky erupts behind me, and pain ripples across my head and right shoulder. I look up and see that a seventh guy is now sliding down the rappelling line on top of me, firing his own SFAR and yeehawing like he's on a roller coaster.

He shuts his mouth pretty quick when I leap up straight past him and grab on to the line myself. An eighth guy is dangling on another cable from another bird across the roof from me, but I raise the Ruger and shoot through his cable so he drops with a shout into the treetops.

My muscles are screaming at me to stop, *stop climbing, what are you doing, don't you know you've been shot multiple times*, but I scale the rest of the cable anyway. The gunner in the gyro's open side door is wrestling with his Minigun, trying to force it to point down directly at me, but before he can, his ankle is close enough for me to reach, and I grab it and toss him down onto the roof of the warehouse.

I climb up to the Minigun trigger and strafe off the rotor or hover propellers or whatever the heck is sticking out of the left side of the gyro opposite me. The rotor bursts into flame, and the gyro spirals away out of my vision.

I put the rifle's muzzle to the back of the pilot's head in the seat in front of me. "Call them off," I yell at him.

The pilot waves his hands. "You nuts, man? I look high enough in the chain of command to you to—"

He's cut off by another bug's Minigun, which explodes through the windshield. The high-caliber rounds tear through both the pilot and me. The big difference being that the pilot slumps lifelessly in his eviscerated chair and I just fly back onto the floor of the compartment, bloody and afire with pain but still conscious of the fact that my gyro has started to spin out of control and spiral earthward.

Through the open side door, I see we have already dropped below the opposite bug, the one with half a rappelling line dangling from it. But still, it's close—maybe even close enough. I launch myself out of my bug as it falls and grab on to the fraying end of the cable. The last remaining gyro is turning toward this one. They really don't care how many of their own people they kill, do they?

Unfortunately for them, my momentum when I grab on to the line causes me to swing forward in a high arc. I let go and launch at the pilot behind the cockpit glass.

I cross my arms in front of my face, smash through the windshield, clip the pilot, and keep on going until I reach the gunner compartment in back. Knocking the gunner, screaming, out of the bird stops my fall, and I land with my hands basically on the Minigun. I sheer off the tail of the third whirligig with it, and now the bug I'm in is the only one still in the sky.

I lost the Ruger jumping from my old gyro to this one, so I just rip the Minigun right off its mount, nuts and bolts clattering to the floor. I rest its barrels against the pilot's head. "Get us out of here. Now."

"Y-yes, sir, M-Mister B-Bloodshot, sir. W-w-whatever you say."

"Why does everybody keep saying 'Bloodshot'? What, is that code for something?"

"Uh, yeah, man. It's code—code for you."

I let that sink in. It doesn't do much for me. "Do I have a real name?"

"Probably? But that's way above my pay grade. All I know is you're a rogue asset, and we're supposed to bring you in."

"Yeah? Whose asset am I? Who do you work for?"

"We're—we're Project Rising Spirit. A defense contractor. We build weapons, and, uh, we use them."

"Is that what I am? A weapon?"

"You just single-handedly took out an elite capture-kill team in less time than it takes me to take a dump. What do you think, genius?"

"Genius thinks you shouldn't mouth off to the guy with the Minigun to your head."

"Sorry. Terrified. Hard to stop talking."

Still, he's right. My head is overloaded with revelations, and I need time to figure out what to do with all this new information.

The gyro passes over an almost completely dark section of terrain, with no house lights or streetlamps visible. A few oblong white shapes mill about below—a cow pasture.

"All right, put down here. Nice and easy. And I'm watching your hands on the controls. Don't do anything to warn your friends."

When we're safely in the muddy field with cows batting their tails at us, I tie the pilot firmly to his chair and gag and blindfold him. I guess I could try knocking him out with a blow to the head, but I'm still getting used to my strength and worry I might bash his skull in.

Holding the Minigun in both hands makes me feel badass, but it's heavy as hell and too bulky to carry far. The pilot has another Beretta in a side holster, and that seems like enough gun for me right now, so I dump the Minigun and stick the pistol in my waistband. I hop out of the bird and run as fast as I can for the tree line. I have no doubt that Project Rising Spirit has a way of tracking wherever their bird and its pilot are.

And next time, I bet they're going to send way more than eight guys after me.

THREE

Kalea and Clark's day starts out pretty normally. Their mom wakes up around dawn and goes into the kitchen to scoop ground coffee into the maker, pour in water from the carafe, then turn it on. It's funny, their mom looks like a combination of them—green eyes, brownish-blondish hair, thick glasses—even though it's really the other way around. Kalea gets up an hour later and answers some texts on her phone before going downstairs to get some cereal.

The cereal she takes out of the cupboard is Honey Nut Cheerios; I can tell only from the flash of brown and gold on the box from where I'm hiding, looking in through her back kitchen window. Amnesia is weird. I can recognize a Honey Nut Cheerios box from yards away based on its color pattern alone. I can recall the make and model, caliber, and rate of fire of most firearms within seconds. I know that babies cry when they're born. I know that Lilly Wachowski is a famous movie director who made *The Matrix* with her sister. When it comes to most general knowledge categories, I'm a champ. When it comes to knowing who I am or who my parents are or where I live or where I go to school, or if I go to school, tough luck. Goose egg. This sucks.

Both Kalea and her mother take turns trying to get Clark out of bed. Their mother comes in and opens the shade. That doesn't work. Then

Kalea kicks the door open and yells at him. That doesn't work. Mom comes back and flips the lights on and off until finally he emerges out of bed, groaning, and staggers toward the bathroom.

They're all still here, which means I'm not too late to prevent what I am pretty sure is going to happen. It took me three hours to walk from the cow field, knowing Kalea's address from her TMI cell phone. I kept off the roads and in the woods as best I could, skirting the edges of motion-sensitive lights in backyards and hiding in the bushes when a stray cop car passed.

Mom has a mostly ignored toolshed full of rusting tools and cobwebs in the back of her yard. I went inside and sat down, leaving the door a little ajar so I could see through the windows into the rear of their rather small house—the bedrooms and kitchen, mostly.

I suppose, to most people, what I'm doing would come across as creepy. I don't have much of a defense, except that it's pretty hard to watch out for somebody without actually, you know, *watching* them. I am just happy they were there and unharmed when I arrived. My working theory is that having lost me, PRS is going to circle back to them.

Still, why should I stick my neck out for two random kids I just met? I don't know. Partly, maybe, it's because they're the only people I've met who've shown me any sort of kindness. Of course, they're also the only people I've met who haven't tried to kidnap me, so that's a low bar. Maybe it's more that there's something inside that makes me want to believe I'm a good person, even though I don't really know who I am. And the best way to maintain that belief is to act like a good person. Does desperately wanting people to think I'm a selfless person make me selfish? Seems like a chicken-and-egg thing.

I struggled to stay awake through those last few hours of the night. I have an irrational fear that if I fall asleep, my memories will be wiped again, and Kalea will find me sprawled out in the toolshed, freaked out that I had followed her and was watching her through the windows, but I'd have no idea who she was anymore.

Also, I'm starving. My stomach aches like it's trying to devour itself. This is a hunger that seems way more intense than it should for this time of morning. I wonder if this is a side effect of my healing. Replacing shot-out tissue and stitching up broken blood vessels didn't just create matter out of nothing. My body was using its own mass to work miracles, and that mass has to be replaced somehow.

At 8:25 a.m. Kalea and Clark are putting on their jackets and grabbing their school bags when what I have been waiting for rolls into the driveway. It's an SUV with tinted windows and no license plate. Out of it step a man and a woman wearing dark suits, mirror shades, and comms in their ears. I can see the flash of white on the man's right index finger. Tape securing a metal splint, I'm going to guess.

Why, hello there, Not-Rodriguez. So not-happy to see you again.

Not-Rodriguez and the other not–ambulance driver walk to the front door in their freshly pressed three-piece suits, and I creep out of my hiding spot. I press myself against the side of the house by the living room window just as Mom unlocks and opens the front door.

"Good morning, Mrs. Derby?" Not-Rodriguez says. "This is Special Agent Layton, and I am Special Agent Van Hook. May we come in? It's about your children." I peer around the side of the house. They both flash ID cards and badges faster than anyone could read the name of the agency printed on them.

"My—children?" Mom's voice goes up two octaves. "What's the problem?"

"Ma'am, if you don't mind, it'd be better to tell you inside."

Mom lets them in. "Kalea? Clark? You've got visitors." They all gather in the living room, which is just on the other side of the wall I'm crouching against. I stand up between the two windows so I can hear better.

"Hey, kids," Agent Van Hook says, "why don't you have a seat?"

"I'll stand," Kalea says, steel in her voice. Good girl. "Who are you claiming to be?"

"I'm Special Agent Van Hook, this is Special Agent—"

"Special agents of what?" Clark asks. "What agency? Are you with the CIA or the FDA? Food inspectors or spies?"

"Clark," Mom says, chuckling uneasily, "maybe let them get a word in edgewise."

"No, that's all right, it's a good question," Agent Van Hook says.

"You're a smart boy. Smart enough, you know you should be totally forthcoming with us."

"I have seen a *lot* of movies," Clark says. "I notice you didn't answer my question."

"Can't get anything past you," Agent Van Hook says.

"Oh, so this is a 'we ask the questions here' kind of deal, huh?" Kalea says.

"You've seen a lot of movies too?" Agent Layton deadpans.

"You know," Mom says, raising her voice, "I think *I* would like to know what part of the government you work for."

"Centers for Disease Control and Prevention, ma'am, Office of Readiness and Response."

"Oh," Mom says. It's more of a gasp than a word.

"Is it true that around dusk yesterday, you two were in the Greenwood Glen?" Agent Van Hook asks.

No answer until Mom clears her throat.

"Y-yeah," Clark says. "So? We go there all the time."

"So then you must have noticed the clearing with all the knocked-over trees half-blasted to ash," Agent Layton casually says. "That must have really stuck out for you as kind of unusual, due to your familiarity with the area, isn't that right?"

"Clark! Kalea!" Mom cries. "You never said a word about that to me last night."

"Then—I'm just gonna take a wild stab here—your children did not tell you about the teenage boy they found there. The one with the red eyes and the unnaturally pale skin coloration?"

"My gosh, I just don't believe you two," Mom groans.

"Is . . . is he all right?" Kalea asks softly.

"'All right' is a very subjective value judgment," Agent Layton says.

"He, uh, didn't make it," Agent Van Hook says.

"Oh," Kalea says, her voice cracking. That she's sad at news of my death makes me feel good for some reason. Then feeling that makes me feel bad.

"Why did he—look like that?" Mom asks. "Was he sick?"

"Possibly," Agent Van Hook says. "That's why we are identifying everyone who had contact with him and bringing them into the hospital for tests. We have the EMTs who picked him up in quarantine, under observation, since last night. The results are . . . not encouraging." He keeps going over Mom's horrified moan. "So we're going to have to ask you to come with us for some tests."

"Where are you taking them? Sinai? That's where I work—"

"No, we have our own facility in the federal complex downtown. You kids should grab some overnight things—toothbrush, whatever you sleep in, that sort of thing. Don't worry, you won't be gone long. Purely precautionary."

I remain crouched, coiled like a spring, in the mud of a flower bed below the window, ready to move at the first sign of Kalea or Clark or their mom being in serious danger. I don't dare move too soon or give away my position. I'm not yet sure what Project Rising Spirit's play is here, so I can't know what mine is either. Do they have eyes in the sky? I don't sense anything, but that could just mean their drones or satellites or whatever they are could be higher in the air than my machine telepathy.

I hear the siblings' footsteps tromping upstairs. The agents remain in the living room with Mom, making small talk. Mom asks and gets told she can't come with them because there's too much risk of contamination. The agents assure her that they'll keep her updated as to her kids' location. What's the connection between the destroyed trees and this mysterious illness? Unknown at this time.

I'm pretty sure Mom isn't in any immediate danger. If PRS were going to ice the whole family in the house, they would have done it by now, no contact-tracing cover story required.

So I return to the toolshed and a rusting snowblower I'd noticed earlier. It's got a fading nylon strap that I unhook and take with me into the front yard. I crouch low so I can't be seen from the house.

I drop on my back and slide under the SUV. The truck is a beast, long enough that I can haul myself up by my hands and brace myself with my feet on the frame above me. But I'll still need some support. I wrap the blower strap around my waist and hook it to the frame above me. It's got enough ground clearance to keep me above the road so that my shoulder blades won't get torn up by the asphalt.

The front door of the house opens, and out comes everybody. Mom walks her kids to the SUV, but the agents don't let her kiss them goodbye. "Contamination," they keep saying, like a verbal tic.

They get inside and drive off, and I'm pretty well braced. If I weren't as strong as I am, it'd be a challenge to stay above the blurry gray ground below me. But I am as strong as I am.

The fumes from the engine don't smell too great, though, and small stones keep getting kicked up from the tires and hitting me in the back. Then the SUV pulls off into the woods and bumps and grinds over rocks and rainwater-filled puddles, and it's all I can do to hang on for dear life.

The car stops in a clearing that used to be a drive-in movie theater, the panels of the giant screen having fallen off in patchwork gaps, rusting speaker posts facing it, waiting through an intermission that's never going to end. I was hoping they were telling the truth about having a facility where the EMTs were "recuperating" and the SUV would drive me right to it, so I might be able to sneak around and get some answers, but I am beginning to get the impression that the universe doesn't like me very much and has no interest in making life easy for me.

I unhook myself just as the side doors open and the kids step out. I roll away from them and crouch behind their backs as the agents get out from the front. I take my pistol out of my waistband.

I step out from behind the truck and see the four of them.

But not how I was expecting.

The agents, Layton and Van Hook, stand at attention, as if under military review. Facing them are Kalea and Clark, not under any stress at all—quite the opposite, in fact. Kalea is rather awkwardly holding a Beretta and a Desert Eagle in her hands, taken from the agents, I guess, because of the empty holsters I can see beneath their open jackets . . .

Clark sees me out of the corner of his eye and leaps back with a yelp. Kalea is so startled she drops both guns into the grass.

"It's you!" she cries. "They told me—these two—they said you were—"

"I heard." Clark is still eyeing the pistol in my hand, so I stick it back in my waistband. "All lies. These two killed the real ambulance drivers you called, then drove me out to an abandoned warehouse, where they had an army waiting for me."

"Army?" Clark's eyes dart to the woods around us as if more soldiers could leap out at any moment. "What happened to them?"

"I did."

Van Hook and Layton are still just staring ahead, like they're waiting for a bus. I wave my hand in front of their mirror shades. They turn to me and smile awkwardly, then look away again. "What happened to *them*?"

"Kalea happened," Clark says.

I look to her. She's staring down at her feet, trying to hide behind her hair. "Kalea? Is that right?"

"Yeah. I can—well, for a couple years now, I can, like, 'network' minds. I can link them to my mind—and each other's. The more minds I link, the more complex commands I can give 'em. If I just want their minds to be, well, empty, I can just create a closed circuit between them. No stimuli go in, no thoughts come out. I call it 'Quiet Time.'"

"Pretty cool, huh?" Clark grins, beaming with pride.

"Pretty cool." I nod.

Kalea sighs. "I know, it sounds crazy."

"No, I get it. I can relate. I, uh, can do something similar to machines." I find a phone in Van Hook's blazer pocket. It's a "dumb phone" instead of a smartphone, the old kind you flip open. As far as I can tell, there's only one number on it. Likely a contact number to ring when they had the kids in their possession.

"Gee, it's almost like they were expecting to run into me," I mutter under my breath, then toss it into the brush.

"I knew these guys were full of it the minute they walked into our house," Kalea says. "They had those shades on, but please? Those were the ambulance drivers from yesterday. But I didn't want to do anything in front of Mom, it might have put her in danger."

"Notice she doesn't mind putting *me* in danger," Clark says.

"Can you read their minds, ask them where they were planning on taking you?" I ask.

"No, it's not like you see in the movies. It's not like I can hear thoughts like I'm eavesdropping on somebody while they're on the phone. I can tell, I don't know, the tenor of their thoughts, like the hum inside a beehive."

"Well . . . can you persuade them to tell us out loud what we want to know?"

"Sort of, but not for long, or it'll break the connection."

"Okay, let's try it."

Kalea nods and concentrates, scrunching up her brow a bit. Both Van Hook and Layton make pitiful little groans, as if straining to lift a great weight.

"Who am I?" I ask.

"You're . . . Bloodshot," Van Hook says through clenched teeth.

"I don't know what that means. What is a Bloodshot?"

"You . . . are," Layton says.

"Oh my . . ." My heart pounds. The panic is starting to build up inside of me again. "I mean—where do I live? Do I go to school? Who are my parents?"

Van Hook and Layton are both sweating now. They look at each other. They just gape uselessly at me.

"What purpose do I have?" I ask, exasperated.

"You're . . . you're . . ." Spittle sprays from Van Hook's lips.

"You're our weapon," Layton says.

"You don't own me!" I yell, stepping forward, hands reaching out. I just want to shake the truth loose from them. But suddenly they drop to the ground, marionettes with their strings cut, and they're out of my reach. They lie at my feet, eyes closed, breathing heavily.

I look at Kalea. Clark has stepped protectively between me and her. She has her hands up.

"Why did you do that? You thought they were going to try something? I would have handled that."

"It's . . . not them . . . I was worried about," Kalea says, and I know what she means.

"Sorry."

"You're upset. I don't blame you. I . . . this isn't my first experience with something like this," Kalea says. "What now?"

My stomach growls loudly.

"Breakfast?" Clark asks.

FOUR

"More."

Kalea and Clark look on in awe as I finish off my eighth egg sandwich and my twelfth helping of hash browns and suck my fifth bottle of OJ dry. There's a mound of scrunched-up food wrappers and empty cups on the tray in front of me. Still, though, my stomach feels empty. It's like a black hole, sucking up and crushing whatever I put into it, leaving nothing behind to let me feel sated.

"Let me go up one last time," I say, and Kalea shakes her head.

"I don't like it. It's stealing."

"C'mon, just let me have the phone again."

She sighs. "This is the last time. You're costing this place hundreds of dollars!"

"Jeez, sis, lighten up," Clark groans. "They're a ginormous fast-food chain. They can take the hit."

"Fine," Kalea says, and puts her phone in my hand. "But this is the last time. That's still my phone." While it's technically true, her phone is just a prop for me.

"Hello again," says the sixtysomething woman in the brown-and-gold uniform operating the register.

I grunt at her and prepare to order my fourth breakfast, but I look up at the menu posted above and see that the options have all changed. Egg sandwiches have been replaced by hamburgers, and hash browns with fries. Salads and fish squares are where pancakes and egg sandwiches used to be.

The clerk laughs as she sees my amazement. "Eleven thirty sharp, we switch over to the lunch menu."

I lick my lips. I want it all. I order it all. Every single item on the menu. The clerk keeps chuckling as she rings me up. "One hundred and forty-one dollars and thirty-three cents. We call that the McEverything."

I hold Kalea's phone against the credit card terminal. It's not doing anything, but the clerk doesn't know that. My fingers on the underside of the phone are touching the terminal, and through them I ask the system to accept the charges. The system does so with a little tingling acknowledgment through my knuckles. Machines not only recognize me, but they seem to . . . enjoy my company? I get the impression they're not doing what I ask because I'm giving commands that they have no choice but to obey. They're doing it because machines like me and want me to do well.

Which is weird. Very weird. But when your memories go back less than twenty-four hours, there's no baseline for normal. I don't have any choice but to roll with it.

The McEverything requires two trays to carry. Fortunately, I have two hands. When I return to the isolated corner booth—I asked the security cameras in here to blur out my face and my companions', but I'm not taking any chances—Clark and Kalea are whispering, and he clams up as soon as I sit down.

"What?" I ask Clark. He's not a machine. He's not happy at all to see me. I can tell from his eyes he's a little afraid of me.

Hard to blame him. I'm a little afraid of me too.

"Nothing," he mutters, looking at the table while I dig in. Four-, six-, ten-piece McNuggets, all gone in seconds. I don't even bother to grab more mustard-sauce packs. The underrated Spicy McCrispy fried chicken sandwich. The double-stacked Big Mac with its pickley sweet-and-sour sauce. Amazing. I could go on. I will go on. This Quarter Pounder has "cheese bacon" on it. What is cheese bacon? Who cares? It tastes amazing.

I'd be completely lost in fast-food ecstasy if Kalea didn't blurt out, "Clark is worried about what's going to happen to Mom when these goons figure out we gave them the slip."

"She's in danger," he says.

"She was in danger the day she gave birth to me," Kalea says bitterly.

Clark puts his hand over hers. "C'mon, don't say that."

"I've been thinking about this a lot too," I say between mouthfuls of Filet-O-Fish, "and I think it is safest for her if we stay as far away from her as possible. They didn't try and take her in along with you. They want as few people to know about this—me—as possible. They're probably just going to watch her house, see if you come back. Besides, all they care about is using you to get to me."

"Not necessarily," Kalea mutters quietly.

"You think they know about . . . what you can do?"

"I don't know how they could, but it seems like a strange coincidence. For both of us to have . . . powers. The speed, the strength. The healing. The talking to machines."

"The bottomless appetite," Clark says.

I move on to scooping a fudge-covered sundae into my mouth. "You know what power I'd really like? The power to remember who I am."

"I might be able to help you with that."

"How?"

"Well . . . not me literally. But I know a group. Kids who help out psiots like us."

"Psy-huh?"

"Yeah, psiots. Indigo children. ESPers. People born with unusual, unexplained abilities. Corporations and governments want to find us, control us. I used to be part of the main network of kids fighting them. They're not happy I didn't stick around. But they shouldn't hold that against you."

"No, Kalea, not Generation Zero again." Clark sighs.

"Shush. Thing is, the only way I have to contact them was too dangerous for me to keep in Mom's house. So we've got to get it out of my locker at school."

We leave the fast-food joint and head down the block until I find a car parked by the curb with a totally electronic ignition and security, no physical keys required. All I need to do is look at it, and it unlocks and shuts down its antitheft tracking system.

I can feel Kalea's disapproving gaze on the back of my neck before I turn around and see it with my own eyes. She's not like Clark, though. She's not scared of me. Just . . . disappointed. This feels worse.

I have this impulse to hold the car door open for her, like, *I know you don't approve of this, but it's not like you're going to walk to your school.* She gets in without meeting my eyes. It doesn't feel great. But I still don't entirely understand my impulses. Even when I'm not directly being shot at, I have this very clear sense of where to go and what to do. I don't need memories of responsibilities, wants, or desires to make decisions. All I need are clear mission objectives. When I have those, I will do whatever I need to achieve those objectives. This isn't my car? So what? I need it to get where I'm going without being tracked.

I know Kalea doesn't like it, but I don't have any choice except to follow my impulses. Until I get my memories back, my instinct is the only thing I have to go on to know what is and isn't me.

In fact, as I climb behind the wheel of the stolen car and Clark gets in the passenger seat beside me, I realize I haven't felt this confident since I woke up. Everything seems very clear to me now. I am Bloodshot. Some company called PRS wants me because of these psiot abilities. I am trying to find a network of psiots to help me stay out of their clutches.

Sure, the psiot abilities to heal myself and talk to machines are kind of a random power set, but how am I supposed to know how the Power Fairy works? Maybe giving people logically linked powers is just something comic books have brainwashed us into thinking is a thing. Here: You can breathe underwater *and* shoot fire out of your eyes. Enjoy.

I drive to the school, letting Kalea guide me from the back seat. I could easily tap into the car's GPS, but as long as I can hear her voice, I can pretend she's not mad at me.

Thelma Archer Memorial High is set back from the main street along a dedicated road that winds past a football stadium. The first-period gym classes are blearily jogging around the track that rings the field. Boys and girls alike are wearing gold shorts and white T-shirts with a grinning Tyrannosaurus on them ("Go Rexes!").

"Oh, no, stop!" Clark suddenly cries out, and I slam on the brakes, rattling us around inside the car. I immediately start scanning the surrounding trees for hostiles.

"What do you see?" I ask.

"They sprang standardized testing day on us early this year," Clark groans, pointing at a black van parked by the front entrance to Archer High. Emblazoned on the side is a white logo: AccuChieve.

I give Clark an annoyed look. "Please save freaking out for actual threats."

"It *is* an actual threat! We sixth graders will have to do it over in middle school too. You get a bad score, you can mess up the rest of your life."

I come almost to a full stop on one side of the van to block any view of our car from the school entrance. Kalea opens the door and prepares to get out. "I'll be right back."

"Wait," I say, and speed up so she has to close the door again.

"What's wrong?"

"I did a quick search of AccuChieve online. It's a subsidiary of Project Rising Spirit."

"I told you!" Clark cries. "I told you standardized tests were totally evil!"

I pull into a parking space on the far side of the football stadium lot, where only a few gasping gym students can see us.

"So . . . they're already here," Kalea says. "Should we come back later tonight?"

"After we check in with Mom," Clark says.

"No, I'll go in," I say.

"What?" Clark cries. "You? No offense, man, but you look like an angry ghost."

"Sure, I do now. But there's something I've been wanting to try." And I had wanted to try it ever since I saw my body stitching my wounds back together. I have a picture in my mind of a boy, about sixteen years old, sitting next to Kalea on the edge of a pool, wearing red trunks and a red lifeguard jacket. I hold up my chalk-white hand, and suddenly a darker brown pigment floods across my arm and spreads up to my elbow and down to my wrist.

Clark's jaw drops, and he scooches across his seat away from me, against the door.

For this next part, I have to close my eyes. In the picture the boy at the pool is smiling, the sun behind him, backlighting him, but I can make out his sandy brown hair, the divot in his chin. I can't make out his eye color, but I know he has irises, unlike me, and so I give myself green eyes, same shade as Kalea's, which I can picture quite well. My muscles and limbs tremble and shift to match the picture in my head. It doesn't hurt, but it doesn't feel all that pleasant either; fortunately, it's over in less than a minute. I open my eyes and look in the rearview mirror: Just as my body changed itself from damaged to healed, I was able to get it to change from my usual appearance to this other guy's.

I'm pretty proud of myself. Kalea wears a big grin and has her arm over this guy's shoulders in the photo, and I guess I picked this look because it'd make her happy.

But then I see Clark is now as pale as I used to be twenty seconds ago.

"Dude," he breathes. "Not cool."

"What?" I turn back to look at Kalea. "What's wrong with—"

She looks even worse than her brother does. "Why did you choose to look—to look like him?" There's a wounded edge to her voice. I've offended her somehow.

"I, uh . . . I just shifted to the first thing that came to my mind. I guess . . . okay, now that I think of it, I guess before I could control my powers, your phone . . . It was the first thing that came to my mind. You know, this guy was in your Favorites, and in your photos, and I don't have very many memories to go on—"

"It's okay, I guess." Kalea holds up her hands. "I guess I didn't realize a photo of him was still in my phone. You didn't know."

"And I still don't."

"That's Mason," Clark says, "and Mason's a real piece of—"

"*Clark*," Kalea snaps. "Can't you pick another, uh, 'look,' or . . ."

My stomach growls at me, and my heart sinks. Every time my body repairs or modifies itself, it burns way, way more energy than I expect. Am I going to have to stay within walking distance of a McDonald's for the rest of my life? "I, er . . ."

"Look, forget it. Let's just get this over with. My locker's 126, up on the second floor. Combo's thirty-two left, forty-one right, eight left. You need to write it down?"

I shake my head. She describes in detail what I'm looking for inside the locker. I don't really understand why it's so important, but it's not really my place to question. I get out of the car.

"Be careful," Kalea says, sticking her head out the window. "Mason hasn't gone to this school for a while now. And he doesn't have a twin brother."

I nod hastily. Maybe I should have thought this plan through a little better. "What's his last name?"

"Miller."

I nod again and start walking toward the school entrance like I belong there.

FIVE

I sense the metal detector standing in the school foyer before seeing it through the glass doors at the school entrance. And, of course, I still have a Beretta shoved down my pants. I also see a matronly uniformed security guard sitting at a table next to the detector, flipping through an actual paper newspaper. I could tell the detector not to notice my weapon as I pass through it, but concealing the bulge in my waistband from her is another story. Neutralizing her would be no problem, but it would likely get messy. And the idea of beating up rent-a-cops beyond retirement age makes me feel gross inside.

I should return the pistol to the car, but I can already feel the external security cameras on me, registering me as Mason. Instead I let it drop into the garbage can at the bottom of the steps leading to the entrance, using my body to block the camera. It's not a perfect solution, but it's the best option to make sure some random kid doesn't find it later.

The guard doesn't look up from her paper as I push through the glass doors. "Mason, welcome back! I had no idea you were visiting us today."

"Yeah! Uh, my parents are in town, so I thought I'd . . ."

I don't get to finish my lie. The metal detector whoops and lights up as I pass through it.

The guard doesn't look up. She just picks up a small plastic basket off her table. "Keys, wallet, phone."

I don't have any of those things. And I'm unarmed. So what set the detector off? Strange. "I left them in my car."

"In your unlocked car? You trust humanity more than I do, kid. Turn around."

She looks up for a second as I do so and examines me from the table for concealed weapons. "I keep telling the school board to replace that old hunk of junk, and they keep telling me it's not in the budget. Go on now, Mason. Don't forget to pick up a visitor's pass from the front office. And it's great to see you again! You look great after, er, you know . . ." She looks around to make sure no one's watching, then loudly whispers: "After your troubles."

"Okay, thanks." I absolutely *have to* get this story out of Kalea.

The entrance to the high school holds what amnesia forces me to assume is a standard collection of trophy cases, student art on the walls, and mascot-themed sports banners ("Go Rexes!"). A plaque on the wall facing the entrance shows the face of a fortysomething woman and says the school was recently renamed after a US congresswoman who passed away while doing missionary work in the Himalayas.

The corridor comes to a T at the Thelma Archer plaque, and I see the glass-lined main office on my left. I head in that direction as if I'm going to get the visitor's pass, but I keep walking right past it when I round the corner and head for the stairs on the right.

Two adult men in baggy navy-blue AccuChieve windbreakers are coming down the stairs as I go up, and one of them has a bandage over a broken nose and a few open minor scratches on his face. I somehow manage not to do a double take and squeeze the banister extra hard as I go past them and up. Of course the beat-up AccuChieve guy doesn't recognize me. Why would he? I look like Mason Miller.

But I recognize him. He's one of the mercs I tangled with on the abandoned factory roof last night. All those scratches and his broken nose are souvenirs of when I smashed in his visor.

My mind starts to run wild after the implications of this. I have to rein it in. I am Bloodshot, I remind myself. What does Bloodshot do? Bloodshot does the mission. And the mission right now is not Accu-Chieve; the mission is Kalea's locker.

Rows of lockers line the second-floor hallway, interrupted in regular intervals by closed classroom doors. As I walk up the numbers to Kalea's, I glance inside the classrooms through the windows on the doors and see students hunched over their desks, filling in answer sheets with number two pencils while flipping through identical black-and-white test booklets. A teacher sits at the desk at the front, a stopwatch in one hand, scrolling through Instagram on her cell phone in the other.

Still. The test isn't the mission. The locker is. Number 126. Even if she hadn't told me the number, KALEA is on it in puffy glow-in-the-dark letter stickers. I turn the combo lock to thirty-two left, forty-one right, eight left. It opens. Inside are a few textbooks, a few manga tankōbon, a few YA fantasy novels. Taped to the inside of the door is a page ripped out of a magazine with a photo of a K-pop singer so handsome he looks like he was genetically engineered.

On the upper shelf, partially hidden behind old tests (invariably graded A), I find it: a plush cloud, smaller than a bed pillow, bigger than a doll, with wide eyes full of love and a grin cocked to one side, a bright sun on one white edge. On the other side of the plush, the cloud has another face: the eyes have narrowed with anger and the mouth is scowling. The edges of this side are dark, gunmetal gray, and instead of a sun there's a lightning bolt in one corner.

Why Kalea wants this cloud plushy so badly I have no idea, but if she needs it to help me, I don't really care why. It barely fits in my back pocket. I close her locker door and flip the combo lock a few random turns. Mission accomplished, and rather speedily at that.

When I look up, there's a man standing on the other side of the door. An inch shorter than me, boyish sandy hair, deep laugh lines around the mouth. He must not have a cell phone on him, or he wouldn't have been able to sneak up on me like that.

"Hey, Mason!" he cries out, and slaps me on the shoulder. "How's it going? Terrific to see you again. Remember me?"

"Uh . . ." I say, but fortunately he immediately rescues me.

"Mr. Dysart. Say, I hope you're not in too much of a rush. I was wondering if I could get a quick word with you in my office, if that's not too much to ask."

"Uh . . ." Over Dysart's shoulder I can see the two guys in Accu-Chieve windbreakers pop up at the top of the stairs down the hall. Even unarmed, I could probably take out as many of these people as I need to get away. But that would absolutely tip PRS off to my location.

"Sure, of course, Mr. Dysart," I say.

"Great," he says. "Right this way."

The AccuChieve windbreakers recede down the hall in the opposite direction, and I follow Dysart back down the stairs and into the main office suite I ducked past on my way in. He might have seen me through the glass wall. He leads me into an office marked J. Dysart, Guidance Counselor.

"Have a seat," he says as he closes the door behind us. He sits on the edge of the desk and bears his everything's-all-right teeth at me. "How you feeling? You went to—where was it again? Did it help your, you know? Your ideation?"

It's beginning to sink in how mind-bogglingly stupid I was to choose this disguise. I might as well have just walked in as Bloodshot; I would have attracted less attention.

"Oh, yeah, Mr. Dysart, my ideation! It's, uh, so much improved. Like night and day really. That place you mentioned, it totally helped me out."

Mr. Dysart nods vigorously. "Oh, that's great. That's so great to hear. Just remember: It doesn't matter what social media says. *Everyone* has power. The poster is corny, but the poster is right."

He gestures to a shiny new poster hanging in a corner. It shows a racially diverse bunch of teenagers with a wide range of body types—including a redhead in a wheelchair—laughing in a fancy high school's courtyard, clearly ideation-free. "EVERYONE HAS P.O.W.E.R.," the copy cheerfully says, spelling out:

Personhood
Originality
Worth
Empathy
Remarkable Qualities

In the lower right corner of the poster is a swooping bird symbol in a circle and a note saying that it was paid for by something called the Harbinger Foundation.

"Yes, sir, Mr. Dysart, I, uh, I know that now. I'm so much better, it's . . . hard to put into words how much."

"Great. Just fantastic." Dysart crosses his arms over his chest. "You know you don't go to this school anymore, so you needed to have picked up a visitor's pass from Mrs. Abiola when you came in, right?"

"Right. Yes! True. Sorry about that. My bad. I am in a little bit of a rush, is the thing."

"Going through Kalea Derby's locker. Can I see what you got out of there?"

"Yeah, absolutely." I sit up slightly, pull the plushy cloud out of my back pocket, and hand it to him.

He's as puzzled as I was seeing it. Turning it over in his hands, he says, "You two work out your . . . I mean, you're back in touch again? Friendly?"

"Yes, sir. In fact . . ." I am going to need to convince this dude of my cover story if he's ever going to let me out of here without my knocking his ass out, which I would really prefer not to do. "Well, I don't know how much the family would want me to say, but both Kalea and Clark are in the hospital."

"I'm sorry to hear that."

"Yeah, it's some, uh, well, I'm not even sure. An environmental thing? That happened out in the woods while they were shooting one of Clark's movies? She called me and asked me to bring her that plush as, like, a comfort thing. That's how I knew the combo on her locker."

"Uh-huh. And she didn't ask one of her friends who actually goes here because . . ."

"Like I said, they don't want the news going around. The family's kind of freaked out."

"Right." Dysart is kneading the plush cloud very carefully, feeling, I'd guess, for hidden drugs. He doesn't find anything but a squeaker that makes a little bleat that startles him. And me. "If I call her parents, they'll confirm that?"

"I don't know if they know she asked me. I think call Kalea? Pretty sure she has her phone on her."

"All right." He sets the cloud plush on the desk and walks out of the room. "I'll be right back," he says, and closes the door behind him.

Part of me wants to bolt right out of here. In this tiny concrete room, I am a sitting duck for PRS. But I keep my cool.

He's gone longer than I expected. My eyes wander around the office, and something on his desk blotter catches my eye: a thin stapled booklet. I grab it.

CEWA21, it proclaims on the cover, *Cognitive and Emotional Wellness Assessment for the 21st Century.* The fine print says, "CEWA21 is administered by AccuChieve LLC under contract with the Ohio Department of Education."

I flip through the booklet. In plain type it asks a bunch of numbered questions with two possible answers each:

3.) Is every point on a circle
A) an ending point or
B) a starting point?

17.) Is the sun new each day?
A) Yes
B) No

37.) Are the way up and the way down
A) the same or
B) different?

49.) Can you expect the unexpected?
A) Yes
B) No

What the heck? I don't know what I expected to see when I opened the test booklet. There's no way PRS is administering standardized testing to public school kids for innocent reasons, even just for a paycheck. The actual questions are all paradoxes or word games with no "correct" answer—even the ones that seem obvious become a lot less so the more you think about them. (It's the same sun every day, but because the day is new, and the sun marks the beginning of the new day, doesn't that make the sun new too?) What exactly is the state of Ohio supposed to learn by forcing a kid to pick one of two equally good choices? For that matter, what is PRS? Or is the point just to traumatize kids by making them sweat out having their personalities judged on a series of totally arbitrary choices?

I turn the next page, and my eye falls on the question up top:

102.) What is more real to you:
A) your dreams or
B) your waking life?

And suddenly silent fireworks start going off on the edges of my vision, and I'm not in the guidance counselor's office in Thelma Archer Memorial High anymore. I am in a forest and it's dawn and I'm looking at a person that seems to be made of light

—no, not light, fire—

—no, not fire, lightning—

—and I'm shouting and they're shouting but the air itself is humming and the lightning suddenly explodes outward from the figure and the trees ignite and it's like standing in the middle of a lit birthday cake and I point a pistol at the figure and then the lightning suddenly springs toward me and I'm back in Thelma Archer Memorial High and I'm on the floor of the guidance counselor's office. How long was

I out? Long enough to slide off my chair. A nanosecond? Twenty seconds? Ten minutes?

Okay.

I think I just had my first real memory.

SIX

I'm back in my chair long before Mr. Dysart returns. "All right, Kalea confirmed your story. Just, Mason, next time get a visitor's pass, okay? The safety of the kids here is my first priority, and it's not like you left on, you know, the best of terms."

"Again, really sorry, sir, just wasn't thinking." I point at the plushy cloud on his desk, and he hands it to me.

"Hope whatever Kalea's got turns out to be nothing. She sounded pretty good on the phone."

I wave goodbye to the security guard and go back outside and fish the Beretta out of the trash can with my back to the cameras. Back in the car, I toss the plush cloud to Kalea in the back seat as I climb behind the wheel. She clutches it to her heart. "You let Mr. Dysart catch you?"

"Sorry, sue me. Maybe you should've mentioned this kid was voted Ex-Student Most Likely to Come Back and Shoot Up the Place."

"You were the one so gung ho to look like him. Can you go back to looking like yourself, please?"

"Not quickly enough." I lock eyes with her and effortlessly shift from Mason Miller's form back to what Clark calls my "angry ghost" form: white skin, red eyes, and all. She visibly shivers. My stomach grumbles. "What'd this guy do to you that got you so upset, anyway?"

"None of your beeswax," Clark barks.

"I never said he did anything to me," Kalea snaps. "But it's not important right now. We need to get to a high, isolated spot . . ."

"What about the castle," her brother asks her.

"Yeah, that could work. Squire's Castle, in the county park. I can tell you the way—"

"No need." I wave my hand at the steering column, and the car starts. I nod at the GPS, and a point appears in the middle of a mostly green map: 14.5 miles north, about a half-hour drive. I put both hands on the steering wheel but hesitate to move forward.

"What is it?" Kalea asks.

"Do you know other . . . psiots? Ones with different powers? That aren't telepathy related, I mean?"

"Maybe. Why do you ask?"

"I think . . . for the first time, I think I remembered something. Of the time before you found me. I was in that same wood where I was, but I was fighting someone—someone who could generate, or control, lightning."

"That's 'electrokinesis,' Holmes," says Clark.

"They set all the trees on fire, then blasted me . . . and that's where the memory ends."

"Why would you be fighting another psiot?" Kalea asks.

The question makes my spine squirm. I pop the brakes and drive off as if I can peel away from having to answer it. "How do you know the other psiot didn't start it?"

"'Lightning can heat the air it passes through up to fifty thousand degrees Fahrenheit,'" Kalea reads off her phone. "That's five times hotter than the surface of the sun, apparently." She holds up the web page. "Powers wiki."

"Can we trust that site? Bunch of wannabes," Clark scoffs.

"It'd explain why those trees all around you got flash-fried without setting the rest of the forest on fire," Kalea says.

I don't say anything. I just drive to where the GPS tells me. On the way we pass a supermarket. I stop in to fill the trunk with all the snacks I can find: Pringles, Twizzlers, Doritos, Slim Jims, Famous Amos cookies,

Fruit Roll-Ups, energy bars, bottles of blue Gatorade. If my body is going to be crying at me every time I use it for something more strenuous than walking, I want to make sure I have plenty of provisions on hand.

"The Bloodshot Diet." Clark laughs when he sees my arms full of grocery bags. "Eating crap and kicking ass."

Squire's Castle is really just the gatehouse part of a castle, a tall tower like a chess rook and some battlements and a big, wide arch that an iron portcullis used to block. Still, dropped on the edge of trees and a picnic lawn in a sprawling county park, it's pretty cool all the same. As the car rolls up, I have a sense of driving back in time.

"We should probably wait until dark before we try contacting my friends," Kalea says.

"Snack picnic!" Clark shoots his fist straight up. "*Yes!*"

We eat garbage food sitting on a picnic table. It's the middle of the week, so while people come or go in cars and bikes or walk dogs on foot, we mostly have the place to ourselves. After eating a whole roll of red ribbon licorice, Clark starts running around in circles, yelling, high on sugar. Kalea and I watch and laugh at him.

Out of nowhere, she says, "Mason Miller didn't do anything to me. I did something to him."

She looks into my face for a response, but I just sit and listen.

"You know the #PowerParty hashtag? It started to really be a thing a year or two ago. When you hit our age, that's when your psiot powers start to develop. So something people do at sleepovers and parties or whatever, you know, when no parents are around, is dare each other to show off what they can do. Film it, try to make it go viral. A lot of them are basically magic tricks or, like, Ouija board stunts. Some of them, I bet, are altered in computers. The ones that really take off, though . . . are harder to just explain away. Like . . ."

Kalea hands me her phone. The social feed cycles rapidly through the highest-rated videos under #PowerParty. In the first one, a bunch of kids are standing around a marble-topped kitchen island in a posh suburban house, clutching red Solo cups. They lose their minds with screams and OMGs as a curly-haired boy sends his eyeballs under his eyelids and all the drawers open and out fly silverware and steel whisks and such. He shudders as the metal utensils spin in a silver typhoon over the countertop before stabilizing into stacked tiers, like the layers of a wedding cake. Forks and spoons and knives start doing a spinning kick-dance, Disney musical style. The video abruptly ends when a pale-faced, long-haired brunette watching this display faints dead away to the floor.

"My friend Yvonne Wilshire had one, and I was the only one at my school who could really, like, do anything. I networked everyone's minds and made them, like, do handstands and recite Doja Cat lyrics in unison. The video made it to the #PowerParty hashtag, but it didn't get many views. I get it; something like that could have easily been faked. But the people who were actually there, I mean, they knew. They knew I took control of them. They knew it was real.

"It freaked some of the people who go to my school out, but mostly everybody there thought it was cool. But Mason Miller, who I knew from lifeguarding at the rec center, who is just, you saw him with his shirt off—I mean, come on, right?"

"He's a good-looking guy," I say through gritted teeth.

"I mean, he was into it. He was into me. We started dating, sort of, in, like, a silly tenth-grade sort of way. I could hardly believe it, a guy like him would be into a girl like me. I guess that's why when Yvonne told me she thought he was cheating on me, I believed her almost instantly. I guess she was into him, or maybe she was just mad I was so happy. You know how people get.

"Yvonne . . . she planted this idea in my head, and I couldn't get rid of it, you know? The thought of Mason with someone else just ate me up inside. I couldn't think about anything else. So when we were at the movies, I forget what it was, some superhero thing, his hand was in mine, and I thought, *Let me try. Let me see what I find in there.*"

She falls silent. "What'd you find?" I ask.

"I didn't understand what I was yet, you know? It's not like on TV, you know, where you just close your eyes and scrunch up your nose and hear people's thoughts like it's their own private podcast? It's not like that at all. It's not even what I can do.

"I network people's minds, and when I threw open Mason's mind, it's like I . . . threw open a window and this big breeze came in and knocked all his thoughts out everywhere. The girls he fantasized about, the mean things he thought about teachers behind their backs, the mean things he thought about his *best friends* behind their backs . . . and the real reason he was into me.

"He desperately wanted powers of his own. I mean, more than anything else in the world. He was just glued to those #PowerParty videos. All he wanted out of life was to be special. His mom wouldn't leave him alone about it. And he wasn't even that into me! He thought maybe, I don't know, that by being near me he could figure out my trick, right? Or that my power would rub off on him.

"Thing is, like I said, I network minds. Multiple minds. And I accidentally gave those things, Mason's private thoughts, to everyone else in the theater. They all knew those things. They didn't know why they knew, but they did. And he knew. And when he looked at my face . . . he knew it was me who did it. He didn't know how, he didn't know why, but he knew I did it.

"He ran out of that theater so fast he dumped his popcorn all over me. He basically had a total nervous breakdown. He had to finish out school at a clinic somewhere. Then his parents moved out of the state. I never saw him again."

She takes a deep breath. "I was scared and alone and I didn't have anyone to talk to. If I hadn't found other people like me . . . who could explain to me what I was, and how I could protect myself . . . I don't know what I would've done without them. Those are the same people I am going to contact for you tonight."

"How did you find them?"

"You don't find Generation Zero. Generation Zero finds you. Turns out they saw my #PowerParty video. I spent a summer with them at the current hideout in . . . the Rockies, I think. I wasn't entirely sure. They've got to keep moving around because the government is always looking for them. Capture them, study them. PRS, I guess. But I'm luckier than a lot of kids. I realized I could use my powers to wipe the memories of everyone who was at the party. I made sure to delete my video. When summer ended, I could come back and resume my regular life."

"Until I showed up. Sorry about that, Kalea."

She shrugs. "Not a big deal. I know there are tons of psiots who can't hide their powers. People who look . . . uh, you know, unusual, like you. No offense."

"It's okay. I've seen a mirror."

"And if I can't help people who don't have the advantages I have, I mean . . . what kind of person would do that? Psiots would be the monsters a lot of people think they are."

Night falls. The streetlamps ringing the parking lot all glow on at the same time. We eat a dinner of extra sugars and naturally flavored meat-like substances. We tell Clark it's not safe to call Mom five or six more times. The crickets start strumming in the darkness. Kalea complains she's getting eaten alive by mosquitoes. They're ignoring me. I wonder why. A self-regenerating body should be an all-you-can-eat buffet to a bloodsucker.

"You want to see something cool?" she asks me out of nowhere.

"Who doesn't?"

"Don't check the temperature." Well, as soon as she says that, her phone instantly chirps in my head with the exact current temperature, but I keep that number to myself. "Just listen to the crickets."

They chirp everywhere and nowhere, surrounding us unseen, before lapsing into silence for a spell.

"When they come back, count them for fourteen seconds."

"Why?"

"Because—" Clark starts to say, but his sister shushes him.

"Don't ruin it. Just do it."

When the woodland strings section returns, Kalea starts counting off the seconds under her breath. I start counting the chirps. When she gets to fourteen, I've gotten to eighteen.

"Now add that to forty. And that's the current temperature. In Fahrenheit, obviously."

"Huh. Yeah. Fifty-eight degrees. That's exactly right. Okay. That is cool."

"See, you don't need machines for everything." She beams. "The crickets have slept all winter as larvae, and now that it's getting warmer, they come out singing for mates. Longer the summer goes, the more desperate they get, so the faster they sing."

"They wanna get *biz-zay*," Clark says offhandedly. "Nature's dating app."

"Cronus taught me that last summer," Kalea says. "He knows all sorts of weird survivalist stuff like that. He kind of has to."

When I hear Cronus's name, my scalp gets warm. I don't want to think about why. "He your new boyfriend or something?" I say just as I think I probably shouldn't.

"No," she says. She's staring off into the distance. In the dusk I can't really see her expression. It sounds like the question doesn't bother her, but also like she wasn't exactly not expecting it either.

"Kalea, I was thinking—would it be possible for you to scan my mind? Even if you only got impressions, there might . . . there might be some of 'me' you could get out of there, you know?"

"No," she says again, in exactly the same way, and now I get even hotter.

"Jeez, sorry." I get up off the picnic table before I even know what I'm doing. "I thought maybe you wanted to help me."

I start to turn away, but she grabs my arm. "No, Bloodshot, sorry. I meant—it isn't actually possible for me to scan your mind. It's not that I, uh, tried before or anything, but—it's kind of involuntary, I'm just aware, at all times, of the minds around me. And yours . . . isn't one of them. I reach out to your mind . . . and there's just nothing there. Nothing I can pick up on, anyway."

"Don't worry, dude," Clark says, "you still seem super smart to me."

I mean, I know I have a mind. I'm not insecure about that. But . . . is psychic shielding another random power granted me by the Power Fairy?

A bad thought comes to me. "That doesn't make me . . . weird to you or anything? Does it?"

"No! Quite the contrary. It means . . . what happened to Mason is never going to happen to you. I can let my guard down around you. Be myself. It's kind of awesome, to be honest."

I nod, and she laughs, letting go of me. "Oh, good, you *can* smile."

Once the sun sets all the way, Kalea declares, "It's time," and hops off the picnic table. She walks to Squire's Castle and motions for me to help her up. I lift her by her hips. She digs her sneakers into the jutting masonry and climbs up the rest of the way through an arrow-slit window into the turret of the main spire. I do the same for Clark, then follow up on my own. The conical turret on the castle's tower is hollow inside, but there's no direct access to it from the ground. That hasn't stopped kids from covering the walls with scratched graffiti and littering the floor with cigarette butts and smashed beer bottles.

"Cool clubhouse," I grunt.

Kalea snorts and sits in a lotus position in the middle of the floor, crossing one leg over the other. "It's all I've got in this nowhere town. For what I'm doing I need height and quiet. And this." She holds up the plush cloud I got from her locker. "I can get . . . lost, out there."

"Out there?"

"In the clouds." She holds the plush in her lap with both hands and squeezes it tight. "I need the tactile sensation, the soft fur, the squishiness, so I remain anchored to the grou . . ."

Her eyes are still open, but her head lolls to the side, like she's fallen asleep midword. I step forward, reaching out to her, but Clark stops me with a hand.

"Freaky, right? But that's how she does it. Touching the cloud keeps her brain connected to her body." Clark sighs. "Before she figured that out, she could stay like that for days. Freaked Mom out. Sent her to all these hospitals for, like, sleep disorders because that's what she thought it was. But then, finally, Generation Zero found her. I'm the only one she told about them," he adds, beaming. The little brother let in on the big kids' secrets. "After she went to Gen Zero camp, Mom just thought she was cured. And we like it that way."

"Yes, Cronus, it's me, Cloud," Kalea says in a strong, assertive voice unlike any I've heard out of her mouth before.

"Cronus is in charge of Generation Zero," Clark whispers. "I've never met him. She says he's really cool, a slightly older kid—like seventeen or something."

Her head is still resting on her shoulder. "I've come across a psiot that needs your help. PRS has already tried to nab him. They've tried to nab me and my brother just for knowing about him. No, I don't think they know about my powers, not yet. Here, I'm opening the relevant memories to you. You see? Yes, that's him. Yes, he's with me now. I'm sharing my location with you . . . You will? Yes. Absolutely. Thank you. Thank you so much, Cronus. You're the best."

She squeezes the plush cloud extra tight in her hands and straightens her neck. She blinks and shakes her head. "All right! Well, I thought I'd have to argue for you a bit more, but Cronus says he's sending a first-contact team right away. Thirty minutes or less."

"Like a pizza," I say suspiciously. "Convenient. Their headquarters nearby?"

Kalea shrugs. "Doesn't need to be. Not with some of these kids' powers."

The longest twenty-eight minutes of my life ensue—at least in my memory, ha ha. The tower room is tiny and smells like month-old dried booze. I want to wait for them outside in the fresh air, but Kalea tells me to sit tight—that's what Cronus said.

Whatever help Cronus is going to give me better be worth all this bossing around.

SEVEN

When Generation Zero arrives—wait, no, that's not right. They don't "arrive." They don't come in through a door or even crash through the roof.

They're not here, and then, all of a sudden, they are.

There are three of them—a really young Black girl, about Clark's age, with a wild curly mane and a scowl; a white kid slightly older than her, with a shaved head and an Indiana Pacers jersey two sizes too big for him; and the oldest is a Latina girl wearing a cowboy hat, denim jacket, plus boots to match. They appear in the tower room so abruptly none of us have time to act surprised.

Cowgirl is clearly in charge. Kalea runs up and embraces her. "Oh, wow, Telic, he sent you? That's fantastic. This—this is the one I was talking about. This is Bloodshot."

Telic doesn't budge a muscle, even to return Kalea's hug. "I don't need you to tell me who he is," she says. "Animalia?"

The youngest girl steps toward me, and—

—and—

—and I don't really *see* what happens. A grayish mist suddenly envelops her, streaking out at me, but it smashes into me as hard as a giant fist. Back I go, into the arrow slit behind me, and through it. The stone around it crumples around me. I feel my shoulder blades scream and my ribs crack and suddenly I am in the air and out of the tower and falling with the masonry down to the concrete ground and I am bouncing across it in pain and in a *lot* of freaking pain—

Telic is suddenly over me as I lie looking up at the night sky. Her snakeskin bootheel digs into my already-cracked ribs. I can feel my body trying to stitch the busted bones back together again, but it still hurts more than anything.

"What'd you do with Pulse, Bloodshot?" she yells at me.

"What is a Pulse?" I yell back, and lash out at her with a fist, but suddenly she's not there anymore.

I really wish she were because then she'd be in the way of what I'm seeing right now, which is the tower exploding outward, and a foot and a leg and a torso the size of a small house are now climbing out of the cascading masonry of the spire. Hopefully Kalea and Clark are okay, but I don't see them. I get to my feet, and Telic is next to me out of nowhere again, striking my ribs with an open palm. They burn with pain. They'll never heal straight this way, no matter how fast my body works. I'm pretty sure she knows that.

Telic comes close to my ear. "You haven't met Animalia yet, have you? She's pretty amazing. Her psiot trick is projecting solid psychic shells of whatever she can imagine around her own body. And the thing about this kid is, she watches a *lot* of anime." I spin around and lash a kick out, but I hit air and see a denim blur moving far away from me.

The air is full of rock dust from the now-collapsed tower, and out of it steps a horrific titanic zombie many stories tall, with rotting skin and exposed muscles and bones and, thank goodness, a smooth nothing where its private parts should be. I've never seen anything like it before, and I am very glad of that fact.

Telic is now on my other side, hitting me in fresh ribs. I throw a jab at her face—or wherever her face should be but isn't. She's just to the left of me, kicking me square in the chest, knocking the wind out of me, sending me to the ground again.

"Pulse? Where is she?" Telic asks.

"Are you speaking in code?" I gasp. I see movement out of the corner of my eye. Kalea and Clark rush toward me from the parking lot, yelling. How did they get to the parking lot? Time and space have abandoned me. Logic too.

"Headspace!" Telic yells out. "Keep them away from here!"

This time, I actually see what happens. A head-shaped warp in the night appears between Clark and Kalea, and Pacers-jersey guy leans out of it and grabs my friends' hands, and then suddenly the cleft in reality collapses in on itself, and all three figures wink out of existence.

What the hell is happening? It's like fighting fairy tales. Give me gun-toting goons any day.

At least Telic turned her back to me to yell at Headspace. I get up, scissor-kick cocked, when a giant titan foot slams into my midriff from below, and I get a very brief idea of what it's like to fly, sailing up and over the nearby treetops, turning over and over.

"What are you doing?" I barely hear Telic cry below. "I had him handled!"

Animalia yells something, but now I'm dropping out of the sky, smashing through tree branches and cutting and bruising as I try to grab onto one to break my fall, but they all snap off in my hands. I land, and I land hard, on a packed-earth walking path, and on impact, screaming agony ripples up and down my broken ribs like someone smashing down on the keys of a grand piano with their face.

I should get up and off the path and out of sight. I really should. I flex my fingers. Stretch my arms. No digits or limbs are broken. I am able to stand up, though my torso feels like someone poured crude oil all over it and lit it on fire.

I look at my tombstone-white hands as I pull myself into the woods and get an idea. I lean against a big elm and concentrate, and I am able to shift my color into the mottled mahogany of the bark of the trees and pale green of the poison ivy at my feet. I sit down on the roots of the elm with my back against the trunk and tell my body to hurry up and heal already.

Why the heck did these kids attack me without so much as a hello? Telic said she already knew who I was. And whoever I am, she doesn't like me very much. Did Kalea set me up? No, her and Clark's faces looked as surprised as mine probably did.

Could . . . could Cronus somehow know I have feelings for Kalea? No, no. For one thing, that's totally insane. For another, I don't know if I have any feelings for Kalea, not really. She's literally the first person I've ever met.

I reach to my waist but don't find the Beretta. Must have fallen out either when I got drop-kicked by Superzombie or in my subsequent fall through the trees. No huge surprise.

"Animalia, eye in the sky!" Telic yells in the distance, and with an earsplitting howl, flapping above me is another cartoon horror, a giant crow-like thing with the white-spiked hair of an anime warlock.

Boots crunch on the path beyond my view, and I take a peek around the tree: Telic is there—how is she so fricking *fast*—taking a few steps off the trail, looking around like she doesn't know where I am. But she finds the Beretta in the ferns and takes it in hand.

"Last time Pulse checked in with Cronus, she said you were on her heels," she calls out. "Don't tell me you don't know what happened to her. You take her to the Nursery? You kill her? Why don't you just tell us? You usually take more pride in your work, Bloodshot!"

Okay, wait, so this "Pulse," she's a person. Another psiot—a Generation Zero member. That sparking lightning figure in my lone memory—could it have been a girl? Could be.

"Listen, all my memories got wiped yesterday!" I call out. "You have to listen to me, I don't—"

Telic turns and shoots my Beretta right at the sound of my voice, and I just barely pull my head back before the bullet calves a bunch of bark off the tree.

"*Telic, stop!*" I hear a voice cry out. Kalea.

"Cloud, I need you to stay out of this," Telic calls. "What'd you do to Headspace?"

"I put him in Quiet Time. You have to talk to me, not just yell orders! I know you and Cronus and the rest of Generation Zero can be really, I don't know, supermilitant psycho or whatever, but how can you do this to another psiot?"

"Another . . ." Telic laughs. "Oh, wow. Are you serious? You think he's another psiot? Is that the story he told you?"

"He didn't tell me any story. It's like he just said. We found him in the woods. He doesn't know anything. His mind—I checked. Or . . . tried to, anyway. It's completely blank."

"It's a trick. It's a PRS trick."

"Telic, he saved me and Clark from PRS!"

"*Cloud, he is PRS!* He is their best weapon against us! A relentless, remorseless psiot hunter! He's like a bogeyman for ESPers because none of us can read his mind! Do not let your guard down around him. This kid is not your friend."

"Sure, I heard about the psiot hunter at camp, but . . . PRS is after him too."

"Have you *seen* them try and capture him? Or did he just *tell* you that?"

Cloud—er, Kalea hesitates. I know she knows she never saw my fight at the old factory. Just the bullet holes in my shirt. She struggles to voice a response, and Telic is totally focused on her now.

"Pulse was on a mission for Cronus, and he tracked her down! She last made contact three weeks ago, and we haven't heard from her since! Cronus doesn't want you to end up like her. Look—my mind is open to you. Raid my memories, learn what I know about him directly from my brain if you don't believe me."

I see my chance. I charge out from behind the tree and rush at Telic through the ferns. She doesn't even flinch my way. I lower a shoulder and plant it right in her solar plexus. The breath flies out of her lungs, and she crashes on her back in the path. When she tries to sit back up, her eyes glassy, I smash a fist across her jaw, and she goes down.

"Are you all right?" I ask before I look at Kalea and can see with my own two eyes that she is most definitely *not* all right, but not for any reason I can perceive.

"She—she was showing me," Kalea is saying, blinking tears from her eyes. "That's the only reason you could get the drop on her—she was in my mind . . ."

"She was showing you what?"

"Showing me you! What—what you really are."

"No, c'mon, Kalea. You know me. You know what I really am!"

"They—Generation Zero—have security footage of you—stalking psiots—fighting psiots—subduing psiots—killing . . ." She puts her hands to her head. "And you've—*I've* been helping *you*?"

"Yes, thank you, and I've needed your help, Kalea, and I still need your help—"

"Look, Bloodshot," she whispers through tears, "look at what you've done."

She said she can't manipulate me the way she can other minds, but she's not receiving now, she's transmitting a scream in the form of images, of sounds—overlapping each other so rapidly that I don't have time to breathe.

I'm in a gym locker room. A teenage Black boy with spider braids and chains and an ear full of studs is bent over, tying his shoelaces. He hears me coming. He looks up.

He doesn't say anything, but as my shadow falls over him, he squints, and I feel a slight twinge in a few random parts of my body—my left hip, my jaw, my right big toe. But that's it. He looks surprised, but not for long because my chalk-white hand lashes out and smacks him across the face.

He stays awake just long enough for me to smash his head into the lockers behind him, and then the memory ends—his memory.

"That was Spike," I can hear Kalea say. The crazy thing is that Kalea and the woods are still around me, but they're flat, two-dimensional, like the backdrop of a school play. In front, in the foreground, is the important stuff.

The bad stuff.

There's a teenage Asian girl in front of me. She has a ponytail and a white dress with flowers sewn around the collar. We're in a windowless room wallpapered in children's drawings. A big boat with animals going into it—Noah's Ark? A man getting off a camel to help another man fallen by the side of the road—the Good Samaritan? Am I in a Sunday school? She's picking up pieces of paper and flats of finger paints and thick markers off knee-high tables and putting them on shelves. I'm helping her. We're the only ones in the room, and we're chatting.

Then we're not. Fear darkens her face like a sudden storm cloud covering the sun. I've done something to tip her off. She fades from my view as if a giant eraser rubbed her out.

I must have been expecting this because there are still paints in my hand. I throw them outward and cover the room in a multichromatic spray—in the air in front of me appears a blue-yellow arm, a purple-yellow shoulder, and a pink-black patch on a back, rainbow splashed. She's trying to sprint for the door.

I reach my arm out, and from a sleeve holster a Taser pistol pops into my hand. I fire at the fleeing disembodied back, and it is embodied with a scream. The rest of the girl comes into view, and she drops, twitching, onto the floor.

"That was Shadow," Kalea says, and now someone else is screaming. It's Clark. He's belting his sister with his hands, yelling.

"Kalea, stop it, what are you doing? Stop shame-bombing him, he needs our help!"

"No," Kalea says, pushing her brother away. "It's Bloodshot! The Nightmare Hunter. He's the worst sort of psiot, one who tracks down other psiots for his masters at PRS! None of these kids Telic showed me were ever heard from again!"

I'm at a party in the woods. A bunch of kids around a keg are drinking from red Solo cups, and what little light there is is coming from little bonfires made from a pile of cardboard six-pack cartons set ablaze. I'm drinking with the rest of them. There's a lot of talk about the future. Impromptu high school graduation party. I'm chatting and laughing up a storm. Everyone here thinks they know me.

They don't. I'm waiting for one white girl to leave. She wears fishnets and combat boots and smoky eyes and a leather jacket, dark-blue hair combed over her eyes like she can hide from the world. She's got ripped jeans and a black T-shirt with white lettering that says STRONG FEMALE PROTAGONIST. She bids farewell to the others and heads out through the woods alone.

I follow. The trees get closer and closer together, and the sounds of the party get more and more distant behind me.

To my surprise, she stops first. She turns, sees me. Smiles.

—Hi, Bloodshot.

A blue fire ignites behind her eyes.

—Yeah, I made you a few hours ago. I can sense electrical impulses, you know? And you're lit up like a Christmas tree.

The fire branches out from her eyes, flaring out across her face like a mask of light.

—I just wanted to get you a safe distance away from my friends before I asked you to dance.

It's like I can see her nervous system suddenly light up, like she's all glowing nerves and nothing else—lightning shoots out of her fingers and flickers across the forest floor like a Tesla coil.

—What do you say, tough guy? *Let's dance.*

Just like before, my retinas are overwhelmed by light, and I can't see anymore. I stagger back. When I put my hands to my head to massage the throbbing, I feel the wetness around my eyes. I've been crying.

"That was Pulse," Kalea says. "Seems like she's the only one you haven't nabbed. She beat you. Fried your memories. And got away. What happened to her? Tell me!"

"*I don't know!*" I yell.

I step toward her, and she leaps back like she's been shocked. "Stay away from me!"

She grabs Clark by his jacket and pulls him away, running back down the path. I feel something crucial slipping from me, like I'm bleeding out or can't breathe, but I can't make my legs move for fear that might cause the final break, the final straw that scares her away altogether.

Once I do finally put one foot forward, there's a great distant shriek, and a giant cartoon bird swoops down and grabs Kalea's and Clark's shoulders in its talons and flies away with mighty flaps.

I hear a scrape on the path behind me. I turn around to see Headspace gathering up Telic's unconscious body behind me. He gives me the finger.

"Don't go too far, psiot hunter," he says in a Midwestern drawl. "We're coming back with reinforcements."

Reality shimmers around his head, rippling out in layer after layer of visual distortion, like the heat mirage coming off burning blacktop. He and Telic are gone, like forgotten ideas.

All of a sudden, I can't hear anything except the crickets. Chirping seventeen times in fourteen seconds. The temperature dropped a degree. The stars blaze down on me from a completely black sky. There isn't even a moon.

For the first time since my awakening, I am completely and utterly alone.

EIGHT

I decide not to stick around to see if Headspace makes good on his threat. I run through the woods and don't stop until I twist an ankle leaping over the metal guardrail of a highway and fall down a steep slope into a shallow bog. Frogs leap into the brackish water, and grackles take flight with a caw. I sit in the damp squish and catch my breath.

So this is what it's like. To *be* chased. From what Kalea just shared with me, seems like I'm much more used to being the one *doing* the chasing.

I get up slowly. Is that all there is to life? Hunting, or being hunted? I can't say either is a lot of fun. At least when you're the one doing the hunting, there's a feeling of control. What you decide matters.

I make my way through the swamp. It takes all my strength to pull my boots up out of the sucking mud with each step. I see the bulk of darkened buildings through the trees and head in that direction, if only to have something resembling a destination in mind.

The sting of Kalea's rejection still lingers, but maybe it's a good thing, really. No, I know that sounds like I'm trying to convince myself. But it was my desire to keep her and Clark safe that made me stick around them in the first place. Put a target on my back. Allowed both PRS and Generation Zero to find me.

But now she hates me too. Good. Right? Now I have no one holding me back. No obligations. I can just . . . take off. Do whatever. Let Gen Zero and PRS duke it out. Not my problem. Both that PRS stooge and Telic called me a "weapon." An object. Something made to be used by an actual person.

Well, forget that. I'm through being used. I don't care which side wins, gun thugs or psiots. They're both crazy and deserve each other, as far as I'm concerned. I mean, sure, the psiots are just kids, and PRS has all the guns and government behind them.

But so what! Then it's inevitable. The kids are doomed. I don't have to actively go out and hunt them for the authorities, but I don't have to join their little Rebel Alliance or whatever it is either.

I can just, you know. Strike out on my own. With no ID, no memory, no family, and skin the color of Grandma's fine china. Sure, I can give myself a human skin tone, any human skin tone, really, but with effort, and it'll make me so hungry I'll have to clean out an all-you-can-eat buffet afterward.

I stifle a laugh at my stupidity. Yep, and with all that and the right attitude, I can become the first melanin-free president of the United States. And, of course, I am already starving again as I heal from the beating Superzombie/Animalia gave me.

I reach the fence surrounding the property. Based on the smell and the mud compound beyond the barbed wire, it's a small farm of some kind. I climb up and swing over. The barbs hurt when they tear open my skin, but I'm used to bleeding by now, and the lacerations are half-healed by the time my feet hit the ground.

A few sheep wander out of the nearest structure and blink at me, then go back inside one of a trio of barns. They have no fear of me whatsoever, which is both strange and very appreciated. I could get used to this. Maybe I could become a shepherd. Are shepherds still a thing?

Painted on the side of the barn nearest me is a child's crude mural of kids holding hands and hooves with farm animals. "Unity Fields: Cultivating Enduring Life Skills Through Farm Experiences" is printed underneath. I see pigs, goats, and even a large llama.

I stagger inside that barn. Leaning against the wall near the door is a big sack labeled "Livestock Probiotic Feed." The top is partially ripped open; inside, a big metal scoop is stuffed into a big pile of brown pellets.

Before my brain finishes the thought that, hey, maybe this isn't such a great idea, my body tells it to shut the heck up, and my hands are shoving into the bag and cramming animal feed into my mouth. It's got a sour, nutty taste, like a breakfast cereal that's trying too hard to be good for you. A sheep shaped like a wine cork hears the crunch of the bag and waddles up to me. I'm not some greedy bastard. I give a handful to the sheep, who sucks it down with its slimy, lipless mouth; then I swallow a handful for myself. A couple of goats figure out what's going on and join the party, and the llama too, and between the lot of us, we polish off the whole bag in maybe fifteen minutes. Not the best or most dignified meal I've ever had, but it shut my hunger up, which is all I care about.

My usefulness to them over, the livestock trot away and go back to sleep in the mud of the yard. That gritty feed was as dry as all heck, so I have to find a hose outside to wash out my mouth. Back in the barn, I find an unoccupied stall with poop-free straw. I sit down in it with my back against the wall, and all of a sudden, my limbs feel like they're ten thousand pounds. I still haven't slept. I still worry that if I do, my memories will get wiped again, and when I wake up, I'll be right where I started. Nowhere.

I go over what memories I do have again to maybe reinforce them so I can't lose them so easily by sleeping. What do I know? Sounds like I, the Psiot Hunter, tried to get the jump on this Pulse, and she fried my circuits, so to speak, and wiped my memories. Didn't Telic say she'd been missing for three weeks, though? I couldn't have been lying in that clearing for that long before Kalea and Clark found me. But what did happen to Pulse? Generation Zero doesn't have her, and if she knocked me out, why would PRS have her? If I could somehow track her down on my own and save her, maybe I could bring her back to Kalea and prove to her I'm not the monster she thinks I am.

I spit out the last few remaining flakes of animal feed. Just this morning I was enjoying a McEverything, and a few hours ago, my friends and I were laughing in the park.

I shake my head. Dummy. You're getting nostalgic for stuff that happened literally today. What are you thinking? Kalea is a trap. Forget her. She's gone now. You have to be independent of everybody. No connections. It's the only way to keep yourself safe. And everyone else safe, for that matter.

A strange sound makes me start. I look around, but it's only when I lower my knee that I see the cat. Mostly reddish brown, with black blotches all over its fur, including over one eye. It's sitting in the straw of the barn and looking at me. It cries again, a little strangled half meow, half squawk.

I wave it away, but instead it stands and walks closer. Cats. Why are their favorite people always the ones who don't want anything to do with them?

The cat sits again and stares up at me.

"I'm bad news, you know," I say out loud. "Everyone seems to think so. Nobody who sticks by me has anything good happen to them. Including me."

The cat puts one paw up and taps my knee a little bit.

I shrug. "It's your funeral, fleabag."

The cat jumps into my lap and stretches its back, kneading my legs with its claws. I can feel its purr throughout my entire body. Against my better judgment, I reach out and stroke its furry head. The purring gets louder. It rubs its nose and mouth across my fingers.

"Don't say I didn't warn you."

As the cat curls up in my lap, I lean my head against the wall of the barn. I close my eyes. Is it safe to sleep?

Pulse. She's the key. If I could just find her, I feel like I could make this whole thing right.

I learn I can sleep. But I guess I don't dream.

A sudden scream awakens me. I don't even know if *scream* is the right word. Just a piercing tone, high and sustained, that couldn't have possibly been made by anything living. Yet it's coming from within my mind.

Just as it fades, gunshots. Three extended bursts.

A girl screams.

"Tango down, tango down!" The man's voice is distant, muffled.

I bolt upright. The cat, startled, bounds out of my lap and into the darkness of the yard. I look around. I don't see anything except farm animals ignoring me.

But I hear the crunch of sneakers on gravel.

A thud, a cry, a bigger thud.

"I got the little one!" yells a much closer man.

"Get off me!" screams a voice I recognize. Kalea's.

Struggling, grunting, cursing.

"Tranq her ass!" cries a woman's voice in the distance.

Thupp! I don't hear anything that sounds like Kalea anymore.

I stand up. I'm pretty sure I know what's going on.

"Kalea's iPhone," I ask out loud, "where is Kalea?"

Where Kalea is is forty-six degrees Fahrenheit, or, if you prefer, 7.8 degrees Celsius.

I jog out of the barn.

Where Kalea is is eight minutes past oh-two-hundred hours, Eastern Daylight Time.

In the yard I break into a run. A curly-horned ram is zonked out in a small doghouse-shaped structure, which I jump onto, the big boy awaking with a bleat; then I spring off and over the barbed wire fence to the hill beyond.

Where Kalea is is forty degrees forty-one minutes north, eighty degrees fifty-six minutes west.

I run up the hill, digging my bootheels into the wet earth, sprinting toward the top, hands like blades cutting through the air.

"Thank you, Kalea's iPhone," I say.

The phone doesn't make a reply, but I have an image of a round yellow head with a blushing face in my mind.

“Whoa, whoa, look: Blondie tried to call somebody.”

“Who?” asks a hollow voice, as if muffled by a tin can. “Our guy?”

“I don’t know, some 1-800 number. Doesn’t look like it went through, though.”

“Well, don’t stand there looking at me with your mouth open, dumbass,” growls Scary Voice. “Turn it off.”

“Okay, Red Cell. Sorry, Red Cell.”

Click.

Silence.

Too late, gun-toting goons.

You were dumb enough to make yourselves my mission.

Now there’s nowhere you can hide from me.

NINE

About four klicks down the road from the petting zoo, I find a roadside saloon, the Iron Horse. It's late. The guitar solo coming from the jukebox inside is louder than the handful of remaining patrons. Three big dudes in chains and leather jackets are on the porch, smoking cigarettes and drinking pint glasses by a row of formidable motorcycles. They're the old-school kind, requiring a physical key for the ignition.

A bald biker with a Civil War general's massive bushy beard is facing me as I approach, and he watches me walk the last half mile. He stops talking when he sees me turn into the dirt parking lot, and his two friends see his face and hear the crunch of my boots on the gravel and turn around and face me just as I walk right up to them.

"Shee-it, boy," the tallest, hairiest one says at the sight of me, "that's some makeup. You a mime or something?"

"Which one of you has the fastest bike?" I ask them.

They look at each other. "They're all pretty much the same make," says the third guy, who's wearing green sunglasses at two a.m. for some reason, "not that it's any business of yours."

I nod. "I should probably apologize for this, but I'm not really good at that, and I'm in a big hurry, so," I say, and then punch the guy who spoke in his nose, shattering his glasses and laying him flat on his back.

The biggest guy cries out and reaches for me, but I step between his hands and uppercut him just below his solar plexus. His breath isn't completely done exploding out of his lungs before I grab him by his hips and flip him upside down and piledrive him headfirst into the porch, splintering the wood.

Bald Boy's shadow falls over the front of me, a knife coming out of his belt sheath, so I lash my foot back and into his jaw. He's stumbling back as I turn around and ram my fist into his throat as hard as I can. I feel his trachea collapse beneath my knuckles. He drops the blade, and I snatch it in midair. It's a pretty slick high-carbon steel hunting knife. I point it at him as he gurgles and gasps. He's breathing, but he can't get air down into his windpipe.

"Listen up," I say very calmly. "You are going to suffocate in less than a minute unless I save you. Which bike is yours?"

He hesitates, choking, turning blue. He bumps up against the porch post. He clutches at his neck, but it doesn't do him any good.

"Hey. Buddy. Look at my face. This isn't optional."

He sputters out blood and spit and points at the third bike from me.

"Keys."

He reaches into his right-hand pocket, but his arm is shaking, so I pull them out myself.

"Hold still." I grab him by one shoulder to steady him against the porch post, and I stab him in the trachea right below where I made the break. Breath wheezes through his body from the hole instead of his mouth. He drops to his knees, gasping gratefully. In the doorway I can see other patrons approaching, their faces struggling with whether to get involved.

"Thanks. I wish I could say I'm going to bring your ride back in one piece, but . . . I'm not."

I get on the hog and fire up the ignition just as the other bikers rush out of the bar, followed by a bartender with a hunting rifle. I gun the bike forward onto the porch, making them scatter before I smash through the railing and roar out onto the road. I hear one futile shot behind me.

I open the throttle all the way, and the trees and streetlamps on the side of the road flatten into a blurred ribbon. Just because the connection to Kalea's iPhone was cut off doesn't mean I can't still track her using its GPS. Ever since I reached the highway on foot, they've moved her and, presumably, any other captives they nabbed with her. I don't have much time.

—

Where Kalea is is thirty-seven degrees Fahrenheit, or, if you prefer, 2.78 degrees Celsius.

Where Kalea is is eighteen degrees Fahrenheit, or, if you prefer, negative 7.7 degrees Celsius.

Where Kalea is is zero degrees Fahrenheit, or, if you prefer—

"I do *not* prefer, Kalea's iPhone, thank you." Kalea's local temperature has been dropping rapidly for the last eight minutes, even as her speed remains constant at around seventy miles per hour (or, if you prefer, 113 kilometers every 100 minutes—metric time, why did you never catch on?) in a relatively straight path along what is clearly a highway.

I am easily clocking over 110 mph on my bike, passing at least one speed-trap cop car that tries booking after me, siren screaming, before I leave him in my deafening wake.

My mind reaches out across the same satellite network I am snatching Kalea's signal off of and expands the map. They are transporting her in what is presumably a refrigerated truck, not on an interstate, but on local highways. So this is not a cross-country haul. They are bringing her to a local destination. I scan the map for likely possibilities. The nearest airport is in the opposite direction. Arrows fan out from Kalea's blip on the map. Plenty of abandoned warehouses and factories on the route. Even more jails and police stations. Two private airstrips, one for a twin-prop flying school.

Then I see a blinking red box with the most direct route: Capshaw Air Force Base. At eight thousand acres, a big one. At current speed and distance, Kalea will arrive there in fifteen minutes, assuming that's her final destination.

There's no way those little gyros they sent to grab me have enough fuel for long-distance flight. When it's not tormenting American schoolchildren with standardized testing, PRS is a defense subcontractor. They could be using honest-to-Washington military bases as launching pads for further supply runs.

It's logical, but logical doesn't mean right. Little about the world is logical. I've been conscious for just over twenty-four hours, and I've already figured that out.

But I am not going to catch up to them on my current course, so it doesn't matter whether I'm right or not. I've got to guess their route and triangulate an interception point between here and there. Sure, I could try to grab them after they pass through the AFB gates. Can I take on the United States Air Force and win? Maybe. I'd rather not bet Kalea's and Clark's lives on me finding out the hard way, though.

I find an interception point on the map ten kilometers ahead of the current route of the transport—assuming I've guessed their destination right. I have three minutes to make it and cut PRS off.

I turn off the highway at the first gap in the railing I see and gun the bike into the woods, smashing through a flimsy wood fence and into a backyard, veering to avoid slamming into the aboveground swimming pool on the other side. I roar through other backyards. Dogs bark at me, then flee in yipping terror when I jet through. Flying through an employee parking lot behind a strip mall, I cut through an intersection between endless ribbons of fast-food joints, forcing a bunch of cars to slam on the brakes to avoid hitting me.

I come up on my interception point—an overpass of a local road over the highway—way too fast and squeeze hard on the brakes. I fishtail into the lane next to me, making an approaching pickup swerve and smash into the concrete parapet. The I-beams it was carrying in the flatbed come spilling out, and the furious driver opens his door and tears his trucker hat off his head.

"You son of a—what are you on? You coulda killed me!"

I ignore him. I look over the bridge onto the highway. The blip is approaching fast—in fact, it should almost be on top of me. Night is about to cross over into dawn, and all eight lanes below me are moving fast, bumper to bumper.

She's in a refrigerated car. There are scores of semitrucks and tractor trailers approaching me, passing under my bridge, but I don't see anything that looks refrigerated—no beer truck, not even a Mister Softee.

Meanwhile, the truck driver has got his phone out. He's taking photos of me and the bike's license plate. "I already called the cops, man! You're messing with the wrong guy!"

Kalea's blip is almost on top of mine on the map. Then, just as we're about to converge, I see it:

A long dark-blue semi with the blazing white AccuChieve logo on it.

Its cab is passing under the bridge as I lurch the bike around in the other direction and gun it right at the pickup driver. He screams and dives out of my way, leaving me clear to drive up onto the I-beams spilling out of his flatbed and launch over the chain-link fence lining the bridge.

The AccuChieve truck is already halfway out from the overpass by the time I'm airborne. I swear I'm not going to let it get away from me.

So I leap off the bike.

My hand grabs the rear edge of the trailer as I hear my bike bounce and crash into the car behind me. The latch for the back doors is too far below me to reach, so I haul myself up onto the top of the truck.

I'm gasping for breath, on my back, in a perfect position to see the buglike gyro descend out of the graying sky above me, the Minigun mounted under the cockpit spinning to life. I am aware of radio chatter erupting all around me.

"Did you see that? Bogey just jumped onto the back of the—holy—it's Bloodshot! I'm not takin' any chances!"

I am on my feet and sprinting toward the front of the trailer just as the Minigun whines to life and spits death at the spot where I once was.

"Eye in the sky, ceasefire, I repeat, ceasefire! You damage the assets inside that rig, and Red Cell'll make sure your life ain't worth a bucket of warm spit! Let the ground crews handle it."

Ground crews?

The Minigun's whine cuts short sharply, but all of a sudden,

I am flooded by light from down below. A quartet of formerly innocuous-looking passenger vehicles, all different makes and models, have floodlights mounted on their roofs that all train on me at once. The shadows of arms with assault rifles fall over me and open fire just as I reach the edge of the trailer and drop down between it and the cab, the fusillade missing me completely.

Riding now on the flat platform between the two front sets of wheels, I see the floodlights on the pace cars darting wildly, trying to pick me up again. I could try to climb back up and into the tractor and replace the driver. But that would leave me open to several seconds' worth of fire.

Three spiraling wires—red, blue, and green—connect the front of the trailer to the back of the tractor. I yank all three of these out at once with one hand. Hydraulics hiss and hot air burns the side of my face, but I pay it no mind, not when I am about to do something even stupider.

I crouch down and reach under the trailer, where a raised plate attaches the trailer to the tractor. Comms chatter continues in the background, but I barely pay attention to it:

"Red Cell, should we open fire? He seems to be trying to hide under the trailer."

"Negative," breathes the same hollow voice as before. "Might hit the tires or damage the assets. In about a half klick, we should be able to turn off the highway, and we can light his ass up away from any pain-in-the-ass witnesses."

I don't need a half klick, boys. There's a hole in the side of the plate for a large key to be inserted. I don't have a key, but I do have a high-carbon steel hunting knife. I unfold it and find the blade just fits into the slot, letting me crank the plate lower until the pin attaching the trailer to the tractor is released.

"Wait—what is he doing? No, no, no, tell me he isn't actually trying to—"

Unyoked from its burden, the tractor cab zooms out from under it at seventy miles an hour, nearly taking me with it, but my hand passes the flailing green coil and I grab onto it just as the front of the massive trailer drops onto the ground, spitting up a cascade of orange sparks. The rear buckles, the wheels squeal, and the back pinwheels into the trailing SUV with the floodlight and the guns. A voice on the radio screams and goes silent as the vehicle explodes into shrapnel.

I grab the red cable too and hold on for dear life as the trailer starts tumbling, over and over, off the highway and down an embankment until finally it stops with a crash, right side up, in a stream dribbling out of a metal cistern by the side of the road.

I let go of the cables and drop on my side into the rust-colored water. My head is spinning from the sudden upside-down, topsy-turvy trip down the slope, but I manage to put one foot in front of the other, hugging the side of the trailer. Out of the corner of my eye, I can see the gyro swooping down, and I remember it won't risk opening fire and hitting the trailer itself.

I reach the back of the trailer just as the rear doors pop open, and two guards stagger out. I grab the edge of the door nearest me, smash it into the head of the first one out, and drop him into the shallow water. The other tries to point his XM7 rifle at me, but his head is spinning too, so I smash him in his sternum, grab the rifle by the strap, and slam him headfirst into the ground.

"Wait—wait!"

I hear her before I point the rifle into the back of the trailer. A woman with glasses and dreadlocks pulled back in a scrunchie is sitting up on the metal floor. She's got both hands up.

I start to say something, but what I see behind her distracts me. Mounted along the trailer, from end to end, are eight cylindrical meter-tall containers, four on each side, with small viewing windows set at different heights. Through the windows I can see five currently occupied—with Telic, Headspace, Animalia, Kalea, and Clark. Their eyes are closed, as if they're asleep.

I step over the fallen woman. She flinches, but I ignore her and proceed to Kalea's tube. I grasp the handle to open it, but the woman says, "Ray! Don't!"

It hits harder than any bullet—the name. "Ray?"

"The assets have achieved full cryopreservation. If you open the stasis chambers, expose them to room-temperature air, that could cause irreparable cell damage. The younger ones, in particular, won't survive."

"You can thaw them from inside here, though?"

She swallows. "I mean—I—"

I shoot over her head, and she yelps. "Why would you do that to me?! Ray, you *know* me, I—"

I point the muzzle of the XM7 at her. "Remind me."

"Nina? You don't—" Her jaw drops. "Oh, is that—is that why you've turned against us? Are you—oh, this is all a huge misunderstanding."

Nina flinches as I place the end of the still-hot muzzle on her forehead. "Show me how to free them."

"You—need this key card." Nina jiggles the ID on the lanyard around her neck. "And voice recognition."

"Do it."

"Ray, listen, that's a really bad idea."

"Thanks for your input. Do it or I'll kill you."

Nina looks into my red eyes and doesn't see any doubt there. With a wince she rises to her feet. She limps over to a console covered in flickering screens. She shows a barcode on the bottom of her ID to a laser reader, and a beep sounds.

"Perlin, Nina. Revive assets."

A hiss from the tubes, and a countdown appears on one of the screens. Fifteen minutes. I groan. In combat, fifteen minutes is a lifetime.

I can hear the screech of tires up on the embankment, shouts. Chatter on the comms converging. The rest of the mobile ground crew has circled back and is preparing an assault on my position.

Nina watches my mind work through my face. "They'll be here long before this countdown ends. You should just surrender. It's the best for everybody. Including these kids."

When I don't say anything, she takes that as license to keep talking. "Red Cell—Dodge is with them. He's never been your biggest fan. If you stay with me, we can talk, we can figure out why you've been acting so—erratically. If it's a . . . memory issue, we can fix that too. You've been talking to Cronus, haven't you? Ray, that kid is out of his mind. Whatever he's told you are lies. If you stand down, I can protect you. If you keep acting like a mad dog . . . somebody's going to try and put you down."

My mind races. My eyes fixate on the ID card around Nina's neck. In addition to the barcode, it has her name, her face, and the title "Field Medic" on it. "Anyone out there got one of those cards that can operate the console?"

"No, only me. Field medical decisions can only be made by field medics. You see? Your father's not a complete monster. Not what Cronus says he is."

My . . . father.

I can hear the PRS goons trying and failing to slide down the embankment silently. I see the light shining down from the gyro overhead outside the open trailer doors.

I tear the lanyard with the ID on it off Nina's neck.

"If anything happens to those kids in the next fifteen minutes, I am going to hold you personally responsible. And if you haven't noticed, I am extremely persistent."

Nina sighs. "Ray, it doesn't have to be this way."

"Funny how the people shouting orders always say that. You're lucky you have a bum ankle, or I'd make you come with me."

She doesn't look too thrilled by that info. "I'm pretty sure it's broken."

I stick my head out of the back of the trailer and see the gyro overhead. I blow out its spotlight with one shot. Cursing on the comms.

Before I run, I look back at Nina, leaning up against the console. "What's my father's name?"

"Ray Garrison. Same as yours."

I don't know why, but that feels significant. That all this persecution and corruption would have such a direct connection to me.

Once again, Nina fills my hesitation with words. "Do you have anything you want me to tell your father if I see him?"

I think about it. "Yeah. Tell him I'm disappointed in him. Very disappointed."

I sprint out into the night.

TEN

I sprint out of the back of the trailer, running with blade hands chopping the air, zigzagging as I hear sporadic gunfire and shouting behind me. I drop down into the grass and see goons stopping at the overturned trailer. I fire blindly at them. I don't want them hanging out there. I want them coming after me.

Lots of hand waving and yelling when they go inside the truck. Nina must be explaining to them they can't reverse defrosting the Monster Kids without the key card in my pocket. They do not want to hear this. They make unhappy noises. They leave only one guy behind to guard the truck, closing the doors behind him, and the rest duck low in the grass and crawl after me.

Brings a smile to my face, all of that.

Thunder rumbles in the distance as I make my way up the grassy slope in a crouch, holding the XM7 in both hands. Away from the glare of the highway, my surroundings have fallen into obscurity. I can hear the gyro whirring in the air overhead, but without its spotlight it's blind, so I ignore it.

I've been following a hum I've detected at the edge of my consciousness since we tumbled off the road. It gets louder and more intense the closer I get to the top of the ridge, and when I crest it, I see its source: a large electrical substation flanked by steel lattice towers on either side. Wires snake in from the towers above and zigzag in an overlapping labyrinth of conical transformers, pronged switches, three-headed circuit breakers. The whole business is surrounded by a fence garlanded by barbed wire and a sign warning, "Danger! High voltage!" I don't see a gate anywhere. Must be on the other side.

I take my shirt off and wrap it around my hand, protecting it when I rip the warning sign off the electrical fence and throw it into the grass face down. I then throw my shirt over the razor wire, take a step back, and with a running jump, leap over the top of the fence and land in a roll on the gravel ground on the other side.

I stagger slightly as I get to my feet. In the middle of all these wires and electrical equipment, for my machine telepathy, it's like standing next to the speakers at a rock concert. I can sort of hear the music, but mostly I just feel it, the vibration of the waves pounding my body.

Movement out of the corner of my right eye makes me spin in that direction, pointing the rifle. There's a girl standing there, about fifteen, in a STRONG FEMALE PROTAGONIST T-shirt. Pulse doesn't flinch when she sees the rifle, just shakes her head with sad eyes.

I'm lucky the rain starts then, sizzling on the metal of the electrical equipment all around me, because I can see even in the dark that it's passing right through Pulse. She's not actually there. I still feel a chill when she turns and runs through the tall metal arbor of the nearest lightning arrester. She vanishes into the wall of the concrete brick of the control building on the other side of the station.

Various other ghosts flicker out of static and start to pop up in random areas around my vision: a boy on a skateboard, a middle-aged woman pushing an ice cart with a bull on one side, a man with gray temples and a widow's peak standing legs akimbo, arms crossed, looking at me judgmentally.

"Son," I can see but not hear as his lips move.

My heart starts pounding faster than I'd like, so I jam my eyelids shut and shake my head. When I open my eyes again, my sight has cleared, and as far as I can tell, everything I'm currently looking at is actually there.

Okay. Well, apparently, a direct hit from an EMP blast like the one Pulse zapped me with can completely wipe my memory, but proximity to this much juice isn't doing wonders for my nervous system either.

I can see the PRS goons cresting over the edge of the hill, heading for the chain-link fence, and I follow Pulse's ghost to the control building. I shoot the lock out of the front door and kick my way inside. I make my way through the tall, server-like meters and relays, red numbers flickering in megawatts on their sides, until I find the breaker for the electrical fence outside and trip it.

I look back outside. As I suspected, the goons see my shirt thrown over the fence as evidence of my route. Half a dozen are climbing the fence, assuming their padded uniforms will protect them from the barbed wire.

Too bad it doesn't also protect them from the electrified fence when I flip the breaker back on. The rain is not the only thing that makes a sizzling sound. They drop, twitching, back into the grass. They're alive, but that's all they are.

Maybe I should feel sorry for them, but the way I look at it, nobody forced them to become gun thugs for scumbag corporations. They could have joined Habitat for Humanity. But I bet the pay, stock options, and health-care plan at Project Rising Spirit were better. Hope they earned the best medical coverage available. Because they're going to need it.

"Hey, Junior."

The hollow voice is right beside me. All of a sudden I feel a burning sensation in my back. I'm looking at a seventy-centimeter blade sticking through my chest, covered in my blood.

"Remember me?"

I spin around and launch a kick in the direction of the voice. I can feel the solid wall of muscle even through the sole of my boot. I push off it and hit the ground with my shoulder. I roll up into a crouch facing the enemy, and he's leaping back onto his feet, carrying the bloody katana. He's in a baggy black flight suit, with four-lensed goggles covering his face and some kind of pronged breathing apparatus covering his mouth. Weirdly, the blade of his katana is such a dark gray that it is almost completely black too.

"You'd be Dodge," I venture through gritted teeth. My guts burn and my blood is everywhere, but I try to ignore it. I shed blood like sweat.

"Awww. You do remember me."

My eyes dart to the corner of the room. I had leaned my rifle against one of the relays by the door while mucking around with the fence controls.

"No, sorry, I don't. But Nina, the scientist in the truck, talked about you like you were the biggest a-hole in PRS. And you look like the biggest a-hole in PRS."

He laughs so hard his respirator shakes. "You know, I wasn't really buying this amnesia story up until now. But that is exactly what you'd say if you didn't remember anything except how to be you. Which is to say, a pain in my ass."

I rise up to standing. I must have looked in the direction of the assault rifle leaning against the relay one too many times because he looks that way too. "You want it? Go on, go get it. I won't stop you. This'll be fun."

His funeral. I drop to the ground and roll to one side, pop up with the XM7 in my hands, and light him up without a word. He starts to make a move like he's going to try to deflect the bullets with the blade, but of course that's crazy. He takes four slugs square in the chest and drops onto his back with a crash.

Bulletproof vest? Is that why he was so cocky? I take a few steps toward him. There's blood pooling on the floor underneath him. So, no protection. Then what was that all about?

Then his blade lashes out and upward, cutting my right hand off at the wrist.

"*Oh my God, the look on your face!*" Dodge sits right up and slashes at me with the katana again. I am still sort of holding the rifle with my remaining hand and instinctually put it in front of me to guard my body, but he cuts it clean in half, without effort, as if it were a single sheet of paper.

I stagger backward, the blood shooting right out of the stump. I'm shirtless, and I don't have anything to cover it with.

I slip on my own blood and fall back, stopping myself from landing fully on my side by lashing my one remaining hand out. Dodge is rising to his feet, and I'm pushing back, trying to crawl backward out of the control room, and this sick bastard is just laughing his head off.

"Greatest day of my life! The day I beat my dad at flag football, the day I popped my cherry, the day I graduated Fort Bragg . . . I think today pretty much beats them all. Feels like Christmas morning."

Dodge leans over and picks up my white severed hand off the floor and shakes it in his face like it's talking. "'*Oh, no! Ray Jr. has abandoned me, Red Cell, will you be my friend now?*'

"Well, sure, you bet I will, Handy. I like you so much better now that you're freed from that awful Nepo-Frankenstein, Ray Jr. He seems to think he's God's gift to superhealing. But he's learning he's not so special now, isn't he, Handy?

"'*It's true, Red Cell. Now that I'm no longer a part of this gross loser's body, I can see all of his terrible life decisions and crappy attitude for what they are. Don't make me go back to him, Mr. Red Cell, please don't!*'

"I wouldn't think of it, Handy. Don't worry, you'll be safe with me. Forever."

Dodge stuffs my hand into one of the pockets on his flak jacket. I've managed to get to my feet, and I stumble into the doorway of the control building. He points the end of the sword at me.

"Where do you think you're going, little boy? You volunteered to be my chew toy for the evening. And Daddy Dodge loves to play with his food."

I stagger out into the gravel yard of the substation and slam the metal door behind me. The rain is really coming down now. I've lost blood before, but not like this. Spots are starting to swarm in front of my eyes, but I'm not sure if that's from bleeding out or because the sight of it is making my stomach heave like an earthquake.

Then I look across the transformers and circuit breakers and get an idea.

Of course, Dodge slices through the door with his sword instead of opening it like a normal person because he's a giant tool.

"Heeeeeeeere's Johnny!" he yells.

See my earlier tool comment.

I've got my breath back, and I look down at my arm stump. It still hurts, but incredibly it's already scabbing over.

God, I'm famished.

I rush toward him. He takes some swings at me, but I'm fast, and I dip under his reach. I give him an uppercut with my arm stump. I lay him out on his back, but holy smokes, that was a bad idea. I nearly pass out from the pain when the exposed bone of my arm connects with the bone of his jaw.

"I got to hand it to you, Junior," Dodge says as he gets back on his feet. He's kept his hand on the sword the whole time. "You have a real genius for ruining my fun."

He lashes the sword in a wide arc and cuts the lightning arrester tower next to him in half. It falls over and nearly on top of me, and only "nearly" because I leap out of the way just in time.

"Between you and me? I'm kinda disappointed you just got your brains fried to stupid and you didn't truly go native. Means my putting you down tonight is just temporary. And the worst part is, when they rescramble your marbles back at HQ, you won't even freaking *remember* how badly I kicked your ass. I mean, where is the justice in that?"

He leaps up over the fallen arrester, both hands on the hilt, katana raised high, but I'm not there when he lands, sword tip down.

"'Cause you're not a real soldier. Just a freak of medicine with a gun. I keep telling your old man. Guy who heals from every wound without a scar doesn't ever have to learn from his mistakes. And using you in the field to chase down your fellow brat freaks is the biggest mistake of all."

He lunges upward with the blade; I stagger backward, seemingly at random. Hopefully the fear on my face looks genuine. Dodge doesn't seem to notice either way. He just keeps advancing and slashing, advancing and slashing.

"I was the best of my brigade before PRS stuck their needles in me. And what does Doc Garrison have me doing? Glorified au pair, glorified babysitt—"

I spin away just as we reach the three-pronged circuit breaker, and Dodge plants the blade right in it. It cleaves through a considerable portion of the machine, but halfway in, the electricity visibly courses through him and knocks him backward—off the ground, through the air.

And the sword—how can I explain it? The sword is basically vaporized somehow. The gray metal just dissolves into individual shavings and vanishes like a bad dream. It decays to nothingness before my eyes.

I can say that was unexpected.

Dodge is still smoking and twitching, and still somehow laughing. "Good boy," he's gasping. "That was smart . . . You get some actual training, you might actually be worth a damn."

I leap on top of him and put my one usable hand on his throat. Little stubby fingers are already growing out of my rapidly healing stump, but I don't really want to look at them.

"Enough riddles, you bastard," I yell. "Who am I? What am I? What did Rising Spirit do to me?"

"What'd they do to you? Same thing they did to me, kid. They injected you with the bugs that saved your life. The same bugs that killed so many others. You and me, we survived."

He gets his hands out from under me and tears open his jacket.

"I mean, if you can call *this* surviving."

I look down, and I can sort of see the bullet holes I put into his chest earlier.

One has a small eyeball—blue—looking at me.

Another is growing a hundred tiny, flat-topped teeth.

A third is a puckering mouth.

Out of the fourth juts a small finger, not unlike on my own stump, pointing directly at me.

I leap up with a gasp, disgusted. Dodge keeps laughing.

"I'm the earlier model of you, kid. The bugs—the nanites—didn't quite take with me. When they rebuild me after injury, they get the broad strokes right, but the details, the look, they keep screwing up. Or they're just expressing their creativity. Your daddy and all his nerds can't figure out why. They're a real marvel, though, those bugs. They can make all sorts of things."

He holds his hand out. I can see for the first time that he's always had the sword hilt in his hand. Before my eyes the shavings return in a cloud of metal, then stop, straighten, and jut out of the base of the hilt, right before me, into the blade of the katana.

"Like, just as an example, swords that can cut through matter on a molecular level."

Dodge rams the sword straight through my heart. I drop onto my side on the gravel. The rain is really hammering down now, getting in my eyes. That must be why I can't see so well. Not that the whole world is going black.

I can sort of hear, sort of see Dodge looking over me, still enjoying himself. "Each time you or any other wannabe hard case takes a piece of me away, something weird and different grows in its place. I'm losing myself by inches. While you grow back more perfect than before. You can even grow back from this sticker in your ticker, I bet."

I start to shake. There's a roaring in my ears. Why won't he stop talking? I look at the sword in my chest, or try to, but I don't see anything. I close my hands over where the blade should be, and my palms feel cold steel streaked with rain. Is the nanite katana so thin that it actually becomes invisible when you turn it on its side?

Dodge sees me struggling to pull the sword out with flat hands and puts a palm over the hilt, jamming it further in there. I scream.

"Though, I wonder . . . what if I cut your head off? Could you heal from that? Grow a little shrunken head out of the neck stump that blows up bigger and bigger like a balloon? I'd like to see that. I can hear Nina and the other Fresh Kills lab rats bitching about the mess already, but you know what? They could use a challenge."

He puts both hands on the hilt, preparing to pull it out. But then he stops, cocking his head at what might be distant thunder.

"You hear that?"

And then it's above us, a twenty-foot-tall Tyrannosaurus Rex in alternating light-green and dark-green stripes and one fang jutting out the left side of its mouth. Its jaws are opening over Dodge before he realizes it's there, chomps all the way down on him to his waist, then snaps its head back with a roar, hurling him arcing, screaming into the void.

If I am dying, I could do worse for last sights.

But of course, it's not my last sight at all. The T-Rex takes one step toward me, and with a second step, it's Animalia, a little girl clutching her arms together and shivering slightly.

I swallow with difficulty. "It's been fifteen minutes already?"

Telic's cowboy-hat-clad outline transforms from blur to solid above me, looking down. "We woke up in ten. I still can't feel my toes." She cocks her head at the sword. "You want that in you or out of you?"

"Out. But pull carefully. The blade's made of nanomachines and can cut in between molecules."

"Seriously? That's dope."

"Right? I'm totally keeping it."

Telic carefully slides the blade out of my chest. I wince because tissue had already started to heal around the wound, and by removing the katana, she's cutting it open again. Telic takes off her denim jacket and presses it against my chest. "The lab lady in the truck told us what you did. You didn't have to go and get yourself skewered by a PRS horror show to convince me you joined the right side."

"But it helped."

"Oh, it helped a lot."

I put my hands on the jacket on my wound to stanch the red flood. It's sort of working. "Careful, they've got eyes in the sky on us."

"Not anymore," Headspace says as he steps out of one of his crinkles in reality. I hear what sounds like a fiery crash in the distance. He looks blue too.

Relief floods through me when I see Kalea and Clark come out of the portal behind him, even though Kalea is having a tough time looking me in the eyes.

"So," I grunt, "if we're agreed we're all on the same side, what do we do now?"

The three members of Generation Zero look at each other.

"Cronus?" Animalia says.

"Yeah." Telic nods. "About time you met Cronus."

ELEVEN

I wasn't too thrilled to get into one of Headspace's portals for the first time. Like the name says, he grows them out of his face. They're like wispy wrinkles in reality, growing to the size of the average person once they leave his body. If you squint, you can sort of see another location in a small circle in the center of it, all distorted, like looking through a pair of binoculars the wrong way.

I don't have any idea what I am looking at—*where* I am looking at, I mean. When I look back at Headspace, he, Animalia, and Telic laugh at me and dare me to go first. We all retreated back into the substation control room to get out of the rain. But we have to get out of the area as soon as possible. Dodge is no doubt making his way back from wherever Animalia-Rex chucked him.

Still, I hesitate. "How do I know you aren't gonna dump me in the middle of the Atlantic or something?"

"Naw, man, I wouldn't do that to you, we're tight now," Headspace says in his flat Midwestern drawl. "'Sides, I ain't never been over no ocean. I can only port to places I already been to, or in my field of vision. My brain—it's like a homing pigeon. It can warp me back to somewhere in my memory—in space, not time."

"And . . . you were able to warp into the castle in the park because

Kalea was there. With her powers she could share the memory with you like it was your own."

Headspace nods. "It's a trick that even freaks me out. If we had Cloud's psychic network up and running on all our ops, Gen Zero would be un-freaking-stoppable."

He grins at Kalea, but she is still lurking on the edges of the group, avoiding eye contact. Clark scowls, and he takes his sister's hand.

"Damn, girl, I didn't mean to put you on the spot." Headspace waves a hand at her. "I know you all about that normie life."

"And we shouldn't call it 'normie life' either," Telic interjects quickly. "We respect everyone's choices to be in or out of our movement. We force people to stay in Generation Zero, we're no better than Rising Spirit."

"And *that's* why we're *losing*," Animalia singsongs, and Telic shoots daggers at her with her eyes. There's an old argument there.

I change the subject by pointing at the still-floating wispy mirage-portal thing. "Since I'm a first-timer, can you at least tell me where I'm going?"

"No," Headspace says with a grin.

"C'mon, tough guy, you can do it," Animalia says.

"Wherever you're going, I promise, we'll be joining you seconds later," Telic says.

"What, you don't trust us?" Animalia giggles. I've never seen her even crack a smile before, so the giggle is extra unsettling.

"Fine," I say. "But if this is some hazing BS and you zap me onstage at a strip club or in front of an oncoming train or something, I swear there will be payback."

"Ooh, payback, I'm so scared!" Animalia laughs.

"Seeing is believing," Headspace says, bowing and gesturing me toward the portal with both hands.

I still have the nanite katana in my hand. Without thinking, I try to thread it into the belt loop in my pants, and of course the atomically thin blade promptly slices right through it and drops to the ground.

Clark laughs. So do I.

"Wait, if it can really cut through molecules," Clark says, "why doesn't it just, like, cut right through the ground all the way to China?"

"Molten core of the Earth might stop it by turning it into slag. But maybe not." I pick it up and look at it. "But it's made out of nanites. Intelligent machines. I wonder . . ."

I concentrate slightly. The electrical interference from the substation all around me has tamped down my ability to sense and converse with machines, but now, up close and personal, I sense the blade not as a single object but as a densely packed swarm of hundreds of thousands of tiny machines—nanites—that I can talk to as I would any other device.

"Rest," I say out loud, and the blade just dissolves into the cloud of shavings I saw before. But now I see they enter a small slot that has opened up in the otherwise ordinary hilt. Once the last particle of the cloud disappears, the small hatch slides shut.

"Cool," Clark breathes. "Like lots and lots of tiny hermit crabs."

"You're stalling," Animalia says, and points into the portal.

"All right, all right, keep your anime on." I shake my head and step into the space—my eyes jam shut as I hit it, to my shame, an involuntary response.

—

The weirdest thing about traveling through Headspace's head space is that it doesn't actually feel like anything at all.

—

When I open my eyes, the first thing I see is a startled seagull flapping off a blue-green railing and into the night sky, spooked by my sudden appearance. The cool sea breeze hits me, and I am looking at thousands of glittering lights, earthbound stars. Once my eyes adjust, the lights coalesce into an island's worth of skyscrapers. Below me is water, a wide harbor with a couple of ferries and barges nosed by tugs. I turn to the source of the light behind me and see the blazing head of a torch, glass and metal. To the right and below me I can see the rest of the giant statue holding it, crown and gown and all.

The portal remains, and as the others file through, one by one, I admire the view. Have I ever been to New York City before? Who knows. I feel like seeing it for the first time from here is a real gift.

Headspace comes through his wrinkle in reality last, then closes it. "If Generation Zero makes its headquarters inside the Statue of Liberty," I say, "I've got to admit I am super freaking impressed."

Telic grins. "I wish. No, we make multiple nonlinear jumps before arriving at HQ just in case PRS stakes out any of the jump stops, tries to figure out how to trace us to our home base."

"When's the last time you were in the torch of Lady Liberty, kid?" I ask Headspace. He looks winded. He sits down on the base of the torch and takes a deep breath.

"It's all 'porting.'" He taps his temple. "Just had to see it first, down there in the Battery." He takes a bottle of Poland Spring out of a side pants pocket and swigs. "Jump that far, you're gonna have to give me a sec before the next one."

"All this zigzagging works?" I ask Telic.

"It did until the one time it didn't. We ported to what we thought was a safe house near Cloud, only PRS had a strike team waiting for us. They hit us with Screamers before we knew what was what, and this chalk-skinned psycho who used to be PRS's biggest asset had to come save our asses."

"Screamers?"

"Neural disruptors. You'll know them when you hear them. They disrupt synaptic flow so bad you'll have a tough time remembering your name, much less how to use psiot powers."

"Damn, you really do have amnesia, Bloodshot," Animalia says with a slow grin. "Screamers used to be your best friends."

I remember the piercing sound that woke me when Kalea's iPhone was alerting me to her predicament. If that was the tail end of a Screamer's cry, I never want to be on the receiving end of a full blast. "How'd PRS make that safe house, you think?"

Headspace shrugs. "We used it once too often, I reckon. I used to go get Slim Jims from the convenience store around the corner, and the security cams could have picked me up. PRS runs face-recog bots twenty-four seven, scrubbing any available live feed for our beautiful faces."

I frown, trying to process this. "So . . . they set up shop in the neighborhood of wherever Headspace might have been, just to see if any of you pop up? Then they unleash the hounds? They have scramble teams just floating around the country to respond to that?"

"Don't hate us because we're popular," Animalia deadpans.

I'm still trying to make sense of all this when I'm suddenly aware of Kalea at my elbow. "Hey, can I talk to you for a second?" Still no eye contact.

I look at Headspace. "Give me like five," he says, waving us away.

Kalea walks around the balcony to the other side of the torch, where we have a commanding view of two islands dotted with old brick buildings. A big orange ferry, windows lit up so I can see that it's mostly empty inside, cleaves the water between the islands. She just stands there fidgeting and looking at her toes until I say, "What's up?"

"I just wanted to say, you know, that I'm sorry." The sea breeze has her hair and flaps it out to one side. She sniffs.

"Sorry for what?"

That inspires some eye contact. "For . . . leaving you behind. For believing every terrible thing Generation Zero said about you."

I shrug. "Really, Kalea, it's not a big deal."

"No, I really think it is!"

"Like I said, I don't remember who I was before this. Why should you trust me when I don't trust me? I . . . I certainly believed every terrible thing that they said."

"I wanted to believe you. I did." Kalea brushes her hands over her eyes. "But . . . you're different. I can't network with your mind. On the one hand, it made me want to be close to you because . . . I could. Safely. I couldn't accidentally interface with you like I did with Mason. On the other hand, it means you're like a closed book to me, across a room, with a cover I can't open. So it's scary too. I never experienced anything like it with another psiot before."

I nod. "I got a pretty good idea why."

"You do?"

"I'm not a psiot. I'm something else."

"What are you saying?"

"I got, like, a million tiny minds inside me, fixing me, healing me, letting me talk to machines. You can't control them because there are too many consciousnesses for you. It's what lets me hunt psiots so well. And . . ."

Kalea's still looking at me. "And?"

"And it sounds like my own father did that to me. And I am not at all happy about that."

Clark appears around the torch. He has flattened his back up against the torch because he can't quite look over the edge of the railing. "Headspace is ready. Time to go."

"All right, sounds good." Kalea takes my hand. "Thanks—for understanding. When PRS showed up out of nowhere to grab us, my first thought before they hit us with Screamers and I couldn't have any more thoughts . . . well, I thought, *I should have trusted Bloodshot.*"

"Smartest thing you've said since I met you." I smile, and she smiles back.

"Bleeagh," Clark says.

TWELVE

Nothing can prepare me for where Headspace drops us off next.

Or should I say when?

I appear without warning in front of a herd of waist-high lizards rushing toward me on their hind legs, fangs bared. In less time than it takes to think, the hilt of the nanosword is in my hand, and the blade is forming with a tinkling like cracking ice.

Then enough time to think passes, and I can see now that the attack herd of raptors isn't moving. I can see the chips of paint missing on one and a spray-painted dick and balls on the scales of another.

They're also being shepherded along by a robed man with long white-blonde hair and matching beard, holding a wooden crook high. I mean, it's supposed to be wooden, but it's fiberglass, just like the rest of the shepherd and his raptor flock, frozen in place.

I hear giggling and turn to see that the rest of Generation Zero has materialized behind me. Telic and Animalia are pointing at me and laughing. Kalea at least has the decency to hide her smile with her hand. Headspace just looks tired.

"Boy, they really got the drop on you, Bloodshot," Clark says. He coolly appraises the tactical situation. "If they could actually move, you woulda been dino food."

"Hardy-har-har." I release the blade nanites to return home to their hilt. "What is this place?"

Telic points. I follow her finger to see a large gate dotted with ticket booths, none of which seem to have intact windows. Over the entrance loom the words PROMISED LAND.

"It's, like, I dunno, an amusement park, but for people who are really religious?"

As the girls lead me through the park, I see a lot of typical state-fair rides, like the Tilt-A-Whirl and a minicoaster for toddlers, but everything's painted with happy-looking dudes in big beards and robes. And also cartoon brontosauruses.

Kalea laughs at the confusion on my face. "Look, if you believe in the literal truth of the Bible, and that God made the world in a week and all that, then humans and dinosaurs had to have lived together at some point."

"Well, you weren't there," Animalia says. "How do you know they didn't?"

"Gee, I don't know, maybe because that's literally what every scrap of scientific evidence says?"

"Quiet," Telic grunts, and the other girls instantly obey her. "I got a bunch of dirtbags trying to make me extinct right now. I couldn't care less about what happened six years ago, or six thousand years ago, or six million. All I got are now problems."

"I think they just know kids really like dinosaurs," Clark says. "Though I guess not enough to keep this place in business."

Hanging precariously from rusting cables and graffiti-scrawled pylons over our heads are four-person cars shaped like flying pterodactyls, leather wings spread wide. A flash of movement in that direction draws my attention skyward, and for a minute I think maybe the fiberglass fliers have sprung to life.

But the truth is much stranger. There's a boy perched on the head of one pterodactyl. He's about nine, with long black hair and wearing nothing but a tattered pair of jean shorts. I wonder if he's cold up there. I have to squint a little to see him as if he were backlit, even though the sun is actually behind me.

Telic sees him too, so at least I'm not imagining it. "Seraphim!" she calls out to him. "Let Cronus know we're almost there, okay?"

Seraphim nods, and the glowing corona around him shifts. Incredibly he seems to sprout wings made of light, and he takes to the air in a mighty flap. He's heading toward the large structure in the middle of the park, a giant wood-and-fiberglass boat with a log-cabin-like structure on top of it. I don't need to see the two-by-two fiberglass statues of lions, tigers, bears, and triceratops tumbled over out front to know it's supposed to be Noah's Ark.

The glowing, flying kid disappears into the Ark via the little house above, while we have to go in through the bottom gangplank between the massive bulk of a pair of gender-opposite woolly mammoths. I can tell one is supposed to be a girl because there's mascara on her giant eyelids and a big pink fiberglass bow on top of her hair.

"They're so gender normative in this place." Kalea sighs.

The interior of the Ark is hollow but far from empty. Someone has dragged torn-up rugs from elsewhere to line the floor. Sleeping bags and toys and candy wrappers are everywhere. I get the impression there's supposed to be a bunch of kids here too, but the minute we appear, I see one disappear in a floating cloud of pure darkness and scurry to the edges of the hull. Seraphim emerges from a hole in the top deck but floats at what he must think is a safe distance from me, silently flapping his wings.

One kid hasn't run. He can't be much older than eight, in superhero-branded footie pajamas and a close-trimmed Afro. His eyes and nostrils glisten from a recent cry. He keeps trying to put his thumb in his mouth, but he is enveloped from head to toe in a semitranslucent force field frosted and thick like his Coke-bottle glasses. The thumb keeps banging into the force field before it reaches his mouth, which isn't improving his mood much.

"Go away, Bogeyman!" yells Seraphim from the rafters.

"Yeah, get out of here, Bogeyman, nobody wants you here!" yells a voice inside the floating ball of darkness near the hull.

"Bloodshot's different, he's on our side now," Telic yells out, but that only inspires the kids around us to yell more. They climb out from inside soiled sleeping bags and from behind battered dressers. Some have purple skin and some have horns. One, a tall, skinny Asian girl, is forming a fireball between her two hands. I am pretty sure she really wants to throw it at me. They're all yelling some version of "Bogeyman, go home." One of the older kids picks up a toy cement mixer and throws it at me. It comes at me faster than I expect. I'm lucky I dodge out of the way because it literally goes through the hull of the Ark, making a tiny truck-shaped hole.

I shoot that kid a look and recognize his curly hair. He's a bit older, his clothes are stained and tattered, and he looks like he hasn't showered in a while, but he is the same kid who made cutlery dance in the #PowerParty video Kalea showed me yesterday. Six-point-two million likes, all for running from place to place for the rest of your young life. Quite a trade-off.

"That's enough!" a voice yells. A kid older than any of the others, except maybe Telic and Kalea, emerges from a side door. He holds a small kid in a onesie in the crook of his arm, then sets him on the ground. As soon as he sees me, though, the tot scampers straight up the wall of the Ark on his hands and feet.

"It's fine if you go up there, Ben, but make sure you stay where I can see you," the older kid says. "I don't want to go chasing off after you again."

"Nice welcome, Cronus," Telic sneers.

"Yeah, well, I keep telling the gang what you told me—that Bloodshot isn't the Bogeyman anymore . . . but the gang's finding it a little hard to believe." Cronus walks halfway toward us, then stops and looks me up and down. He is a pretty regular-looking kid: blonde hair, blue eyes, white tee, jeans, red jacket. He's a little grimy, like he doesn't get to shower all that often, which, considering where he lives, isn't a huge surprise. "I'm with them."

He walks over to the kid in the middle of the room in the force field. "And little Castle—Isiah, here—had bad dreams all night after we told him that the once-and-future Bogeyman was paying us a visit . . . and now he can't lower his defensive bubble." He crouches down before Isiah. Between them is a plate of uneaten waffles drowned in syrup. "You need to eat, buddy. Come on. Now that he's actually here, he's not so scary, is he?"

Isiah looks at me and my chalk-white skin and red eyes and blood-caked and shirtless chest and then looks at Cronus like that's the dumbest question he's ever heard.

"Uh, like, air can get inside that force field so he can breathe and stuff, right?" Clark asks his sister.

"Apparently."

"But how?"

"How the heck should I know? I don't know how I read minds."

That plate of waffles in front of Isiah is looking pretty good. I'm damn hungry, as I usually am. "You know, you're making a big mistake by not eating those waffles," I tell him. "They can give you even better protection from the Bogeyman than that force field." I kneel down in front of the plate. Isiah doesn't flinch. He's pretty confident in his force field's ability to protect him. "You know these are poisonous to my kind, right?"

I pick one up and just pop it right in my mouth, a bomb of carbs and sugar I desperately need. But then I start choking, grabbing my throat, and spin around and around. The kids stop yelling at me and just watch. Then I fall on my back and twitch a lot, making weird noises until my audience starts to laugh. I do it more, and they laugh harder. Even Isiah forgets himself and starts to giggle too.

The force field drops. Cronus picks off a piece of waffle and pops it in his mouth. Then Isiah takes the fork and feeds himself. Other kids rush out and jump on top of me where I'm lying, tongue stuck out, and start hitting me on the chest and arms. It doesn't really hurt at all until that one girl with the flaming hands gets a shot in and singes me pretty good. Cronus and Telic and the other kids break it up, but they're smiling, and now every kid in the Ark has forgotten their fear of me and is dancing or yelling or acting out in some other way with that unbridled exhibitionism little kids have.

I get up and see that Cronus is looking at me in a different light. He offers his hand to shake.

"I really want to believe this is real," he says. "Don't disappoint me."

"It is and I won't."

"Good to hear." He turns to Kalea and smiles. "Cloud. Great to see you back with us. Like the new digs?"

"Hey, Cronus." She smiles, pushing her hair back. "I think I liked that summer camp in New Mexico better. There was a lake." She blushes beet red under his gaze, and I want to throw up in my mouth a little. Gimme a break. What does this guy have that I don't? Other than human skin pigmentation, blonde hair, and the charisma to run a child army, I mean.

"Yeah, well." He shrugs with a grin. "Gotta keep on moving HQ around and around, one step ahead of POS." That's their insulting nickname for PRS, I assume. "Promised Land's got its pluses too. You'll see if you stick around. Are . . . you planning on sticking around?"

"Dunno. I feel responsibility for this one," she says, touching my arm. "I want to see this through, get him squared away."

"What am I, chopped liver?" pipes up Clark.

"Well, you know what my vote is," Cronus says. "Mind if I borrow your new friend?"

"Go ahead," she says. "I'm just hoping there's enough Eggos for me."

"We'll need to do a store raid after that, but I think you're good for this morning. C'mon, Bloodshot, follow me. Let's find you a shirt."

Cronus leads me out through the side of the Ark through an Employees Only door. We find ourselves on a path through a large garden, as ravaged by the elements and vandals as everything else here. Looks like, at one point, there was a mixture of live plants and fake ones, but the elements and neglect have killed most of the living parts of the exhibit, leaving behind the giant prehistoric dragonflies and carnivorous plants and a big cup or grail on an altar. I bet that's a reference to something, but what I couldn't say.

He sits on the altar and looks at me like he already knows everything he wants to know about me, and nothing he knows about me is good.

"So," he says.

"So."

"You really don't remember me?"

"Sorry. People keep asking me that question. I haven't come up with a good answer for it yet. How about that shirt? Starting to feel self-conscious."

"In a minute. Just wanted to make something clear to you first."

"Do what you got to do."

He reaches his right palm out toward me, and the air between us sort of, well, *ripples* is the only word I can think of, and the ground beneath my feet crinkles and burns and disappears, nearly dropping me into an ankle-deep hole.

I leap back and draw the nanite sword. The 'nites haven't completely formed the blade before he reaches out with his left palm pointed at the same spot in the ground, and with the same rippling of space, slag suddenly reappears in the hole until it's completely filled in. It doesn't look exactly the way it did before, but there's now something there where, just a second before, there was nothing.

"I'm not, like, Mr. Science or anything," he says, "but near as I can figure, one half of my brain can break down the chemical bonds that hold the atoms in molecules together, as channeled through this hand." He holds up his right hand and wriggles the fingers. "The other half can stitch those same bonds back together." He shows me his left hand. "Destroy and rebuild, combined in one sexy package. Like the dude with the boom box in that old movie, who wears a bracelet with the letters L-O-V-E on one hand and a bracelet with the letters H-A-T-E on the other."

I bet Clark would get that reference, but it goes right over my head. "I learned I could do it at a power party some kids at my school threw in Seattle. Didn't have too much of a chance to see what I could do with it until you cornered me on the monorail one night when I was coming home late from hockey practice. You looked like the conductor. Until you didn't. I used my good right to blast your arm away, and it just grew right back in front of me. None of this rings a bell?" I shake my head. "Anyway, I just wanted you to know. You regrew your fist right in front of me and knocked me out with it. Next thing I know, I'm in the back of a truck, freezing cold. But not totally frozen yet, so I was able to use my good right to burn my way through the tube they had me in, then out the back, and I escaped. That was three years ago. I haven't seen my parents, my family, my friends since. But I have been practicing. With my powers. You and I ever throw down again, I'll be ready. So don't give me a reason to throw down."

If he keeps making goo-goo eyes at Kalea, I might not be able to help myself, but I'm mature enough to stand up, retract the nanoblade, and put the hilt back in my pocket. "Okay, I get it. Hard for me to get mad at you for being suspicious. But I'll swear on anything you want me to. All I want is for you, Kalea, Telic, everybody, me, to get out from under PRS's thumb forever."

A smile breaks across Cronus's face. "Sure, whatever you say."

"You still don't believe me? C'mon, man, what more can I do?"

"Oh, because you saved Telic and Cloud and whacked a bunch of your guys while doing it?" He chuckles. "That supposed to blow me away with your sincerity? You PRS guys don't care about anybody's life, not even your own people's. I have no problem thinking you'd kill hundreds of faceless goons just to get in with Generation Zero."

"You got a pretty high opinion of yourself."

"It's POS that wants us bad. You met sweet Isiah in there. They want to take him to their HQ, a place code-named the Nursery. There, they can brainwash him, turn him into a killer for the state. Cut his head open, see if they can figure out where this thing they can't control comes from so they can control it."

"And I'm the guy who's supposed to bring them in?"

"That's their standard operating procedure. Then you tried to pull in a psiot who could fight back. Based on how Kalea and her brother found you, sounds like Pulse took you out with her electrokinesis, wiping your memory in the process, but she hasn't reported back in. Any thoughts as to why?"

"I know, man, that's a huge mystery, who wouldn't want to come back to this paradise?" I gesture at our dilapidated surroundings, and the smile falls off Cronus's face. That was satisfying. "But seriously, I don't have any memories beyond a couple days ago. Which I tell literally every single freaking person I meet. It'd be nice if one of you would believe me."

"What do you want from me, then?"

"Pardon?"

Cronus spread his hands. "You've met me. Big whoop. Hope you got a thrill out of it. But I'm not the Wizard of Oz, man. I can't give you memories, or a heart, or send you home. I certainly can't cure people's amnesia. I'm just some kid trying to keep my friends out of the hands of a bunch of gun-toting fascists. You say you won't work for them anymore, and that's great, that's definitely a rare check mark in the win column for us. But sounds like Rising Spirit considers you their property, which, don't get me wrong, that's totally messed up, but it's also a situation I can't do anything about. As long as you're number one on their Most Wanted, you staying here puts my kids in danger. And I just can't have that. All I can do is ask if you want a mostly thawed Hot Pocket and some room-temperature Sprite and then send you as far away from here as possible. And then I have to relocate our little clubhouse anyway in case you get tired of being hunted by your creators and you lead them back here in exchange for them taking you back into the fold."

It's a long speech, and I listen to it without saying anything or making much of an expression. When he finishes, he sighs and shakes his head. "I wish I could offer you more, but I really don't have anything else to give."

"That's not true," I say.

"It's not?"

"No. You have something I want. Something I need."

"What's that?"

"An army."

Cronus laughs. "Those kids out there? You kidding? Other than Telic and Animalia, most of 'em would pee their pants at the idea of getting into any real combat. Or did you not notice how most of them ran and hid from you like you were the Bogeyman when you showed up?"

"But I really am the Bogeyman," I say. "Hiding just means they have good instincts. For what I have planned, I think with a few days' training they can be a difference maker with minimal danger to themselves."

"Make a difference towards what end?"

"Towards a direct assault on this Nursery. Taking it out. Ending the threat of PRS once and for all."

A strange look creeps across Cronus's face, a thing he clearly fears, a thing he forced himself long ago to believe no longer existed:

A thing called hope.

"You're cracked," he breathes.

"You asked me what I wanted. I think you're right. Project Rising Spirit will never stop looking for me. If I'm not on their team, they're going to want to make sure I never play for yours. But I don't want to pick a team. I want to be free to go my own way. And that means wiping out the whole damn game."

"Slight problem with this plan," Cronus says. "We have no idea where the Nursery actually is."

"Not true," I say. "I have a pretty good idea of where it is."

"Oh? Your amnesia suddenly clearing up? Wish you'd mentioned that earlier. It makes me less inclined to trust you."

"I wish. No, memory's not necessary for this. I'm talking about the here and now."

"You're talking in riddles."

"Sorry. It's pretty simple, really: This guy Dodge, he doesn't like me very much. He cut my hand off and stuck it in his pocket. My hand's still full of nanites, and my remaining 'nites can feel their little buddies in their absence in the same way I can track a cell phone or another machine. Except this I can do effortlessly, without thinking, because it's a part of my body."

"Like a phantom limb."

"Not even phantom. Just . . . separated. Because they're little computers, not cells, the two sets of nanites can calculate the difference in distance from each other . . ."

"And we can calculate the exact location of the Nursery once Dodge goes back there. Nice! I knew PRS would slip up at some point. This is just what the doctor ordered."

"Yeah . . ." I draw in a sharp breath. "But . . ."

"Uh-oh, how did I know there was a 'but' in there somewhere."

"We kind of have a timetable to get this done as quickly as possible."

"*We* have a timetable . . . ?"

"Yeah." I can't quite look at him as I say this part. "There's no guarantee . . . there's no guarantee that PRS won't figure out how to do what I'm doing to the nanites, but in reverse."

"And track *you* back *here*."

"You got it."

"Well. We better get started, then."

THIRTEEN

The curtains in Promised Land's main theater are screen-printed to look like the famous painting on the ceiling of the Sistine Chapel. A bearded god reaches down from the clouds to E.T.-touch the finger of a surprisingly distracted-looking Adam. You'd think the first human would pay a little more attention to being created in the first place. But maybe that's the way it always happens: All the important stuff in life happens while you're worried about something else.

When you have amnesia, you really start to pay attention to things like this.

Cronus finds a digital projector I can interface with in the Creation Theater, and he lets me divert power to it from their crappy generator. He then has to get all the psiot kids to come in and listen to my briefing, which makes herding cats look like a walk in the park. I launch right into my speech. They found me a T-shirt with a cactus on it that reads "Pathfinder Day Camp, NM" in twisted rope. The older kids, like Telic and Animalia and Kalea, all pay attention to me, but the younger ones start fidgeting and whispering to each other when I'm barely three sentences in. Cronus hushes them, but one kid starts using his telekinesis to force one girl to pick her own nose, and she gets mad and sets the boy's eyebrows on fire with a single glare. Pandemonium erupts.

I start to get queasy at the thought of leading the Legion of Superbrats into battle. I knew this was a long shot, but I'd like to try to avoid certain death if I can.

Just when it looks like Cronus is about to blow a blood vessel and start blasting these kids with his hand lasers, Clark leaps to his feet and stuffs his fingers into his mouth for a harsh whistle. "Shut up, you guys!" he yells. "Bloodshot is talking. You sick of living on Lunchables and lemonade mix? You wanna sleep in your own beds, in a house with your own parents, under your own roof, that doesn't have, like, stink water dripping on you all the time? Then listen to Bloodshot. He's gonna tell us how we can all finally go home."

It's like he cast a spell on them. They blink and sit back down in the ripped, stained theater seats. I catch Kalea's eyes, and she arches an eyebrow at me. Maybe Clark has some latent psiot powers of persuasion we don't know about.

I don't waste any time. I tell the projector to throw up the satellite images I pulled off the network. It shows the giant jigsaw puzzle piece that is an allegedly abandoned mall in the middle of Nowhere, Idaho, a couple miles from Mountain Home Air Force Base, so that tracks with other PRS sites. "This is where we're pretty sure our friends are being held—that's where my nanites were taken, anyway. See these big, wide parking lots surrounding the place? That means whoever's inside the perimeter has great sight lines in every direction, including up. Headspace and I went up there yesterday to do some recon"—Headspace, leaning against a far wall, shoots me with an imaginary finger gun—"and they have a pair of snipers on the roof twenty-four seven, all with perfect sight lines. If we just show up, guns a-blazing, they'll be able to cut us down before we can reach the front door. So somebody's got to go in first and try to clear the way. That somebody's gonna be me.

"I'm going to have three mission objectives. One, the most important, obviously, is penetrate the mall and find our friends. Where they're keeping them, how many there are, and what's the best way to get them out.

"Two, see if there's another, underground way to let you guys into the building. Sewers, maybe? Tunnels that we haven't discovered yet? Hopefully I'll be able to find plans once I get inside and figure that out pretty quickly.

"Three, soften up resistance as best I can. Disable any Screamers I find, for example. Then, and only then, will I call in the cavalry, which is you guys. Headspace will gather all of you at a highway rest stop about ten miles away, then start ferrying you in. Animalia can probably help with her flying too, ditto for Seraphim.

"Sorry, I know that was a lot. Any questions?"

Isiah raises his hand inside his translucent force field. "Yes, Isiah?"

"Can I go tinkle?" he asks.

Clark buries his face in his hand.

"Can you or may you?" Kalea asks sweetly. Isiah looks baffled.

"Okay, everybody, that's it," Cronus says, getting up onstage. "Now you know what we're trying to accomplish. Let's split up by your team leaders and go through some quick drills." He turns to me and sighs. "Well?"

"Not feeling great about putting these kids in danger, if I'm being honest."

Cronus puts a hand on my shoulder. "They're already in danger. They were born in danger. All I can do is try and keep them safe. But that's just temporary. You're trying to make them free. That's something all of us, no matter what our age, can sign up for."

A grim chuckle comes out of me. "When this is all over, you'll make a great politician, Cronus. They specialize in sending young people to their deaths."

"Gee, thanks."

For the rest of the day, Cronus, Telic, and I try to get the kids to focus on drills, which, as it turns out, have to begin with teaching half of the younger ones how to tell their right side from their left. This turns out to be the most challenging part of our assault planning until Animalia points out that if you hold your hands up with your thumbs sticking out, only the left hand forms an L.

We spread out through the park, dividing all the kids under team leaders—basically, us three—and they practice taking orders, either from the squad commanders or coordinating through Kalea's telepathy. They run for cover really good and can attack with an impressive amount of coordination when given the signal, blowing up rusting Roman legionary animatronics with fireballs and superstrength.

I'm almost to the point of thinking this isn't a completely moronic plan I've come up with when Kalea comes up to me with a puzzled expression.

"I can't find my phone anywhere."

"Did you try looking in the last place you had it?"

"Yes, I did, smart guy. Come on, can't you just use your machine sense to find it? I've got to telepathically coordinate an attack on the Mount Sinai roller coaster. Whichever squad of kids goes up to the top of the fiberglass mountain, grabs a Ten Commandments tablet, and makes it back down first wins."

"Okay, I'll find your phone, if that means I don't have to listen to a sentence like that again."

She snorts and punches me in the shoulder.

Kalea's iPhone pings loud and clear in the direction of the prehistoric garden where Cronus and I had our first heart-to-heart. The closer I get, the louder it calls to me from inside a fiberglass cave on the other side of the garden, the big round stone meant to block the entrance rolled over permanently to one side.

Clark has wedged himself inside the cave between that stone and the wall, knees tucked up to his chin. I don't eavesdrop on his call remotely. When I get close enough to hear his voice, he's saying, "I don't know, Mom, only a couple days at least. No, I don't think they'll let you visit. If it was safe to visit, they would just send me ho—aaahh!"

He says that last part because I stick my head into the cave without warning. I shake my head. "Not good."

"I, uh, listen, Mom, they need me for more tests. I love you! Next time I'll make sure Kalea gets on the phone too. Bye."

I reach my hand out, and he puts Kalea's iPhone in my palm after he rings off. I don't say anything, and he squirms.

"She still thinks we're in quarantine in a clinic somewhere, I swear," he says. "She doesn't know we're here. I was only on with her for a couple minutes! No way that's long enough for POS to trace us."

"C'mon, Clark, you don't know that, and neither do I."

His eyes glisten. "I just miss her a lot," he whispers.

"I get it, man, I do. But that was not smart."

He nods and wipes his eyes with the back of his sleeve. He's never looked so young to me. With all his Hollywood-film-school fancy talk, I forget he's just a boy.

"Please," he croaks, "please let me stay."

We text Kalea and Clark's mom to drive not so far from Squire's Castle, where I had my first little scrap with Generation Zero. That way, Headspace can get us pretty close to the rendezvous point without completely exhausting himself. The sports car I stole before going to the school is still in the Squire's Castle parking lot, in a space far from where yellow hazard tape has encircled the collapsed gatehouse. It's only been a couple days since I swiped it, so I guess that's not that surprising.

I drive, Kalea gets in the passenger seat, and Headspace and Clark get in the back. We had to wait until dark, of course, and I can't really see Clark in the rearview mirror, but I can hear him sniffling a little bit. I can see Headspace's face in the mirror. He doesn't react to Clark's tears with mocking or sympathy, just stoically stares out the window like the good soldier he is.

"Why you so upset, big guy?" Kalea turns back to him, smiling gently. "You've been complaining this whole time about wanting to go back to Mom."

"I know," Clark says, wiping his nose on his sleeve, "but I wanted to go back with you. I wanted things to be like they were before."

Mom's white Kia hatchback is already waiting for us when we arrive at a small lot surrounded by picnic tables and a brick firepit. I'm not picking up any unusual electronic chatter. If PRS has eyes on Mom, they haven't bothered following her here. Mom explodes out of the little car, and Clark runs out to embrace her before I even fully come to a stop. Kalea is right behind him, and all three of them are hugging each other and weeping in the glare of my headlights. I can't hear what they're saying, but I don't need to. Clark clings to his mother's legs like a toddler, and I can see the disappointment on her face when Kalea tells her the bad news. Kalea takes a step back to return to us, but Mom grabs her sleeve. Kalea puts both hands on Mom's shoulders and explains the deal to her, and Mom breaks into sobs, shaking her head. Pretty soon, though, it sinks in that Kalea has made up her mind, and Mom has no power to stop her. Kalea gently pulls away from Mom and gets back next to me in the passenger seat. Clark follows, but instead of going to her, he comes to the driver's-side window.

"You'd better take good care of my sister," he says, stone-faced, "or I'll find out. And I'll come after you."

"I was planning to anyway, but now I'll make doubly sure." We awkwardly shake hands, and he goes back to Mom. She and Kalea exchange blown kisses, and Mom gets into the Kia and drives off with Clark.

"You leave your phone with him like we said?" I ask Kalea.

She nods. "I feel a little naked without it, not going to lie."

"It's for your own safety. Makes you too traceable."

"Yeah, I know, I get it. Still sucks, though. Gonna miss *Pokémon Go*."

Headspace has been snoring loudly from the back seat for the last couple minutes. Doesn't look like he's faking it, but just in case, I keep my voice down. "I still don't like how PRS was able to ambush you and Telic and the others so easily at the safe house."

"You think they were using my phone to track me?"

"I kind of hope they were. There are worse options."

"Meaning what?"

I glance up at the rearview to make sure Headspace's eyes are closed. "Listen, how quickly could you scan, like, everyone in Generation Zero? With your powers, I mean."

She scrunches her nose up at me. "Quickness isn't the problem. They're my friends. I wouldn't violate their privacy like that."

I groan. "Hey, listen, Kalea, I think it's great you have morals and you're a good person and all that happy crappy. But there's something sketchy about this situation. I just want to make sure that nobody is secretly playing both sides, you know? Particularly when I'm the guy about to walk into the Nursery by myself. Because up until now, PRS has been really well informed about our plans."

She crosses her arms. "It's intrusive."

"Well, yeah, of course it's intrusive. It wouldn't be any use if it wasn't. All I'm asking is, just, you know, do a quick drive-by through everybody's cerebrums, see if there's anyone thinking about back-channeling intel to their real masters at Project Rising Spirit. I don't care about any other deep, dark secrets, or, I don't know, weird ideas anybody has. It's my ass hanging out here, and I don't really want it to get shot off."

She looks into my eyes and melts a little. She reaches out to touch my shoulder with a smile. "You're scared."

"What? No! It's called caution. It's called planning for a successful operation. I'm not scared."

Her hand moves up my shoulder. Her fingers play with the short hairs on the back of my neck.

My heart is beating really fast.

"You want *me* to save *you*," she singsongs.

"You got a problem with that?"

She shakes her head. Her hand still on the nape of my neck, she leans over and kisses me, wet and warm. I feel it all over my entire body.

"I like you when you're vulnerable."

I go to kiss her back, but Headspace stirs in the back seat, coughing, his eyes opening. "Whoa. I must've dozed off. Sorry. You guys ready for me to take you back?"

Kalea settles back in her seat and turns to me. "Are we?"

"Yeah, sure," I say, voice cracking. Why can't my nanites fix *that*? "We can just leave the car here. And that, uh, thing, I asked you? What do you think?"

Kalea nods slowly. "I think I can make it happen."

"Well, thank you."

Headspace frowns. "Make what happen?"

"It's a secret," Kalea says, and gets out of the car.

—

Cronus gave me a sleeping bag in one of the offices in the park administration building. I try to lie down and get some rest before I shove off to the Nursery, but I just stare up at the water-stained ceiling tiles. I'm not scared, I swear. Just anxious. I am rushing toward an endpoint to my current predicament, or an endpoint to me. Part of me doesn't even care which one of the two actually happens, just that it hurries up and gets here, now.

When dawn first glows through the blinds of the office windows, I decide it gives me permission to stop pretending I'm ever going to be able to fall asleep. I go out into the park. It's rained a little bit, and everything is glistening in the dawn light, like it's all freshly born. The sun rises over the fiberglass T-Rex and Noah's Ark, and for a few glorious minutes, Promised Land doesn't look ridiculous and cheesy at all, but majestic. Sacred.

I sit on top of a picnic table, watching the sunrise. I'm so absorbed, I'm not aware of the person sneaking up behind me and putting their hands over my eyes until it happens. I cry out and grab their wrists and swing them right out in front of me.

It's Kalea, of course. "Dude, c'mon, leggo!" I let her go, and she staggers back, rubbing her wrists and cursing. "Careful, people are going to start calling you paranoid."

"People are actually after me, so I'm not technically paranoid. Sorry. I'm used to you having your phone. It announces you're near like a bell on a cat's collar."

"At least you didn't say a cow's collar. So, anyway, I did that thing you asked."

"And?"

She blushes. "I tried to dip into everyone's minds really quickly, but just like I was afraid of, I pulled up way more than I wanted to. Like, way too many of the boys think about kissing me. And a couple of the girls."

"Glad you can't read my mind then. Any of your admirers moles?"

"No. I didn't find a single instance of anyone thinking about going to PRS or trying to find PRS. No mole chatter whatsoever. With one exception. Telic agrees with you; she thinks there's a mole too, also because of how easily they captured us." She grins bashfully. "But she thinks it's me. I'm not too surprised about that. I've never been gung ho enough for the psiot rights cause for her."

"Is Telic right? Are you the mole?"

"If I say no, isn't that just what the mole would say?"

"How do I know how moles think? Maybe you're doing some kind of inscrutable three-dimensional chess thing to convince me you're on my side."

She smiles and wraps her arms around my neck. "And how can I convince you I'm on your side?"

There's a swarming in my head that I'm pretty sure doesn't come from nanites. "I don't think I care whether you're on my side or not. As long as you're by my side."

She chuckles. "Who knew the Bogeyman could be so incredibly corny." She bops my nose. "And sweet."

There's nothing more worth saying, so I lean in to kiss her.

That's when Cronus clears his throat behind my back. I turn to see him, Telic, Animalia, and Headspace. Animalia is making a gagging motion with her finger down her throat. Kalea and I giggle like idiots.

"After Headspace ferries you over, he's got to start ferrying over the rest of us to the rendezvous point," Cronus says, blushing, too embarrassed to look us in the eyes. Tough-guy revolutionary kid can't handle kissing. It's adorable.

He rips a burner phone out of its package and activates it. I can hear its distinct transponder ping in the ear of my mind. "When you think you're ready for us to move in and attack, you send 'O-K' to this phone, and 'N-O' if it's time to abort. You got it?"

"Got it."

"Good. Well." Deep breath. "Guess there's nothing more to say, is there?"

I shake my head. No. There isn't.

FOURTEEN

Headspace blips and blaps me on a zigzag teleportation tour across the continent, from cacti in a ravine in Nevada to a snarl of mangroves in the middle of a slick bayou in Louisiana. We stick around there just long enough to see an alligator sunning itself on a nearby log fall off it and into the brackish water. Next, a rooftop in a city somewhere, with tall buildings riding crazy hills up and down and a red bridge astride a bay in the distance. San Francisco?

I don't have time to ask. Next, we're there, outside the Nursery in purple near-dawn. Even this far out, in the tree line ringing the parking lot, I can see the forms of the snipers moving around the mall roof. Sloppy. They should be concealing themselves, but out in the middle of nowhere, it's hard to blame them for not staying on their guard.

I point in the sky above the gunman nearest to us, relatively speaking. "Right there, you got it?"

"Yeah, yeah." Though we practiced for a couple hours back at Promised Land, I know he's never tried this aerial maneuver in the field before.

"You sure?"

"I'd rather not talk about it, let's just do it, okay?"

"After you."

He puts a hand on my shoulder but doesn't port. Instead, he clears his throat. "Listen, Bloodshot, it's been a long time since anybody stuck their neck out for us. Thank you. My little sister graduates eighth grade next month. I really want to be there, and for the first time in a long time, I think I might be."

"I hope you are too. But let's maybe try and survive today first, huh?"

Headspace nods. Space folds around us. When it unfurls itself again, I am about twenty feet in the air above one of the snipers. I have enough time to curl up into a ball as I drop. Just as I'm on top of him, I snap my feet out and land right on his head, smashing it into the ground and shattering his helmet. He doesn't get up again.

I hear a kind of strangled cry to my right. The other sniper must have wandered over to gab with his pal right as I appeared because he's unslinging his AX308 rifle and raising the scope to his eye.

I am just about to dive behind a big doghouse-high air-conditioning unit when reality uncurls like a translucent flower and Headspace flies through, sideways this time, having teleported after dropping me. He's still got all his momentum from the fall but is now moving horizontally instead of vertically. He slams into the sniper's chest, and they both go down cold.

I grab the sniper rifle out of the prone guard's hands and knock him out with the stock to his head. I could take it with me, but it's got no suppressor and I need to be as quiet as a church mouse. I throw it aside and help the groaning Headspace up with one hand.

"Whoa, that was some rush," he says with a grin once he's recovered.

"Perfect. Go get the others, wait for my signal."

He vanishes midnod. I tie up the guards with the straps of their rifles and toss their walkies over the side of the building. I can feel my severed hand still. It hasn't moved for well over a day. Two floors below me. I find a hatch that drops me down into a mostly empty security office—just a few stray power cords where long-gone equipment used to be plugged in. I crack open the door and find a jet-black hallway running behind the various stores, identified by names on the doors: Spencer's, Auntie Anne's, and so on. I see an unlit exit sign over double doors at the far end of the hall and go through it. I find myself in the mall itself, metal gates closed and locked over empty shops. Pale starlight filters through the big glass skylight overhead. I don't detect any security cameras or cell phones, just my hand down on the floor below. In a crouch I creep down the nearest staircase to a dry fountain surrounded by browning spider plants.

Now I can sense my hand above me somehow. Did I go down one level too far?

Then I lose the signal altogether.

All of a sudden, there's a shadow above me, and I'm spinning on my heel away from it as a massive form drops from a balcony above and lands with a crash on the floor beside me, shattering the floor tiles. It's—what is it? It's twelve feet tall and looks like it's got a giant generator or an engine of some kind as a torso, hydraulic shafts for arms and legs, and clawlike metal skeletons for hands and feet. Its head is much too small for the rest of its body, and in a second or two, I realize this is because its head appears to be a radar gun, whirring and clicking at me like a bird.

I draw out the hilt of the nanoblade and let it form as I step forward. The monster matches my advance with steps backward, and it's always one lunge away from the blade. I get frustrated, which is dumb, so I switch tactics, which is dumber, and brace myself for a spring forward, sword over my head.

The second I drop into a crouch, it sees an opening and backhands me in the ribs. Then it picks me up, spins me around, and sends me through an abandoned sunglasses kiosk. My hands lash out to grab the tarpaulin covering it as I go flying by, and I just succeed in pulling the whole thing over on top of me.

While I'm trying to get the stupid thing off me, I see the sword land on the floor ten yards away. It slides right through the floor as if it were made of hot butter. Only when the hilt hits the tiles does it stop its downward momentum.

I feel the ground shake under my cheek before I can hear the footsteps of the junk monster pounding toward me. I somehow find the reserved strength to push myself up and the kiosk off me. I roll to one side, grabbing the tarp in one fist as I go, and I am on my feet before the monster smashes its fists into the tile with ear-ringing crashes.

I manage to loop one end of the tarp over its left fist and use it to yank myself inward and upward inside its grasp to its upper torso. I bash this thing's radar head over and over again with my foot until it snaps off and goes flying away in a shower of sparks.

Finally its free hand gets ahold of the back of my shirt and pulls me off, bouncing me across the ground like a basketball. By the time I roll to a stop and get back up, it's already freed itself from the tarp and found its radar gun head on the ground, as if it can see without its single lens for an eye.

With both claws it holds the radar gun over its, uh, shoulders. Out of the base of the thing, below the radar gun, a series of cables and tendrils snake out and go inside the sensor and pull it back down to rest on top of its torso like a crude neckless head. I can see a cloud of nanites briefly swarm around it as it does so.

So. What is this, another prototype Bloodshot? I'm not sure if these eggheads stayed awake in biology class, but this isn't usually how evolution is supposed to work, sending the older generations to take out the newer models.

Still, I'm more than willing to school any fools if I have to. The junk bot punches its left fist into its right claw—adorable—and rushes me. I start rushing at it in return but dodge to one side just before we're on top of each other so I can push off the railing of the nearby staircase with one foot and leap over the thing. The only sound it makes is the whirring of hydraulics as its arms reach out and fail to grab me. It doesn't make any cry—it doesn't have a mouth—so my own breathing and grunts as I move sound deafening in my ears. Two somersaults through the air bring me within reach of the floor where the nanosword hilt is sticking out. I grab it as I start my pinwheel descent, land on knee and foot, and yell, "Over here, Junky!"

It turns around and, seeing the sword in my hand, seems, as near as I can tell, to advance on me with a little more caution, though it keeps advancing nonetheless. I have its movements timed pretty well, though. Now I can see the armor plating at the center of its stomach and all the power cables rushing to it from other parts of its body.

I wait until it's nearly on top of me before I strike. It throws out a jab with one fist, but I'm pivoting outside its arm, bringing my blade down and cutting it in half with a crackle of lightning. It's not human; it doesn't react to losing a limb any more than it would to hearing an unkind word. It throws a cross with its remaining claw but doesn't get anywhere close to my hand before my sword streaks upward and severs its arm at its piston elbow.

The thing tries to retreat then, but its step back is nowhere near fast enough. I leap forward and plunge the nanosword, for which nothing is truly "armored," into the armored plate in the center of its chest. Its legs immediately start twitching and whirring spasmodically. When I twist the hilt and turn the blade horizontally, it starts to fall to one side.

When I bring the sword out in a flat plane and cut its torso in half, the robot falls into two pieces.

The crash of its landings is still ringing in my ears and the empty mall when I lean over to open what remains of its chest plate. I am curious what power source brings to life this bargain-basement killer robot.

What I see is a small compartment swiftly filling up with several streams of black sand. The little pile grows more and more distinct, five small piles and one really big one, until the various streams merge with each other and start forming bones, blood vessels, muscles, and tendons. For its final trick, it completely covers itself in chalk-white skin. With less time than it takes me to breathe again, the nanites have re-formed themselves into my missing hand.

A long, extended golf clap begins, a hateful sound. It summons my attention to the central atrium of the mall, where, standing under pale moonlight seeping in from the giant skylight overhead, is a man in a gray suit with slightly lighter gray highlights. As he comes forward, it becomes clearer that I've seen his face before: high cheekbones, slicked-back widow's peak with white temples, deeply recessed eyes, an almost comically strong jawline.

"Ray, do you recognize me? I know you've been through a lot the last couple of days, but I am hoping you do."

I can't say he's actually triggering any memories, but his face is immediately recognizable.

Because it is my own.

"Hello, Dad," I say.

FIFTEEN

He walks toward me, the heels of his fancy dress shoes ringing through the wide halls of the empty mall. I still have the katana out, but as he approaches, I can see he isn't armed and I know he doesn't have any electronics on him, so I start to feel a little foolish. I command the nanites to disappear back inside the hilt again.

"Hope you didn't mind my little experiment," Dad says, nodding at the collapsed junk bot. "I was curious to see if you could reconnect with your nanites after their short-term memory had been wiped. You see how few nanites we actually need to animate that kind of rudimentary 'human' form? My first few experiments with nanorobots all ended up this way—rude, crude, and unsophisticated. But it was the necessary stepping stone to reach you. To teach them how to reconstruct human material."

"What was Red Cell? A detour?"

"Red Cell is many things, but a detour he is not," Dad says. "In this work there are no detours. When you know as little as we do, every failure can be ten times more illuminating than any success."

"Culminating in me?"

Dad puts a hand on my shoulder. "Son, no one of us is a culmination. We're all just stones that form one path that goes ever onward.

I believe several related sciences need near-genius-level breakthroughs before you can truly be thought of as completed. Our most exact computer models suggest the Bloodshot program will not reach its fullest potential until approximately 4001 CE, if you can believe that." He slides the hand down my back and gives me a little hug. "C'mon, follow me. You're the guy with the questions. I'm the guy with the answers."

He leads me toward one of the big side corridors that lead to the restrooms, through the deserted food court.

"How do the psiots fit into the program?" I ask him.

Dad sighs. "The psiots. They do and they don't, son. They do and they don't." At the end of the hallway is an elevator that opens as we approach. The inside is gleaming chrome, with no noticeable buttons or seams, decades ahead of anything else I've seen in this mall.

"What you need to understand is what Project Rising Spirit is, and what said spirit is rising to. Some people think we are simply a defense contractor, which is simultaneously accurate and misleading. Some people think we are a technology think tank, which is similarly inadequate."

The doors in the elevator close, and the lift starts to descend. For a long time.

A really long time.

"PRS, son, is in the *future* business. Getting to tomorrow first. Today. Yes, we are heavily involved in warfighting, but that is only because warfighting has always driven progress, not because PRS is especially bloodthirsty. We let the bloodthirsty bankroll our research. Life and death, my boy! They have a great way of focusing the wandering mind.

"Psiots and their abilities have been around for centuries, some would say since the beginning of humanity, though their existence has been something churches and states have long wanted to suppress or demonize. In the last couple decades, though, psiot abilities have been manifesting in children younger and younger. For this, the brightest minds, yours truly included, have only theories, no explanations.

"Nevertheless, those who hold our purse strings wanted our research group to focus more on tapping into the resource that is the psiots, and given the potential benefits nanotechnology could bring to that research and given I am the world's leading authority in nanotechnology, PRS encouraged us to . . . branch out."

The elevator shudders to a stop and the doors open. We step out into an enormous football-stadium-sized concrete chamber filled with rows and rows of blinking servers. Dad keeps walking and talking.

"Edwin Drake? You know who he was, son? Of course you don't, it's a rhetorical question. Nobody does. That's the point. He worked for a company called Seneca Oil. Seneca refined petroleum for lantern oil, oil that was literally just bubbling up from the ground. But it was Edwin Drake who was the first person to think, *Heck, why should we just wait for whatever Mother Earth deigns to dribble out to us on the surface—let's drill beneath her, and find the stuff, and take it, and put it in barrels.* First person to do that! Invented the modern petroleum industry. Designed the process that allowed the modern world you see to spring up around you. But nobody knows his name. He should have died rich and happy, but he never bothered to patent his drilling apparatus. Other people seized and exploited the vast opportunity for wealth that should have been his.

"Those 'other people' were the founders of Project Rising Spirit, veterans of the Opium Wars who took the name from their adventures in the East. They stole what they wanted from Edwin Drake and left him to rot by the side of the road. In the end, the state of Pennsylvania had to grant him an annual stipend to keep him from dying in poverty. And PRS just kept on seizing the future wherever they found it.

"You see, son, I have spent the last few years trying to guarantee I am not going to end up like Edwin Drake. The nanomachines were my discovery, and it certainly took me long enough to develop them into something PRS could actually use."

Whatever. I'm getting the impression he's stalling me. I already know he's boring me. "And that's the purpose of this place? The Nursery?"

"More or less. For security purposes my operation has been split up across multiple locations. But yes, 'the Nursery' is this facility's code name."

"Are Pulse and the others here?"

He stops and just smiles wonderingly. "You . . . really care about them, don't you?"

I scowl. "Why wouldn't I?"

To my surprise, he puts both hands on my shoulders and pulls me in for a big hug. "Oh, son, you do not know how proud I am of you right now. This operation couldn't have gone off any better if . . . well, if I had planned it, except that I did plan it. I had no idea it'd work this well, though. You have completely changed your attitude about psiots. I mean, completely. The mindwipe of the short-term memory in your networked nanite consciousness is, as far as I can tell, wholly complete. Then, all I had to do is put you in the path of the Derby girl, that skinny blonde bleeding heart. Psych Ops really picked the right one to find you. She was all you needed to suddenly bleed for the suffering psiots of the world. It's nothing short of a miracle."

I wriggle out of his grasp. "Don't talk about Kalea like that, or I'll—"

"Or what? You'll stab me? Through the heart, with your scary sword? No. I don't think you will."

"You think I'm scared of you?"

"Aren't you?"

With the hilt in both my hands, the nanoblade forms an inch from his nose so fast he drops the smug look immediately.

"What do you think?"

"Careful, son," Dad whispers. "I thought you wanted to see where Pulse and the others are. Just a little bit further."

I lower the sword slowly, but I don't dismiss the blade entirely.

He leads me past row after row of humming, blinking servers into a large oval room with walls mostly covered in giant flatscreens showing various maps and streaming blocks of ever-changing data. At an almond-shaped island in the middle of the room sits a bunch of people in PRS jumpsuits hunched over computers. Their spines visibly straighten when they see Dad enter the room, and half of them leap to their feet when they spot me, katana in my hand or not.

"Now, now, everyone take it easy," Dad says to them. "Just keep working. You all know Bloodshot. Despite any rumors you may have heard, my son is very much still on our side. Isn't that right, Junior?"

I don't say anything.

"What you're looking at here is the main PRS control center for our satellite network—and, well, one particular satellite. Carol?" He turns toward a young woman with straight brown hair just sitting back down in her chair. "Could you call up the maintenance feed for, um, I believe Camera Three, inside HC01?"

"Yes, sir." Carol's fingers dance across her desktop, and the screen directly above her head shifts from an Earth map to grainy, low-res footage of . . . of what, I'm not sure.

Dad studies the puzzlement on my face. "You're looking right inside satellite HC01. It's orbiting, well . . . over the middle of Australia, from the looks of it." He nods at another screen, which still shows a world map. I can see several satellites being tracked, with flight paths scattering them across five continents.

"You're keeping Pulse . . . in a satellite?"

"Sure. You don't see her?"

I squint at the interior sat view. I am looking at a row of tubes, and inside each tube is what looks like a potato with a bunch of wires hooked up to it, like those old-school science projects that prove you can generate electricity with the acidic electrolytes inside a spud.

"Pulse is the third one from the right, I think."

I try to look even closer, using the nanites that make up my eyes to enhance the image.

It's sinking in that I am not looking at a potato.

"The human cerebellum," Dad is saying, "up until this point, at least, was seen by medical science as a minor organ, a bridge, if you will, from the lower motor functions ending in the spinal column below it to the higher thinking processes handled by the cerebrum above it.

"Now, even though we still don't one hundred percent understand how the psiot brain works—hell, we don't even know one hundred percent how non-psiot brains work—we have figured out that the cerebellum's role as the go-between for body and mind is absolutely the seat of psiot powers. By removing the cerebellum from the psiot and keeping it alive with minimal nutrient fluid and occasional bioelectric stimuli, we can preserve that unique psiot power indefinitely . . . and, of course, wonderfully separate from the annoying teenage brats that power used to be attached to."

I thought I was too tough to cry; I didn't think I was capable of it. But I blink and can feel the dampness around my eyes. I knew this was going to be bad, but somehow it is even worse than I imagined.

"Dad, why are you doing this?"

A puzzled expression crosses his face, soon replaced by a smile. "Why . . . would I attempt to establish a monopoly over the single greatest wellspring of raw power the world has ever seen? Is that seriously your question? They're the new oil, son."

"They're human beings."

"So what? Therefore they're inherently good? Like ice cream? Do you really believe that? Humans would be like ice cream only if some ice cream was rocky road and mint chocolate chip and other ice cream was flavored like dog doo or gave you meningitis.

"Some human beings live their lives well, some live their lives bad; both roads lead to the same end. Good and evil, these are concepts the church and the state have made up to pacify us. To keep us from realizing that all there is to life are opportunities, and those lucky or powerful enough to be in a position to seize those opportunities."

"You're a monster," I mutter.

"I mean, technically I'd say I'm more Dr. Frankenstein. That's who that story was really about, after all. I just use the parts I'm brought. Shadow. Spike. Cronus, however briefly. And who's my grave robber? Who's my Igor? Who brought down Pulse, and all the others? Who brought them here so I could cut the only worthwhile parts out of them and discard the rest? You. My bright-eyed boy. Bloodshot.

"You want to see a monster? Look in a mirror."

The tears are spilling down my face now as the screens shift to exterior views of the base.

"You were right to suspect there was a mole in Generation Zero.

You just missed the most obvious answer. We've been monitoring your progress through this little maze of intrigue from the very beginning.

"And we just sent Cronus's phone the O-K signal that you've disabled the Screamers."

"You . . . you what?" Did he just say what I thought he said?

"Here, son, see for yourself."

Suddenly, every screen, all around me, shows Generation Zero emerging from the darkness around the perimeter of the mall. Cronus, fists flashing. Telic, moving so fast from point to point the camera only registers her as a pixelated blur. Animalia swoops down in the form of a squawking blue pteranodon, Seraphim on his golden wings right behind her. Even Isiah, ensconced in his force field, runs at the front, fearless. And then, behind him, in a blue tracksuit, her hair flopping over one eye, looking around for anyone to scan, is Kalea. Cloud. They run across the empty parking lot, and then Headspace's reality-crinkle appears, disgorging him, the girl with the fireball hands, and the dancing-magnet silverware kid. All the others, rushing with purpose toward the mall.

"For years," Dad's saying, "we tried to figure out how to penetrate Generation Zero. Years. Even before Cronus ran it. His predecessor was a real head case, got killed by a SWAT team in Colorado Springs. Long story. Still, we couldn't draw Gen Zero out. But then, someone—who was it? It might have been Nina, even. She had the masterstroke of mind-wiping you even deeper than we usually do. Let them think you'd gone over to the other side. The perfect double agent, the one who doesn't even know he's a traitor. I mean, it's beautiful. You get why, right?

"*They* think they're here to rescue *you.*"

He winces as he says that, touching the back of his head. At first I think he's actually feeling the pangs of conscience, but no, there's a reddish bump at the base of his skull. It's just regular physical pangs.

I can see what, up until this moment, I assumed were parking-lot streetlights retracting open to reveal wasp-hive-shaped machines concealed inside the lantern tops. There's no sound coming from the screens, but I assume those must be Screamers, because once all of Generation Zero is inside the parking lot perimeter, they start flailing and crying and clutching their heads. Seraphim's golden wings disappear, and he crashes to the ground. Animalia turns from a giant robot warrior into a crying girl in a fetal position. Telic abruptly snaps out of her blur and falls to her knees. Then, descending suddenly from the night sky are gyros that disgorge armored men with tranquilizer pistols and zip ties. Cronus blasts one, then another, with his right hand of destruction, but ultimately the Screamers are too much even for him, and he passes out face-first. One by one each psiot goes limp as they're stabbed with sedatives and hog-tied. It's like watching the climax of a human rodeo, and it tears me up inside. When Isiah drops to his knees, clutching his suddenly force-field-free head, I see Kalea behind him, pale and panicked. She's still futilely trying to Quiet Time her attackers; I see it in her expression.

When she drops to the asphalt, tranq darts in her back, I just can't look anymore. "All of Generation Zero, captured in one fell swoop. Your crowning achievement, son. This is the beginning of a brave, new day for Project Rising Spirit. I've never been prouder of you."

I've never been sicker. "What makes you think I'm going to let you get away with this?"

"Oh, I don't expect *you* will." My back is turned to him, and I don't start to turn around until I hear the weird crackle in his voice.

I crane my neck, but it's too late. I can't see him anymore. I can't really see anything anymore, except the hint of a human outline and a pair of burning eyes.

"That's why I'm just going to have to build a whole *new* you," is the last thing I hear him say.

I start to raise the katana again, but there's a thunderclap, and I, uh

I

I

I, uh

I

I

I forgot

What I was saying

Where

Where was I?

PART TWO

SIXTEEN

I awake.

Hers is the first face I see.

"Congratulations on another successful mission, Ray," she says. Her dreads are pulled back in a scrunchie, and I can sort of see the tablet she's holding through the reflection in her glasses. Oddly, her foot is up on another office chair, in a plaster cast halfway up her calf. "Ready to establish baseline?"

"Yes, ma'am," I say.

"Dr. Perlin is fine, I'm not your nanny."

"Sorry. Do I ever remember to call you Dr. Perlin?"

"No. But hope springs eternal. We always end up settling on Nina."

I sit up in the protein-rich nutrient bath I lie in between missions so my nanites can replenish themselves without the necessity of cohering to my body. As I get up, the milky slime washes off my body, and for just a second I can see a glimpse of the me that is me without the nanites: bones and veins and muscles. But then the nanites swarm over me like a parent wanting to shield their kid from the harsh realities of the world, and my chalk-white skin covers my delicate human insides again. How much of me is human and how much is nanites? I've tried to ask Dad, but the whole line of questioning makes him turn green. I guess it'd make me sick too if I gave it any thought. And if I had anything resembling a regular human digestive system and nanites didn't microscopically break down every bit of food and drink I swallow. I haven't gagged, much less puked, since I became their carrier.

I sort of miss going to the bathroom, which I know makes me weird. I couldn't really tell you why. My body doesn't produce any waste materials it needs to expel. Any organic molecule is useful for rebuilding bone, muscle, and skin, and my nanites don't let anything useful escape their grasp.

"What is your full name?" Nina's fingernail hovers over the tablet's screen, ready to check off the box for each correctly answered question.

"Ray Garrison Jr."

"Operational call sign?"

"Bloodshot."

"Who employs you?"

"Project Rising Spirit."

"What is your primary overall mission?"

"To safeguard regular Americans from coming to harm as a result of unsecured psiots."

"What is your secondary overall mission?"

"To apprehend previously unsecured psiots before they can become a menace to themselves or others and bring them in for safekeeping and study."

"What is your tertiary overall mission?"

"To kick ass and look great doing it."

"Ray . . ."

"To accomplish my primary and secondary missions with a maximum of stealth and a minimum of collateral damage, to prevent generalized knowledge about the existence of psiots from leaking out into the general public before decision-makers at the appropriate level of government deem it the appropriate time to divulge that knowledge to them."

"Good. Is every point on a circle an ending point or a starting point?"

"A starting point."

"What is more real to you, your dreams or your waking life?"

A girl's face. Wispy blonde hair swept over the left side of her head past her ear, right side shaved. Green eyes, long lashes. Small nose stud, left nostril. She's leaning on the railing of a balcony. She's looking back toward me, smiling, and then she dissipates into the air, like she's made of vapor. There's a glittering cityscape that she merges into, as if she's made of light. I don't have any reaction to this, like it's natural. Like it's what she wants, to be part of everything around us all the time.

"Ray?" Nina is looking at me over her glasses.

"Waking life," I say.

"Is the sun new each day?"

For some reason, that one gives me trouble.

"Yes?"

"Are you asking me or are you telling me?"

"Telling you. The sun is new each day."

"Mmm." She frowns and speed-types something one-handed on the tablet. I can't read what it is in the reflection of her glasses. Annoying. Makes me feel like a new shampoo that's being market tested.

I nod at the cast on her foot. "What happened to you?"

"I'm the one with questions. Do you have any recollection of any details from your previous mission?"

I think of my dream of the vanishing girl, but that can't possibly count. "No."

"Can you tell me why your short-term memory is wiped after every mission?"

"In case I'm captured or scanned telepathically in the field, I can't give away any actionable intel about Project Rising Spirit, its methods, or ongoing operations."

"Perfect." She pokes the last box on the screen. "We're done."

"Great. My turn. Ankle, what gives?"

"Ah . . ." Nina rubs her brow. "Car accident. Tractor trailer."

"Oh, man. That sucks. You get the guy's license plate?"

She blinks at me and sighs. "You know, the son of a gun just drove off like he didn't even know it had happened."

—

Chef is a genius. Egg-white omelet with feta, sliced cherry tomatoes, and baby spinach. A lumberjack stack of pancakes with two over-easies on top and layered with maple-smoked bacon, Canadian bacon, and chicken sausage. Blueberries atop yogurt. Grapefruit juice. Energy drink. Two-percent milk. Earl Grey tea.

The nanites can snack on their nutrient slime all they like. Me, Ray Jr., I need a bit more flavor.

I'm the only one in the mess hall other than Chef when I set my two trays of breakfast—one in each hand—down at a table and start eating. Dad likes to keep as few eyes on me as possible. He wants me mysterious and a little bit scary to everybody. Half rumor, half urban legend. It's hard to be a fearsome bogeyman shoving a chocolate croissant in your mouth and getting crumbly flakes all over your lips in a cafeteria at five thirty in the morning.

I feel the cold metal of the katana against my neck before the keenness of the blade edge threatens to cut my flesh. I don't see any reason not to finish my croissant, though, sucking the pasty chocolate and pastry flakes off my fingertips.

"Cold! Real cold. Them nanites grow your cojones back, Junior?" With a deep, raspy chuckle through his respirator, Dodge takes the sword off my neck and walks around the table to drag a chair out, turn it backward, and sit on it, facing me. He has two arms and two legs and just the one head, so he must have survived the last mission relatively unscathed too.

"I'd ask if they reconstructed your brain, Dodge, but it's hard to build back what was never there to begin with."

Dodge chuckles, adjusting the four-lensed shades that conceal whatever horrible shapes his eyes have grown into. "Tough talk for a kid who'd be absent one head if I wanted to make it gone. You let me get the drop on you way too easy."

"You just keep telling yourself that, Dodge." In reality, I could sense the nanites in his body as he was coming down the hall into the cafeteria, a low hum like the buzz of fluorescent lights. He's obsessed with bullying me, but I can't quite bring myself to hate him. Life gave him a bad deal.

When Dad first got his hands on the nanites, he tried them out on wounded soldiers. Dodge was supervising his unit's evacuation out of Afghanistan during the first pullout when he made the poor decision to take his helmet off to adjust the photo of his kids inside it right before his armored personnel carrier went over an IED buried in the road by the Taliban as a going-away present. The blast blew apart everyone in the vehicle but him. Still, the explosion propelled him headfirst at the ceiling of the cab so fast it caved in his skull. The impact destroyed enough of his brain that he would have been in a veterans home staring into space for the rest of his life had PRS not gotten its hands on him.

The nanites had rejected every other soldier Dad injected them into, breaking down their cellular structures in a writhing mass of mindless gray goo, forcing PRS to incinerate them in a magma-intensity plasma bath.

That wasn't Dodge's fate, though the way he complains, he might think he got it worse. The nanites reconstructed his flattened brain, let him walk and talk again, but for whatever reason didn't allow him the same level of control over the microscopic machines that I enjoy. His nanites keep him alive, but whenever he needs them to regrow his body, they do so in pretty creative ways: extra limbs, bulbous growths, multichromatic tentacles. My nanites are loyal workhorses; Dodge's nanites are drunken rebel artists who do whatever they darn well please.

So while he's strong as I am and has more practical real-life combat experience than me, it's hard to send him out into the field publicly because if he gets shot up, he can turn into a horrific mutant within the first few rounds of the firefight. Hard to convince people you're the good guys fighting against psychic monsters when the so-called good guys are way scarier than any psiot anybody's ever met. Dodge serves as my primary support in the field but has to lurk in the shadows, stepping in whenever I walk into something hairy.

I wonder sometimes about the family in the photograph that was in his helmet. I can't get much out of anybody, but Nina intimated to me once that Dad let Dodge go back and visit his family, even after PRS had him declared legally dead on the operating table. That meeting must not have gone very well because he lives here at Fresh Kills now. I haven't heard about his family since. I try not to think about how Dodge might have reacted if they rejected him. I've certainly seen what he's done to total strangers.

Dodge unbuckles his respirator. He lights a cigarette and lets out the smoke with a leer in my direction. Idiot. Who knows how the nanites are reconstructing the lungs he's ruining? I get the impression Dodge just doesn't care anymore. Hard to trust someone like that to have your back in the field. I should probably say something to Dad, but . . . PRS is all Dodge has going for him. It's this or the incinerator.

"They tell you anything about the last mission?" he asks.

"Dumb question. You know they don't."

He shrugs with a maddeningly private chuckle. "You never get curious?"

"Obviously. But it's war. Us versus the indigo children. Stuff happens. Better I don't know every last detail. Besides, I like to live in the moment."

"Sure that isn't just 'cause they don't give you any other choice?" He slices his thumb open on the blade of the nanite-thin sword lying on the table between us. He watches the wound erupt in an orange lichen-like growth. He loves that stupid katana.

Oh, who am I kidding. The katana is pretty cool. Maybe I'll get to wield it someday.

"Say, how old are you supposed to be?"

"I was sixteen when . . ."

When my internal organs failed. When I nearly died.

When Dad got fed up with no doctors being able to do anything about my AML—acute myeloid leukemia. My blood had turned against me, abnormal white "blasts" clogging up the marrow in my bones, preventing any good red or white blood cells from getting produced. I struggled for a few months on various exotic, painful treatments. Still, by that point, any other kid, with any other father, would have been dead.

Any other kid wouldn't have had a dad with access to a top-secret nutrient pool full of nanomachines that could reconstruct cells on a molecular level but had rejected every other human host they had been tried on—except Dodge. Sort of.

"You even know how long ago that was, that your dad, uh, 'saved' you?" he asks me. "No windows in this bunker. You don't go to school. You don't have any little buddies to cut class or sneak smokes with. They scrub your noggin clear after every op. You got no way of knowing how time's passing. They say you were sixteen when your dad filled you full of bugs. Okay, fine. But do you know how old you are *now*?"

"Do you?" I get why Dodge hates me. I'm the boss's kid, already privileged, yet I was the trillion-in-one test subject whose nanites bonded with him as soon as Dad injected them into my body. It's like my mere existence is fate giving him the finger. I totally get it.

Doesn't mean it's not totally annoying to have him constantly laughing in my face and making his cute little remarks. He ashes his cigarette right onto the cafeteria floor and makes a little shrug. "What's in it for me to tell you?"

"Well, why don't you tell me what it is you want, Dodge?"

He thinks about it a little bit, then drops the mostly smoked butt on the tile and crushes it with a boot. "A rematch."

"I don't have any memory of us fighting, Dodge."

"Maybe that's because I smacked you so silly it knocked the memory right out of your head."

"Then why would you need a rematch?"

"Because you keep *getting back up*." He pushes back out of his chair with the shriek of its feet on the floor tiles and, nanosword in hand, stalks out of the cafeteria.

SEVENTEEN

"Red Cell and Bloodshot, report to the briefing room," Nina monotones over the PA as I'm putting my trays on the dishwasher conveyor belt. Red Cell is Dodge's call sign, just as Bloodshot is mine. I think they're both pretty dumb, but nobody asked for my feedback.

Fresh Kills's briefing room is a ninety-nine-seat theater with a small white stage and black curtains where you could put on a pretty slick high school production of *Guys and Dolls* if you absolutely wanted to. Dad is already in there when Dodge and I arrive.

"Hey, son. How you feeling?"

"Peachier than hell, Pop. How's by you?"

"I'm getting by. Have a seat. You too, Dodge."

I take a center seat in the front row, nodding at Nina, who arrives on crutches and sits on the aisle. We're the only four people in the room.

"Let's begin." Despite saying that, Dad doesn't begin; he digs an orange bottle of pills out of his blazer pocket and downs a handful without water. His skin is pale and glistens in the harsh theater lights. I'm mildly shocked at how much more white is flecking the black of his widow's peak. Each time I go in and out of the nutrient bath, he seems to have aged months and months, while for me the years stand still.

"You sure you're getting by, Pop?" I ask, but he just waves the question away.

"Gentlemen, the time most of us knew was going to come eventually has arrived," Dad says as the screen behind him lights up with a kaleidoscope of captured phone images and videos of the #PowerParty hashtag: kids cupping fire in their hands, kids levitating their terrified cats off the sofa, kids jumping off the roofs of their houses and making craters and earthquake-level booms as they land unharmed. "As you know, our active-measures people here at PRS created the #PowerParty hashtag to get potential psiots to out themselves on social media. This, in combination with regular standardized testing of the high school population through our AccuChieve division, has produced enormous benefits, increasing our target lists and allowing us to get potentially dangerous psiots off the streets before they cause any significant harm.

"But we knew the risks of such a public strategy were also extremely high. The mainstreaming of #PowerParty, the general acceptance of the mere existence of psiots, can attract nongovernmental opportunists and bad-faith actors, particularly in the media. Our information-control team managed to squash *New York Times* and *Dateline* exposés, but those *Vice* and *CNN* spots went forward despite our best efforts.

"Which brings us to this man." On the screen appears the image of a heavily tattooed man with a goatee, wraparound sunglasses, and a bald pate. He's one of those internet celebrities that no one over the age of twenty-five has ever heard of.

"You know him, old man?" I call out to Dodge.

He barks out a laugh. "Bite your tongue, Junior. That there man's my hero."

"Aaron Twyst," Dad continues, ignoring us, "is a former welterweight boxing champion turned 'positive toxic masculinity' megastreamer. He was obliged to flee the United States when a Nevada grand jury indicted him on three accounts of sex trafficking, namely bringing his underage girlfriends across state lines for the purpose of canoodling."

"Mad respect!" Dodge calls out from the back.

"Shut the hell up, Dodge," Nina yells.

"Twyst has used his millions in internet ad revenue to set up home bases in various countries with a history of ignoring US extradition requests, while continuing to broadcast his wildly popular 'pro-bro' rants. What made him pop up onto our radar was that his media LLC filed trademark claims in various jurisdictions—the United States included—for *Power Party* to be developed as a competitive reality show and filmed on a Mediterranean island he recently purchased from a cash-strapped crypto bigwig."

The screen shifts to show a satellite photo of a marble-white island in the middle of a wine-dark sea, the sand spotted here and there with green scrub. "Twyst's casting agents have recruited a few dozen young potential psiots from around the world and offered them a large cash bonus to fly to the island for six weeks of filming, which begins this coming Saturday. Orbital reconnaissance suggests the security presence is formidable, largely, no doubt, to discourage any American attempts to capture him and bring him back to the States for trial.

"But accumulating evidence and the unusual intensity of Twyst's support lead us to the theory that he is a psiot himself, with mind manipulation and behavior control abilities, and this so-called reality show is itself basically his attempt to surround himself with a number of psiot followers for his own protection and personal amusement.

"Your mission, Bloodshot, is to infiltrate the island and rescue all of the psiots Twyst has gathered there for relocation to the Nursery. Expect heavy resistance, all of which you have full sanction to eliminate. That includes Twyst himself. Our preference, as always, is for him to be captured alive, but not at the cost of your own life or the lives of any of the young people he's lured to his compound."

My heart beats ever faster the longer Dad's briefing goes on. I almost never get to go after an unambiguous, no-doubt scumbag with any moral shades of gray blown away as if by a high-powered wind machine. Sweet.

"There is one more complication you need to be aware of," Dad says.

"*Another* one?" Dodge scoffs in the back.

"We have intel that we are not the only organization interested in Twyst's island."

"Generation Zero?" I ask.

Dad gives me a funny look. Dodge stifles a guffaw in the back. Nina looks right at me; when I look back at her, she pretends she never stopped looking at the tablet in her lap.

Odd.

"Not Generation Zero," Dad says, clearing his throat. "Don't worry about them. You have a bigger problem."

"Harbinger," I say.

Dad nods. "Harbinger."

The Harbinger Foundation is, to you, a nonprofit do-gooder organization directed by a man named Toyo Harada, who claims to have survived the atomic bombing of Hiroshima even though he doesn't look a day over fifty, so he must have been less than a fetus at the time the Big One dropped.

To those who know the truth, like me, though, it's a front for the most powerful psiot in the world to add to his ranks and basically try to take over the world. PRS has been trying to shut him down for decades, but he's as slippery as a cartoon rabbit, with almost as many friends in government and big finance as we have. The main difference between our two organizations is that we grab pretty much every psiot we can find, regardless of power level, while Harbinger is only interested in exceptionally talented or powerful people. Makes sense a guy like Twyst would make Harada's short list.

"We have reason to believe the Harbinger Foundation will be sending a competing agent or agents to the island as well. If the opportunity arises, subdue them for the Nursery; if not, eliminate them. It is quite possible Harbinger will be looking to wreak havoc on the island to pollute the use of the #PowerParty hashtag themselves."

"Man, I would love another throwdown with those freaks," Dodge says. "Don't worry, Junior, as always, I got your back."

"As always, thank you for your input, Sergeant Dodge. Any questions? Let's get to it. Ray, c'mon. I have some time in between meetings. Wanna go bond?"

We take the troop elevator topside to throw a football around. The air is still cool, midspring, and the seagulls wheel overhead, annoyed at our unexpected presence. In the far distance loom the skyscrapers of Manhattan. Fresh Kills started life as a Cold War antiballistic missile base secretly sunk in Staten Island to protect New York City from nuclear attack. It was disguised under a sprawling garbage dump, the smell of which kept most curious looky-loos away. Then, when the obsolete missiles were decommissioned, Project Rising Spirit took over the base and covered the massive renovations by claiming it was an ecological project to turn the landfill into a park. People completely bought it, even though the site is surrounded by a chain-link fence and the public is only allowed in a couple times a year. One thing I've learned in the spy business is that lying to people is extremely easy as long as you're telling them something they want to hear.

That said, Fresh Kills, on the outside, still looks like a pretty awesome park, with its tall golden grass and ginkgo trees just now budding into leaves. Dad goes long, and just to mess with him, I put a little nanite-enhanced snap in my throw to make him run extra far, but even though he says it's no problem, I can hear his labored breaths. So I stop doing that. My tosses are shorter, with longer gaps in between. I can tell by his face that he knows I'm taking it easy on him, and he's not happy about it. But I don't think he's mad at me. He's mad at time.

I grab his next throw to me one-handed and hold the ball close to my chest for longer than I mean to. "What are you waiting for?" he calls out.

"Can I ask you a question?"

"You just did." He grins.

"Ugh, dad joke." I aim my throw square at his chest, and even though he catches it with both hands, the ball keeps going into his ribs and knocks him flat on his back.

"Aw, crap." I run over and give him a hand. He's smiling through gritted teeth. "Sorry about that."

"It's nothing. What's that question you want to ask me?"

"Did something . . . happen during the last op?"

He gives me a puzzled grin. "What do you mean?"

"Everyone's treating me . . . I don't know, differently. You, Nina . . .

even Dodge, in his own super douchey way. Nothing went, I dunno, totally pear shaped or anything last time. Did it?"

"You sure you want to know? You've been pretty explicit about being blissful in your ignorance. Shows you're wise beyond your years. Even when ops go off completely without a hitch, that can still mean . . . you know. Plenty of unpleasantness. What makes you want to hear about this one in particular?"

"Probably because I feel . . . well, there's this emptiness inside. Guilt, I guess. But I don't know what I have to feel guilty about."

"I've got an easy answer to that one: nothing. It was an op just like any other." He slams the football into his hand and starts jogging back. "Go long! I want to see if I can knock you on *your* keister."

I don't move. "Then there's no reason you shouldn't tell me what I did, right?"

"Well, c'mon, sport. You know it's not that simple. I gotta check with our DNI contact, see which aspects of the op are unclassified, which are classified top secret, and which are classified cosmic top secret." Though Project Rising Spirit is a private contractor, it still has to report to the Director of National Intelligence. "Your clearance only goes so far."

"I don't have clearance for my own life, my own memories?"

Dad spreads his arms. "One of the sacrifices we have to make in service to our country."

"'We'? What 'we'? You sacrificed for me. I didn't volunteer for this. I didn't volunteer to get sick. I didn't ask you to do what you did to cure me."

Dad's eyes glisten a little, and my stomach twists. "You think I was just gonna let you die, squirt? Watching you waste away, like that hospital bed was taking a little more of you each day? That I wasn't going to grasp at any straw, no matter how much of a long shot, to try and bring you back? If so, then you don't know me at all."

"Jeez, Dad. I didn't say that. I just don't think, you know, what I'm asking for is all that difficult."

"Well, I'm sorry to tell you that it is. I wish it wasn't, but I don't make the rules. Why are you acting so strange? This isn't like you."

"Maybe because everyone has been treating me weird ever since I woke up," I blurt out, way louder than I mean to. "And this conversation has only made me feel worse."

I turn and stalk back toward the hidden troop elevator. Dad calls my name behind me. I feel bad about everything—about making him feel bad, about him making me feel bad, about me feeling bad without knowing why.

"I'm gonna go call Salma," I yell back at him.

EIGHTEEN

Salma is sipping on a green smoothie through a straw when her FaceTime camera activates. She's sitting in a trendy juice bar, sunlight streaming through a window next to a wall shaggy with hanging mosses and vines, presumably in Toronto, where she lives.

Yes, I know. I have a girlfriend in Canada. Get all your jokes out of the way now.

Her face lights up when she sees me, which never fails to light me up too. "Ray, you're back! You dream of me?"

"Always," I laugh. Technically, it's not a lie. For all I know, I dream of Salma all the time, but my short-term sleeping and waking lives both get wiped away every time PRS restarts me for a new mission.

"Well, it's great to have you back." Salma sort of knows about 20 percent of what the deal is with me. I can't be totally honest with her, for the obvious reasons. She knows I live in some kind of government facility with my dad. She knows I get put under for long periods of time, but we've told her it's because I am not entirely cured of leukemia and need to be put into a medically induced coma periodically. Fortunately, Salma's own blood disease is in near-total remission. Her olive skin glows, her eyes are bright, and her glossy black hair has almost completely grown back.

We had adjacent rooms in the cancer ward of this specialist clinic on Long Island, and when we first met, we were convinced we were the last friend either of us would ever make, and that instantly bonded us. The facts that chemo had robbed us both of our hair and we had both wasted away to the point where if you combined our two body masses, you'd barely have enough for a single person helped too. We fought the cancer wars together, and survived. So we didn't need to bother with a lot of hey-how-are-you, what-have-you-been-up-to chitchat. She's alive, I'm alive. There's nothing better than that. Just her face filling up my laptop screen is enough. We don't need to ruin moments like this with words.

Still, just staring at each other across Wi-Fi would be weird. "Only twenty days to my birthday," she says.

"Yeah, I'm only mildly terrified." That's not a lie. I really am worried about meeting her parents, who I barely remember from the clinic and have only caught blurry waving glances of in previous video chats. It's just shy of three weeks till June 1, her birthday, and I am supposed to fly to Toronto to meet her mom and dad in person for the first time, stay in their guest room, and do tourist things in Toronto, whatever those might be. Her parents emigrated when they were adults and can only really speak Farsi, so if I say anything really stupid, Salma can just edit it out in her translation. That fact is the only thing that mitigates my nervousness somewhat.

"Hey, can I ask you a question?" It's out of my mouth before I can stop it.

"You just did."

"Ha ha, yeah, I never heard that one before. But I was just curious—do you ever think your life is made up?"

Salma blinks. "What?"

I'm wringing my hands together and I can't stop. "You ever wonder, like, maybe everything is too perfect? And you don't have any control of it? Your life is just like a museum, a series of set pieces, and you're just walking through it, observing, but not really, uh, allowed to touch anything? Or rearrange it at all?"

"Oh, jeez, Ray. Do you feel like that a lot?"

"No, I actually just started feeling like this today. But I am feeling it really, really strongly."

"Damn, babe, I wish I could reach through this screen and hold on to your hand."

"Me too." I chuckle uneasily.

She thinks for a second, finishing off the smoothie with one long, loud slurp through the straw. "I was watching this TikTok the other day from this yoga instructor, and she told this story, I think it's called a 'koan,' it's something the Buddhist wise men tell each other to, like, shock themselves into enlightenment or something. It tells the story of a monk who dreamed he was a butterfly. But then, when he woke up, he realized he couldn't be sure whether he was a human who was dreaming he was a butterfly, or this was the dream, now, and he was really a butterfly who was dreaming he was a man."

"Cool. So when did he figure it out?"

"What do you mean?"

"Which was he, man or butterfly?"

"Well, that's the point. He didn't figure it out. You never know. Lots of people have felt like you. Whoever came up with that koan did it thousands of years ago."

"Wow, so deep."

"You're such a jerk." Salma laughs. "That's what I get for trying to help your lame ass."

"Admit it, you love this lame ass."

She leans in and kisses the camera. "I just wish you were here."

"I'll be your next birthday present."

"Yeah. Can't wait."

"What you've got here is Zahn Enterprises' top-of-the-line wingpack, the Osprey," Dodge is yelling over the roar of jet engines as he straps me into a giant graphite arrowhead almost as tall as I am. "You're jumping out of here ten kilometers in the air with no parachute, just this.

You should have about forty klicks of flying ahead of you. Slow down when you have a visual on the island, using this toggle." He indicates a button on the strap on the underside of the wing where my hand will go. "The Osprey is completely buoyant and has about twenty kilos of gear in it, including a mobile Screamer and a long-range sniper rifle. You're coming in on the side of the island with the highest cliffs, low enough so spotters looking for aircraft approaches should miss you. Land in the surf below, using the Osprey's retractable mooring line to hide it in some coastal shrubbery or whatever, so you can come back to your gear if you need to."

He steps back and appraises me, strapped into the wingpack. "You look like a complete tool. Any questions?"

"Yeah, where are you going to be while I'm taking all the risks? Leaving racist comments on websites as usual?"

"Don't you worry about me, Junior. As usual I'm your secret weapon, ready to be sent in whenever stuff goes pear shaped. Also, if Harada personality cultists do decide to show their ugly faces, I'll be a nice little surprise for them. Nina will be your eye in the sky." He nods at her, sitting on the far side of the cabin with a military-reinforced tablet computer and headset. "She'll have full visual of your left-eye HUD and maintain verbal contact throughout. Your communicator is attached behind your ear and to your throat. It uses bone to send vibrations to your ear canal without the need for actual sound. With that diode thingy over your larynx, you won't need to speak out loud either. Just sound out the words in your head, and the comm will send it back to her in spoken language."

Nina mouths into her microphone across the cabin, and I hear her clearly in my ear: "We have a substantial amphibious presence about twenty kilometers offshore. Once you've neutralized the guards and subdued the more hostile psiots, we'll send in the extraction team."

"Copy that," I silently mouth, and Nina gives me a thumbs-up from her seat: She heard me fine.

"You done stalling?" Dodge punches a button on the cabin wall and the bomb bay doors in the floor begin to open. Whale-sized clouds hang below. I can see the misty jet stream speeding across the outline of the plane. There's no land to see. I might as well be jumping into a bottomless gas giant, like Neptune. This high up I can literally see the curvature of the Earth on the glowing horizon. The cold makes me grit my teeth.

I turn back to yell something to Dodge, but he plants his boot in my ass and pushes me out the hatch. "Time to earn your allowance, Junior!"

The hollow laugh through his respirator is almost immediately cut off by the flapping roar of the air around me as I drop, as if he's been carried away by the wind. I should be so lucky.

Most paratroopers have to strap on a full-body wingsuit with an oxygen mask to survive the high altitudes. I'm strong enough that I can hold my breath until I hit a breathable level of atmosphere. For all I know, I'll be meeting resistance the second I make landfall, so I'd rather not be struggling out of a nylon body condom while taking heavy fire.

The clouds pull back like curtains ripped away until finally exposed beneath me is the grand prize: the sea, rolling and rippling away in every direction. The AR, augmented reality, in my left eyepiece kicks in, identifying Twyst's island far in the distance and telling me inside a blinking hexagon that I have about thirty-eight kilometers to go before I see it on the horizon, like I'm playing a video game.

I blink.

A video game.

It *does* feel like I'm playing a video game, doesn't it?

I'm a badass unkillable mercenary who still plays catch with his dad and who has a loving girlfriend. I have a bully I need to deal with, but I find him sadder and more pathetic than threatening. I didn't just beat leukemia; I laid it over one knee and paddled its butt cheeks bright red. I'm not a cancer survivor; I'm a bona fide cancer champion.

All seems too good to be true, doesn't it?

"Hey, Ray," Nina says into my ear, "everything okay out there? Your heart rate is weirdly elevated."

I've started breathing, well, hyperventilating, really, as the water gets closer and closer. It's about an hour before dawn, and I can start to see the moonlight glinting on individual waves. The AR is very strongly beeping at me that I should start pulling up on the throttle now, let the wings level out my descent.

But the waves below look made-up. A constantly undulating fluid plain that doesn't even seem like the sea to me anymore, but a computer-generated texture map. They can do that, right? Inject simulated images right into my brain.

How do I know any of this is even real?

"Ray, c'mon, please talk to me, kiddo."

Altitude alerts join Nina's breaking voice in my ears: My drop will become terminal if I don't deploy the Osprey's wings in the next few seconds.

That would settle the argument once and for all, wouldn't it? If I just let myself drop. You fall into the ocean from ten klicks in the sky, forget it, game over. At that velocity, hitting water is no different than hitting concrete. I'd be a stain on the Mediterranean for a few minutes before what little was left of me sank beneath the waves.

Then I'd wake up in my nutrient bath in Fresh Kills, laughing at myself for believing any of this was possible in the first place.

Or, you know, I'm wrong, and this is real, and I'll never really know since I won't wake up from this at all. My pieces would be scattered too far and too deep across the sea for all the king's special forces and all the king's scientists ever to be able to put me back together again.

The AR is making all sorts of *danger, danger* sounds and blinking arrows at me: Open your wings. Fly this way. Or die.

"Dodge," I can overhear Nina saying, voice cracking, "I think we've lost Ray. He's passed out from the altitude or something. Get ready to deploy in five."

The idea of being replaced by Dodge, even in a dream, fills me with such revulsion that my hands tighten around the wing straps and find the controls. I ease out the rudders on the edges of the wings, and my drop stops being completely vertical.

"I'm fine," I say louder than I need to. "Just had to get used to the controls, is all."

"Oh, thank God," Nina breathes. "Dodge, belay that."

"Yeah, sit your ass down, Dodge."

The warning chirrups subside as I glide into the blinking bracket laid out in the AR. I level out over the waves at approximately 160 kilometers per hour, and soon the top of Douchebag Island pops up on the horizon.

"Ray, I am going to need you to do me a favor, and if I ask you for proof of life, you're going to have to give me some goddamn proof of life pronto, you got that?"

"Sorry, ma'am, I copy that. Won't happen again."

"You mean like you calling me ma'am?"

"Right. Sorry."

NINETEEN

The island comes up on me in two ways: gradually, then suddenly.

At first it's just the idea of land in the distance, barely peeking up out of the Mediterranean.

Then, after a few breaths and blinks, it's right there in front of me, more real than a heart attack, several-story cliffs looming out of my vision. I grip the controls of the wingpack and come in as low as I can without actually skimming the top of the water. At one point, I'm close enough to the surface that I'm parting the sea in a white foam that might be visible to watchers on the cliff tops, so I climb a meter higher.

The AR tracker superimposed over my left eyeball starts blinking at me to slow down about ten klicks out, and within a few minutes, I'm gently gliding to a stop before the rocks and shoals at the bottom of the steepest cliff.

I unstrap myself from the Osprey right before my bootheel hits the algae-slick stones. I pull a silicone-skinned stake out of the side of the mooring line and ram it as deep as I can in the nearest sea rock, then haul myself out of the water and sit on it. I pop the lid open on the wingpack as it bobs in the surf and pull out the PRS Omen, a 5.56-caliber rifle with a built-in bipod, an extendable stock, and a quick-change sniper extension I can twist onto the main barrel, doubling its length. I shoulder-strap the

Omen onto my back, then pull out a belt rung with thirty-round mags. My survival knife never left my belt in case I needed to cut myself free of the pack, and it doesn't mind getting wet. I grab the mobile Screamer—a phased electromagnetic pulse generator to disrupt psiots' ability to trigger their powers mentally—which is about the size and shape of a gaming console but way lighter. I hang its strap off my other shoulder. Finally I take out the grappling gun and kick the Osprey lid closed with a bootheel.

The grappling gun—a ballistic line launcher, if you want to get all technical about it—fires a 150-meter line with a .22-caliber charge nobody's going to hear over the roar and crash of the surf. Hell, I barely hear it when I aim at the cliff face above and fire. The stake seems to sink deep and catch in the rocks above with my first try, or at least it's pretty taut when I pull on it. If I'm wrong, well, then I get to find out if my nanites can regrow a shattered spine. Not something I particularly want to find out.

The gun part of the launcher attaches to my belt, and the winch in the spear above me starts winding the line upward, pulling me with it. I help it out by running up the side of the cliff.

I'm almost at the edge when a guy with his own rifle slung over his shoulder steps up to the edge of the cliff and tosses a mostly smoked but still-lit cigarette into the ocean. I bob my face out of the way so the red-hot end doesn't burn my cheek. I dig my boot into the cliff right before I reach the stake and propel myself up so I am eyeball to eyeball with the guy.

The guard doesn't have time to react to my popping up out of nowhere. His eyes don't even have a chance to go wide. His mouth opens when I grab the front of his flak jacket, but I hurl him off the cliff before he can cry out. Once I have both feet on horizontal ground, I turn and watch him fall. The sea winds steal his scream. He twists and flails until he's falling back-first, and our eyes lock, and he watches me watch him until he hits the rocks. He bounces, his spine now U-shaped the wrong way. He drops into the black water and disappears.

One of Dodge's favorite sayings is that killing is like smoking; only the first time is hard. There's no way he came up with something that smart on his own.

Of course, I have no memory of the first time I killed somebody. I asked all my kills to be purged from memory along with the op itself. Turns out the downside of that is the next time I kill somebody, it's the first time all over again.

I feel my throat tightening. Of course, I have no memory of requesting that my memory of past kills be wiped. That's got to be useful. A soldier without conscience. Not because he doesn't have a conscience, but because he is blissfully ignorant of anything he might have done that would offend that conscience.

Look, I tell myself, this guy works for Twyst. Twyst is an abusive scumbag promoting an abusive scumbag ideology. You take a guy like Twyst's money, you also take the consequences. And if you had actually done the job Twyst's paying for, I couldn't've gotten the drop on you, and you'd still be alive.

Big sigh. Yeah, just keep telling yourself that, Bloodshot, you big tough killing machine.

I drop to my belly on the ground and pop out the bipod under the rifle barrel, then twist in the sniper extension. The Omen scope boasts night enhancement, a laser designator, and a built-in AI that measures wind direction and velocity, adjusting the target reticule in my viewfinder accordingly. It may also be able to make pancakes, but I haven't asked it to yet.

The Greek island's landscape is dotted with ancient sculptures and pillared ruins. I'm behind a crumbling pavilion right now. From here I can see three obvious targets, all armed, all patrolling a different sector of the complex. I fix the reticule on the first head, hold my breath, pull the trigger. Then the next, then the next. Boom, boom, boom. They drop too fast for me to see any blood.

"Bloodshot, status report," Nina murmurs in my ear.

"Southwest quadrant neutralized. Proceeding to interior to find setup point for the Screamer."

"Copy that. Intel suggests Harbinger Foundation operatives inbound. Three-person fireteam. You don't have a lot of time."

"I'm waxing goons as fast as I can, Nina."

"Just saying. No reason to worry. You keep up this pace, we shouldn't have a problem."

Twyst's island is a maze of ridges, rocks, and tropical brush, punctuated here and there by an occasional statue, usually of a hot, ripped dude with a halo of grapevines and a wine jug raised high. I crouch low and make my way toward the center of the island, where I hear a repeated low thrum. On my way I take out two guards walking together by climbing into low willow branches and waiting until they descend the ancient steps where their other buddies lie. I bring the Omen scope to my eye, and the AR reticule finds a spot right above each of their noses. I hold my breath and squeeze the trigger once, twice. Down they go. The idea is to degrade resistance to its lowest ebb before my eventual discovery, which, considering the trail of bodies I'm leaving behind, is a virtual certainty. So far I'd say I'm doing okay.

I make my way to the ridge where the two guards I just dropped lie. My view is blocked by a thicket of olive trees. Beside me is a vine-encircled pillar, its ridged sides pockmarked enough from the centuries that I have plenty of footholds to let me climb to its top.

Finally, I have a good view of the island spread out before me. A fancy villa near the center, with a huge, well-lit area behind it around a reflecting pool. At the top of the stage, a dais has been raised, where a bald man in sunglasses and a floral-print kimono is surrounded by DJ equipment. With his left hand, Twyst is adjusting the bass and treble sliders. With his right hand, he's making time with devil's-horn fingers. Churning in front of him are about thirty people, dancing, shooting each other with foam cannons, jumping in and out of the pool, crowd surfing.

Twyst is playing a heavy bass-lined pop song I feel like I should know, but I don't. If I were a normal teenager, would I have an encyclopedic knowledge of modern pop songs? But they change so often, and I spend so much time asleep. I can't keep up. Makes me wonder, like Dodge says, how old I really am since I never seem to hear the same song twice.

Or, closer to the truth, I feel like kids keep playing the same song, eternally, year after year, with slightly different lyrics and voices. *Partying and dancing are awesome, love is simultaneously the worst and the best thing to ever happen to you, who cares about tomorrow today, it doesn't matter,* et cetera, rinse, repeat.

Twyst's kimono flops open to display the tattoos across his washboard abs. He has bright-blue mascara on his eyes and a giant clown mouth painted across his face with cherry-red lipstick. On his bald head rests a garland of grape leaves. It's the exact same outfit on many of the statues dotting the island. I could try to take him out now, but I'd have a lot of his ticked-off followers to deal with. Best to set up the Screamer first.

On the dark side of the pool party sit various trailers with doors set in them. Dressing rooms for the contestants, makeup trailers, and supply trailers, as far as I can tell through the Omen's scope.

At last, my reticule stops at a three-story tower made of scaffolding, the top surrounded in canvas, overlooking the stage. Must be the sound booth. Assuming all those kids at the dance are my target psiots, that'd be the ideal place to set up the Screamer. The Screamer has its own battery pack, which is fine when I'm dancing with a single psiot, or even two, but up against an entire party island full of psiots, who knows how long the Screamer will have to scream to disable all targets. Hooking it up to an external power source is the safest move, and lucky me, Mr. DJ here has surrounded this island with generators.

Through the scope I see a single occupant in a baseball cap bent over the soundboard. I could take them out from back here, easy, but in the time it would take me to get from here to there, who knows who might wander in there to find the body? Best for me to move in, take the guard out up close and personal, then make with the hookup.

"Found a place for the Screamer," I whisper to Nina, my fairy godmother. "Moving in."

"Copy that."

Keeping low, I make my way to the sound tower. Even though the place is crawling with guard patrols, the topography is so uneven, with rising hills and towering statues, it's super easy to go from cover to cover, shadow to shadow, remaining totally unseen.

I pass the trailers, the doors of which bear *Power Party* logos. The graphics are badly pixelated on foamcore and Scotch-taped to the sides of the dressing rooms. For what is essentially a TV set, I can't help but notice I haven't seen any pro cameras or tall lights anywhere.

Of course, they could be trained on this massive party. I pass between trailers and can see the revelers by the pool: They're all beautiful people, like they stepped off a bus-stop perfume ad. No more than 8 percent body fat between the lot of them. They're smiling, chins tilted upward, eyes rolled back under their lids. Twyst raises a palm overhead to keep the beat, and they follow his gesture, all swaying in the same motion, tentacles of a sea anemone buffeted by the same relentless current. They follow that hand and move with it as if they were hypnotized cobras.

I can't tell if what I'm looking at is criminal, but it sure is hella weird.

The trailers nearest to the giant speakers vibrate in time with the beat. Still, I keep quiet and hear the scrape of a boot on gravel in the distance. I vault up onto the trailer roof and flatten onto my stomach. I crawl to the edge of the trailer roof and peer over. A guard is leaning against the wall facing the sound tower, holding his cell phone with both hands, chortling at some sitcom on the small screen in his native language.

I wait until he's doubled over at a particularly hilarious pratfall; then I drop down behind him and twist the Omen shoulder strap around his neck like a tourniquet. I pick him up and wait until his feet stop kicking. Then I lay him in a bush under the air-conditioning unit jutting out of the nearby trailer.

None of the partiers around the pool have eyes for anything other than Twyst, whose eyes are closed like he's fallen into his own trance. I slip my combat knife out of my boot and clench it between my teeth. I look around and make sure no one is watching, and then I steal up the ladder as quick as a bug up a wall.

The person monitoring the soundboard is in a dark windbreaker and ball cap. Her back is to me. I pull my legs up and take two steps toward her, knife in my hand.

The sound operator drops a pen, and it bounds across the floor toward me. She's looking around for it. Any second she's going to turn around and see me. I need to lunge toward her and end her.

But then she takes off her Pro-Bro ball cap, and the blonde hair spills out. Backlit by the stage lights before her, she looks just like the girl from my dreams, the one on the impossibly high balcony overlooking the endless city of light.

I freeze up just as she turns to look at me.

She doesn't freeze. She grabs something off her console and it's sparking at me, and suddenly the world is filled with light.

Then it's filled with dark.

TWENTY

Faces, faces, all around me. Sun-bronzed beauties and tattooed weight lifters in Hawaiian-print swim trunks. Dozens of them.

Obviously, this is a nightmare, and I recoil, trying to thrash away, to wake up.

But I'm already awake. And I can't thrash anywhere. My hands are cuffed behind me with steel cables that cut painfully into my flesh. But still, when I reel back, I move. I drift around 360 degrees, and on every side of me are beautiful, young gawkers staring out at me, wide-mouthed, like I am the newest baby animal born at the zoo.

I look down, and my eyes are dazzled by the spotlights reflecting off the water under me. Okay. It's starting to make sense. I am lashed to a floating pool chair and have been set adrift in the deep end. I've gone from party crasher to party focus.

One whole quadrant of partiers parts like a tan sea, and out steps Twyst, my Omen rifle in his hands.

"You're awake! Good, 'cause I just want to congratulate you on a job well done, bro. You killed a bunch of people whose only job was to protect us. Hiding in the dark. Never even gave them a chance to fight back. You're a real good goose-stepper. Good at following orders. Giving you a five-star review on Fascist Yelp."

"I'm not so bad one-on-one either," I say. "Want to untie me and find out?"

"Naw, bro, I got a better idea." He makes a show of dumping the Omen in the pool so he can watch me watch it sink to the bottom. "Gonna livestream your confession." He snaps his fingers, and the girl from the tower in the Pro-Bro baseball cap sets up circle lights and a tablet mounted on a tripod pointed in my direction. Even half-blinded in the middle of the pool, I can see that she doesn't look a thing like the girl from my dreams. What was I thinking before? "Your deep state masters in the United States of Amer-i-K-K-K-uh got to know there are free alpha males out in the world they can't push around or intimidate with their mind-virus propaganda."

"Free? *You're* free. What about this lot? They get the same freedoms as you?"

"Sure, bro. Everybody's here of their own free will, aren't you, everybody?"

"We are here of our own free will," everybody says simultaneously.

"Totally convincing," I say.

"What? Everybody here signed their releases before they got here, didn't they?"

"We signed our releases before we got here," everybody starts to say before Twyst waves them into silence.

"Wait a minute." I look around at the slack, TikTok-ready beauty of the kids around me. "Are any of these people actually psiots?"

Twyst shrugs. "They all think they are. Or, I mean, they all want to be. Statistically speaking, at least, a couple of them are latents. I think that dude over there, the one in the *Adventure Time* hoodie, he can, like, create six cubic inches of mashed potatoes with his mind or something. Who knows? It's not important. We all wanna be special, bro. It's human nature."

"It did seem a little convenient that all your 'potential psiots' are reality show–ready hot. Now that they're all here, what exactly do you plan on doing with them?"

"What do I plan on doing with them? Whatever I want, bro." He snaps his fingers, and all the photogenic normies around me drop into a heap on top of each other as if they practiced it. "Bodies, bodies, bodies, baby. I can see them like the keys of a piano. And I can reach out with my mind and play whatever tune comes to mind. Switch tracks, slow 'em down . . . speed 'em up. It let me become a champion in the ring, but before too long, switching off my opponents' nervous systems so I could beat their asses just got boring, you know? I realized I was wasting my God-given talents winning gold belts on pay-per-view. My potential is unlimited."

His eyes start to gleam. "I am the new Dionysus, the new party god. At first, I didn't want to believe it. But then they all turned on me, first online, then the government. That's when I knew. I had to get away from their jealousy, bro. I knew they couldn't stop me, even though they'd try. That's why I got to do some heinous acts to you, bro. Let the normie elites know: Messing with Mr. Twyst is not conducive to positive living. Or living, period."

Suddenly, he breaks out into a laughing jag. "Wow! Listen to me! Blah, blah, blah. Host can't stop talking about himself. Gah! So lame, right? When it's you who's the guest of honor, bro, the man of mystery. I wanna hear your story. Like, for instance . . ."

He nods, and his blonde techie returns, carrying the Screamer down to the edge of the pool. Twyst crouches down and pats the device. "What were you going to do with this little guy, huh? Looks too fancy to be a bomb. You know what I think, bro? I think it might be some kinda brain-zappy power blocker. What do you say, bro? Am I warm? C'mon, bro, you can tell me, just give me a little wink or something."

I stay mum. Unfortunately for me, the Screamer is insulated from technokinesis so psiots can't turn it off remotely. That means I can't turn it on remotely either.

Twyst leers at my obvious discomfort. "Yeah, I thought so. I thought so, bro. You can't fool me. Well, too bad you never got a chance to plug it in." He wags the plug of the dangling cord at me and stands up. "Still, what I can't figure is, wouldn't this thing shut down your powers too? 'Cause you got to be a psiot, bro. You got to be. Because, like I said, bodies are my medium. My canvas. That's why I can tell, you don't got one. Not a human body, anyway. Nothing I can lock on to. I can see why they sent you here to do me in, but I gotta ask, like, what *are* you, bro?"

"I'm just some guy," I say, but my mouth has gone dry.

Twyst shakes his head. "Bull. These normies all want to be special. But you and me, bro, we're the real deal."

"I was sick. As a kid." I know that under no rational circumstances should I actually be telling this jackass this, but I realize that he has the power to tell me some of the things I've always wanted to know about myself. "Scientists—my dad—injected me with microscopic machines that fixed me, and they took to me, bonded to me, after curing me."

"Cured you of what, exactly?"

"AML—acute myeloid leukemia. Bone marrow cancer."

"Bro. Bro. Listen to me. Somebody been, like, catfishing you, bro. Cancer, even after it's gone, sings a song, bro, like a hum. Bone marrow too. And you—you're like a library at midnight, bro. Nothing but silence."

"No. No. My name is Ray Garrison. I am sixteen years old." I am shaking my head. "There are nanites in my bloodstream, but the rest of it is me, it's all me. Skeleton—muscles—brain—heart." I strain against the handcuffs, and the chain goes taut as the bracelets dig into my real skin, stopped by my real bones.

"Dude's losing it. Gotta get this segment in while he's still coherent." I'm barely conscious of Twyst spinning a finger around for his ball-cap-wearing tech to start filming. "Send out the e-blast. Let the Pro-Bros know we go live with a very special guest provided us by Uncle Sam in, uh, let's call it five minutes."

See? I tell myself. The handcuffs know there's a body there. What else would there be? Just a me-shaped blob of nanites? Why, if that was true, I could just de-solidify my body and bones and slip the handcuffs off by—

I hear the splash behind me, but I still can't believe it. I keep my wrists behind me, even though I can feel, I can *feel* there's nothing restraining them anymore.

I am crying. I am crying and I can't believe what's running through my mind: *I am a real boy, I am not a puppet, I am a real boy. I have a girlfriend in Canada!*

I can't stop myself anymore, and I bring my hands and wrists to the front of my body so I can see them. There are no wounds on my wrists, no marks on me.

I can look below into the water and see the handcuffs, unlocked and unbroken, drifting to the bottom of the pool.

I'm not a real boy at all.

I start screaming, and I can't stop. Twyst whirls to look at me, and I look at him like I'm seeing him for the first time, him, the one responsible for this, the one who prevented me from going on with this beautiful dream of humanity forever. I stand up in the floating chair, and I'm still screaming; every phony vein and tendon in my body is standing on edge, and his eyes go glassy with fear. I am ready to leap off my floater at him and show him how much of a disadvantage it is to have real bones because I am going to break every single one of his with my bare hands—

"Bacchae, protect your god!" Twyst cries out, voice cracking.

Three dozen beach-blanket himbos and bimbos all leap at once and, without even bothering to stand all the way up first, cascade in a human avalanche on top of me and drag me off the chair and into the water.

I am strong, but they are many. I kick and punch off as many as I can, but as soon as I get one away, two or three more plunge down through the water to take their place. I don't know how long I can stay submerged before I start drowning, but I have no interest in finding out right now.

Still, they've got their hands on my throat and arms and legs, and I can barely move. In the brightness of the floodlights pointed at the pool, their vivid shadows make it nearly impossible to see. I'm slammed cheek-first into the tiled floor and my lungs start to tighten. I have a brief thought that I can pull the same trick I did with my wrists with my whole body, turn into a floating cloud of nanites, and literally slip through their fingers, but I'm worried about doing that underwater. Would I just disperse like an oil slick across the waves? And besides, there's a part of me that still desperately wants to maintain the fiction I am mostly a human being. Human beings can't just turn into mist and re-form again. What am I, a Dracula?

I lash my hands out to keep them from completely flattening me at the bottom of the pool, and my right fingers wrap around the stock of the Omen rifle resting on the tiles. At last. Something is going my way. Jackass thought that was a flex, dumping it in the drink, but little does he know an Omen is completely waterproof.

I take the rifle in both hands and use the stock as a lever to push up through the mob trying to crush me. I kick through them with my feet and use a free hand to crawl up them until finally my head is above the surface. There are still a few Bacchae trying to gouge my eyes out or flail fists at my nose. Twyst has actually returned to his DJ station and is dropping some hot beats to my aquatic murder. What a total douche.

When I point Omen in his general direction, he drops the headphones he's been holding to one ear and hides behind his deck. But what the AR reticule finds and the built-in targeting computer zeroes in on isn't his useless bald head.

It's the on switch for the Screamer.

I fire. The bullet finds its mark. The Screamer's internal battery switches on, and the first neural shock wave ripples throughout the pool area. Everybody feels it, including me, and we all spasm, like a bumblebee suddenly buzzed past our ears.

But the real screams of agony come from beneath the DJ station, where Twyst's brain is getting good and righteously cheese-grated. Psychically, I mean.

One by one, the kids trying to murder me detach and look at each other with rising mixtures of shame, fear, alarm, and, finally, anger.

"Twyst!" one girl yells. "He—he—"

"PIECE-OF-SHIT MIND RAPIST," one of the biggest dudes yells, and soon they are all clambering out of the pool, looking around.

"Where is he?" the furious blonde in the ball cap yells.

I point helpfully under the DJ rack and whistle.

Twyst is struggling to rise—I must say, rather impressively—under his own power. The crowd lets out a roar of recognition and begins sprinting after him. Somehow he is able to put one foot in front of the other to get away. The mob pursues, ready to give this psychic predator a crash course in consent.

I am forgotten. I swim to the edge of the pool so I can reach out and crank the area radius on the Screamer to the max. The battery will burn out a lot quicker on this setting, but this way there's nowhere on this tiny island Twyst can hide that his powers will work.

I pull myself up out of the water and catch my breath. My instinct is still to act like I have lungs. In the distance I hear shouts and automatic weapons fire. Were Twyst's guards mind-controlled like his "contestants" and have they now joined the pursuit against their former boss, or are they also being pursued? One thing is clear: There's only one psiot on the whole island, and he's been neutralized, so the rest of Rising Spirit can move in.

I start to tell Nina the good news, but then I realize I no longer have the skull comm on me. The Bacchae must have ripped it off during our scrum, so it's among the detritus on the bottom of the pool.

That's when I see the figure moving stealthily between the trailers on the edges of the spotlights' glare. Somebody who isn't after anybody else on the island. Somebody with their own agenda.

"Harbinger," I can't help but say out loud.

TWENTY-ONE

I rush into the darkness, in pursuit of a Harbinger terrorist. I don't have to think about the implications of what happened in the pool. My nanites simply split apart and rebuilt my body. I thought I was the same as I always was, before I got sick, but now New and Improved, With-Nanites. The micromachines simply rebuilt the hurt parts of me when I got shot or stabbed or whatever. The possibility that the nanites have rebuilt me, over and over again, possibly every time I lay in my memory-wipe coma—wait, could it be that the nanites are the ones actually rewriting my memory each time, remaking my mind as fresh and new as my unmarked flesh?—makes me sick to my stomach, a stomach that may only exist as a bellwether for emotion. The nanites don't need a stomach. They break down the food they ingest to the molecule, to be reconstituted . . . well, as themselves. Everything about me is a copy of a copy of a copy.

Is it possible there's no distinct line where I end and the nanites begin? What about my brain? Has it ever been shot and rebuilt? Who is thinking these thoughts?

Who is living my story?

I can't help but ask these questions, but I'm not so interested in the answers right at this instant. Blinded by existential panic, I'm in no state to follow anybody, and I soon lose the infiltrator in the darkness beyond the pool lights.

Remembering where I saw him crouching, though, I head behind more equipment trailers where a waist-high external generator chugs-chugs-chugs power to the now-abandoned rave. At first glance, nothing seems out of the ordinary.

But I take a second glance. Someone has attached a rectangular metal pod the size of my head on the other side of the generator with magnets. I carefully take it off and turn it around. A silently blinking trigger is at the head of several wires of a duct-taped collection of hexagonal metal cylinders stuffed with a waxy, pinkish filling. If I have to guess, and I do, I'd say the metal casing is magnesium alloy ML5 surrounding a plastic pyrotechnic similar to thermite. I'm holding in my hands a firebomb powerful enough to take out this generator, this pool area, this entire side of the island.

The charge is set off by a simple radio detonator, which I can disarm mentally—and I tell it to warn me if someone tries to set it off remotely. I tuck it under my arm and head back into the estate, looking for its friends. And it definitely has friends. Thermite charges are like potato chips: You can't have just one.

I don't find any other bombs as I make my way toward the villa, which is where it looks like the hostages have concentrated their search for Twyst. It's a series of gleaming white cubes stacked on top of each other, facing an infinity pool that shimmers up to the edge of the cliffside, overlooking the Mediterranean. The lights have all been turned on, and I can see Twyst's former thralls through the windows: They're throwing open doors, overturning cabinets, tearing the house apart looking for him.

None of them spot the guy in full black-and-gray camo leaping from an upper balcony and landing in a hero crouch poolside. He's carrying some kind of satchel with him, maybe another bomb. He heads toward a domed pavilion perched on an outcropping of pockmarked volcanic rock.

He's too busy looking behind him to make sure he's not spotted from the villa to notice me sprinting at him from his blind spot. He doesn't know I'm there until I'm leap-kicking into his right side between the pillars of the pavilion, sending him sprawling across the floor mosaic and nearly off the cliff and into the sea.

The satchel falls from his hand and clatters across the ground. It's some kind of blue cooler.

The figure leaps up into a defensive position. He's holding the hilt of a sword, out of which a swarm of nanites plumes until they form a gleaming blade.

As soon as he recognizes me, he rocks back on one heel with a sigh. The sword unforms into a cloud of nothing again.

"Oh," Dodge says. "It's you."

"You bring lunch?" I say, nodding at the cooler. "Got a meatball sub in there for me? I'm starving."

Dodge gives me that look again, that leering smile that makes me feel like a clown. "You wanna see what's in the cooler? You *sure* you wanna see what's in the cooler?"

"Will it end this conversation? Because then I really want to see what's in the cooler."

He shrugs. "Your funeral." He grabs the cooler and sets it right side up in front of him. "You know I enjoy giving you a hard time, kid, but seriously, most of the time, you do solid work. Sure, it looked hairy there for a few minutes, but we knew you could handle Twyst and his teeny-bopper army. As blunt instruments go, you're one of the best. You knock down nine out of ten pins, then they bring in somebody with real finesse, like me, to get the spare. We make a great team, don't let anyone tell you different."

"Finally, my life has meaning," I deadpan.

The cooler has what appear to be two thumbprint-activated locks that Dodge presses his digits against, and the lid hisses open and slides away in a cloud of white vapor.

"Go on, take a quick look—*get off my jock, Nina, he's the one who brought it up, and you're just gonna wipe his memory after this anyway*," he yells suddenly in the general direction of his skull comm before turning back to me. "Seriously, it's humid out here and I got to close this up again before the meat starts going bad."

I look into the cooler. I know I'm going to see Twyst's head even before I lean in, but when I do see Twyst's head in the cooler, neck stump resting in a congealing puddle of blood on the floor of the pack, his eyes rolled up, tongue hanging partly out between exposed lips, I feel a little sick to my stomach. Sure, he was a monster. But do monsters deserve a monster's end? Does anybody?

Dodge swipes the lid with his thumbs, and the lid hisses closed again. "We prefer to capture psiots alive. And nine times out of ten, we do. The eggheads aren't a hundred percent sure that all the psiot's power resides in the brain, as opposed to being distributed throughout the rest of the nervous system. But Garrison didn't want to take any chances with this one. Twyst ever escaped containment, he could tell us all to eat our own sidearms, and we'd do it. Who needs it?

"And you set it up perfectly, kid. Hit the rabbit with the Screamer, and he runs straight for his warren—or his panic room, in this case. He thought it was his little secret, but too bad, so sad, we bribed the architects for the plans to his villa. So I was waiting for him. Snicker-snack. Big, bad Twyst is just another scalp hanging from the belt of the Red Cell–Bloodshot team-up. Now c'mon, follow me, I got a Zodiac down by the rocks. Let's rappel down, blow the charges, and paddle out to the rendezvous point. You're not the only one of us whose nanites are starving."

He grabs the head cooler and stands up to leave, but I show him the thermite charge I picked up. "Harbinger Foundation was never coming, were they?"

Dodge growls and snatches the charge out of my hand. "Where did you get that? 'Cause now I got to go put it back. And I wasn't kidding about being really hungry."

"This island is all scrub and wooden structures. You set off these charges, you're gonna kill most of the kids here. Maybe all of them."

"A-*duh*," Dodge singsongs, crossing his eyes.

"And then in a few days, or hours, 'evidence' will leak to the press implicating Toyo Harada and Harbinger. Make it look like they wanted to shut down Twyst's operation themselves."

"Wow! Check out the big brain on Junior. If you want to be a jerk and not tell me where I have to put this back, fine. I'll figure it out on my own. But if any kids see me and I got to kill 'em 'cause we have a strict no-witnesses policy at PRS, their blood's on your hands, son, not mine."

He tries to walk away from me, but I grab him by the arm.

"How old am I, Dodge?"

He swallows his cockiness all at once. The light goes out of the eyes behind his four lenses, leaving only embers colder than the voice from his respirator. "Boy, you better take your hands off me if you know what's good for you."

"What's the problem? You were all hot and bothered to tell me back at Fresh Kills."

"Sorry, kid, Mommy and Daddy will send me to my room without supper if I air the family's dirty laundry—*I know, Mommy Nina, shut up*," he yells side-mouthed at his comms. "That's the problem with rebooting you as a perpetual teenager. Every single mission, you get your period again for the first time."

I scissor-kick him in the face.

The respirator breaks, and his nose along with it. He falls on his back in the ancient dust and sends up a cloud. "You little bitch! Enough is enough! *I said shut up, Nina!*" He rips the comm off his head and throws it away. "You wanna go, Junior? Okay, let's go. Rematch time. Only this time, your little friends aren't here to save your ass."

Little friends? Huh? Does he mean my nanites? Because they're very much still here.

He leaps straight up to his feet from his back, the nanosword forming with a series of air-cutting hisses from the pommel in his hand. The nanites are already trying to regrow his nose—and badly. They're making some awful miniature elephant's trunk or bat's snout thing. If I didn't want to kick his ass so badly, I might actually feel sorry for him.

"How old am I, Dodge? Sixteen going on twenty? Twenty-five? Thirty? How long have I been doing this?"

He steps forward, swinging the molecular-thin blade at me. They're exploratory lunges, and I don't accommodate him, dancing backward out of range. "Six."

"Six years? So I'm . . . twenty-two?"

He feints as if to launch another attack, and I start to sidestep, but then he stops and sweeps dust up into my eyes with his foot. I'm blinded for less than a second, but it's enough for him to carve an X across my chest with two diagonal swipes. Through it I can see the red circle glowing in the middle of my torso—when that appears, that always means my nanites are working overtime.

He rears back with both hands on the hilt, aiming at my neck, but I'm on to him now. I drop to a knee and claw-strike him twice in the stomach. He groans, doubles over, and I grab his undershirt and flip him over me. He lands on a shoulder and rolls twice but then pounces up on his feet. Unfortunately, he's held on to the nanosword the whole time.

"Dumbass. It's not a math problem. You're six."

I'm focused on the fight. I hear the words, but they don't mean much to me. "Wait, I'm what?"

"It makes me sad that a guy made up of millions and millions of tiny computers is so incredibly stupid." He rushes at me with a snarl, but I shake the confusion from my head and spin out of his way, giving him a swift kick to the back of the head as he goes. He roars and falls to his knees but does a little somersault. The nanoblade disperses into a cloud when he hits the dirt.

"Garrison came up with the nanites to make next-gen soldiers, to increase strength, heal injury, but every single jarhead he injected them into turned into gray goo because all the nanites would do is make copies of themselves or, at lower doses, the nanites would get all creative with human systems, like with me.

"I was the inspiration. Yeah, me. Red Cell. Garrison realized that the nanites wouldn't rebuild me as I was, but what they thought was a better me. So, he thought, why not convince the nanites they *were* human? And, in a nice touch, his nonexistent son, with a ready-for-Lifetime leukemia origin story. Worked like a charm, didn't it? You got to hand it to the doc. He knows how to manipulate people. And tiny robots."

The obvious truth of it all makes it all the more impossible to believe. "You're lying."

"*I'm* lying? No, dummy. I'm the only real friend you got. Nina and your quote-unquote 'Dad' and the rest of PRS, they're the ones who've been lying to you. I tried to tell them, this isn't gonna work, he's not gonna stay dumb forever. Those computers are going to start learning, no matter how many times you keep flushing their short-term experiences down the memory toilet. But the last op, that clearly changed something in you. You've been acting screwy ever since this last awakening. Which is good news for me."

I need to shut him up. I *have* to shut him up. I rush him with an inhuman growl.

Too late, I see a sudden glinting in the air and realize he never dropped the sword; the hilt has been in his fist the whole time. And just as I leap on top of him, the blade has completely re-formed, and he rams it directly through the big red circle in my chest.

It hurts like hell. I catch my breath in a gurgle in my throat.

"I got to tell you, kid, it gets real old, real fast, playing second fiddle to an ant farm with an attitude."

He cuts upward with the blade, and even if I had bones, it wouldn't have mattered. The nanosword cuts through everything—everything—on the molecular level. He drags it straight up through my torso, through my neck, and through my head, and for the first time, my left eye and my right eye are seeing two different things, split apart, and falling downward.

"Truth is, Junior, you've become way more trouble than you're worth."

TWENTY-TWO

My left eye and right eye point in two completely different directions, and I can see both perspectives simultaneously, superimposed over each other, as the two halves of my brain try to reconcile the differing views, trying to merge them into a single image. It's like looking at a big screen with two different projectors showing two different movies, overlapping in the center.

My left eye sees the cooler lying on its side. Left watches as Dodge, breathing heavily, lets the blade of the nanosword dissemble into its component nanites and disappear. He picks up the cooler by its handle and crosses the pavilion and out of Left's field of vision.

But Right can see him grab the thermite charge and amble off, past the infinity pool, back down to the generator where I found it.

It's beginning to dawn on me how ridiculous I've been. I keep thinking of "me" as if I were a single, continuous entity. But in fact, there are innumerable parts of me, networked together with the same identical consciousness. I am splitting the "I" ego of my self between the two halves of my head because visual stimuli are so much stronger than anything else.

The truth is, though, as hard as it can be for a mind trained to be a regular human to process, every part of me is as much "I" as any other part of me. I feel knots in my stomach even when my brain is three feet away from my guts. And in halves. My breath catches in my throat even when I have no lungs or throat.

Maybe I should stop obsessing so much over *who* I am. Simply accepting *what* I am is enough.

And the fact is, I *am*. Red Cell hacked me in half, but suddenly the right side of my face sees the ground receding several feet into the distance as it is pulled upward to, oh, about shoulder height on my body and is fixed there.

I am curious, and the rest of my body indulges that curiosity. As my left eye is suddenly raised upward, the hand that's holding it turns it toward the rest of my body, and I can see the rest of me stitching myself back together at the seams, the nanites briefly visible as they repair the damage the nanosword did to me along the center.

Best of all, I don't even feel a pang of hunger. Must be that I only need to add more nutrients when the nanites have to re-create cells that were destroyed or damaged by crude, explosive kinetic trauma. The nanosword cuts between molecules, so the nanites can just rearrange material that's already there to heal me. No additional matter required.

If anything, the nanosword is the least effective weapon to use against me. Barely even slowed me down by a few minutes. The only problem is the nerve endings build back first, so I have to bite both halves of my tongue to keep from crying out. Why can't those get built last? What's the rush? Maybe Dad did that to keep me from running into traffic. Sure, it won't kill me, but it may hurt badly enough I wish it did.

Now whole once again, I sprint in the direction of where I saw Dodge go and zero in on him at the same spot where I found the thermal charge earlier. He's bent down and cursing under his breath as he tries to rearm the charge attached to the gasoline drum.

I clear my throat.

The look on Dodge's face when he turns around and sees me coming at him almost makes the intense pain of my re-formation utterly worthwhile.

He produces the nanosword, and the blade re-forms by the time I reach him, but I grab the wrist holding the hilt and break it. He screams and lets go of the sword. I grab it in midair. He gibbers incoherently as nano-grown tentacles emerge from the wound and start re-forming his hand into some incomprehensible appendage.

"Sorry, Dodge, but I've been giving it some thought, and I've made a decision. There's just no upside to you."

"There's no upside to *me*?" Clutching his broken wrist, he drops to his knees. "You don't get to talk to me like that, Nepo-Frankenstein. I served my country! I broke my freaking skull open while serving my country. That's supposed to mean something, okay? That means they owe me. *Those bastards owe me!*"

He tries to stand up, but I cut his belly open with the sword. He howls and falls back.

I pick up the thermite charge and make sure he stays on his back with my boot on his sternum. The wound is already beginning to heal at the edges, so quick as I can, I shove the bomb into his squishy guts as far as it will go. He screams again.

"You killed your family when they rejected you. You were going to kill everyone on this island. You're going to keep trying to kill me. I don't see an upside to letting you go. Sorry."

The hole in his gut is already closing around the thermite, skin replaced by a scaly, ridged substance I've never seen before. I bet nobody's ever seen it before. I walk away.

"At least I had a family!" he's yelling, clawing at the inhuman scab but to no avail. "Nobody is gonna love a freak like you, buddy. Ever. At least I *used* to be human! There's no upside to *you*, Bloodshot! You think PRS is just gonna let you walk? Tool around town paying your bills and clocking into work pretending you're a person, instead of the out-of-control science-fair project you are? With nobody watching your back? You're gonna miss me, boy, and sooner than you think."

After about ten paces, I stop and turn back to him. This should be far enough. "Maybe you should've been nicer to me then."

Laughing, he holds up a small device. "You forgetting something? What do you think you're going to do without the detonator?"

"You forgetting something? I *am* a detonator. This is the end of our team-up. Goodbye, Red Cell."

I wordlessly command the thermite charge to go off, and even my superhuman retinas flare out briefly as Dodge is consumed by a nova burst of white light, an earthbound star for a few fleeting seconds.

In the last few moments, there's an inhuman hiss, and a few tendrils flail futilely outward in an attempt to escape the lumpy pyre, but then they're soon consumed by the white-hot flames too.

Pretty soon, it's just a pile of ash on the flagstones, no different from the dust that's lain there since Hercules last passed by. It doesn't move.

Looks like Dodge ended up in that incinerator after all.

I am aware of faces gathering around me from the darkness on the edges of the rapidly dying fire. They're not coming any closer. Which is probably smart.

"Sorry to give you bad news, but you're not out of the woods yet," I call out. "You should get on the horn to your parents, to the press, everybody you know. There are people coming for you, and your only hope is they're not willing to risk killing you out in the open where everyone can see. So tell people what you've seen here. And I mean now."

I take a step toward them, and the would-be reality show contestants scatter into the night. I see the detonator Dodge dropped on the ground when he ignited. I crush it under my boot in case anybody gets any ideas. I see Dodge's skull comm lying on the flagstones nearby. I pick it up and press it to the side of my head, reattaching it to my throat.

"How much of that did you get?" I say.

"Way more than I wanted to," Nina says. "You're making a big mistake, kid. I don't know if they're gonna let you come back from this one."

"You seem like an all-right sort, Nina. I like you. I really think you ought to get another job."

"It's not that simple."

"Then let me simplify it for you: If you're still at PRS the next time I see you, I won't treat you any differently than the rest of them, no matter how I feel about you personally."

"Damn it, Ray. Dodge was scum, but he was right about one thing. They're not going to just let you walk away."

"Feeling's mutual."

I rip off the comm and crush it between my fingers.

Then I run and dive off the edge of the cliff, into the Mediterranean.

I try swimming toward the mainland. One hundred kilometers, give or take.

It takes a while.

To replenish my protein stores, I do it like a whale would do it, swimming underwater and hoovering all the small marine life and seaweed in my mouth that I can. Seawater, my body simply expels through its pores.

The McEverything, Mediterranean version, is a thought that pops into my head, though from where I couldn't tell you.

During the day I dive as deep as I can and swim as far as I can below the waves to avoid detection. Turns out I can, in fact, go underwater for about an hour before my "lungs" start seizing up and I have to return to the surface. The nanomachines must require contact with air to maintain regular functioning.

(Yet I still think of them as "the nanomachines," as if they're separate from me instead of all I am. I don't think, *I must require contact with air*. I'm not ready to fully embrace the real me, not yet. I'm not ready to give up on a Bloodshot that is a self, a person, different from the machine collective.)

When the sun sets again, I stop swimming and float on the water, looking up at the stars in all their infinite glowing combinations. You feel like you can see every part of the universe when the sky is clear like it is tonight.

I feel like I have as many pasts as there are stars in the sky.

There's the Bloodshot that PRS wanted to sell me, Captain USA Man, taking out Uncle Sam's enemies and tossing the ol' pigskin around with Pops until it's time to video chat with my devoted girlfriend.

Then there's "Nepo-Frankenstein," as Dodge called me, the accidental killing machine, an artificial-intelligence-plus-body with the actual age of a first grader but the mental and physical development of a college-bound senior. The last-ditch attempt to control a willful technology by repeatedly lying to it.

Both versions have pluses and minuses, but I'm not a big fan of either. What I'm after is this third Bloodshot, the one they're all scared of back at Fresh Kills, the Bloodshot that must have come to life during my last, mysterious mission. They keep trying to wipe my short-term memory after every op, but that must be producing diminishing returns. Some emotional connections aren't so easily erased. They lurk under my conscious self, waiting for me to access them.

That's the real Bloodshot. That's the Bloodshot I want to be.

On my back, with nothing but the stars above me and the sea beneath me, I empty my mind and try to meditate. I try to make my mind completely empty and hope what I'm looking for will bob to the surface.

A seagull's scream and then another and finally another startle me into opening my eyes. I must have fallen into whatever passes for sleep for me—I mean, even computers sleep if you let them go idle for long enough.

The stars are gone, replaced by a gray sky getting brighter by the slowly rising sun. I roll onto my stomach and look ahead, my feet kicking below me. The horizon at what I'm pretty sure is north is dominated by a green strip of land.

My attention is brought to my right side by another cry, this one quite human. I turn and see a squat, rusty tugboat bobbing a short swim away from me. A tall, skinny man is standing at the prow in khaki pants and a life jacket, close-trimmed Afro whitening at the temples. He waves half-heartedly at me, as if not entirely believing what he is seeing and embarrassed to be trying to get a mirage's attention.

I wave back, and his hand lowers. He seems almost disappointed that I'm real.

I swim toward the boat. The man picks up an oar, and at first I think it's to help me up, but he clutches it defensively across his body as I clamber aboard. "We don't have any more food and almost no water," he says in English in an East African accent. His thick, intense eyebrows give his face a very serious cast. "Nothing left for you. You understand me?"

I nod. I see now sitting on the main deck are about a dozen people across three generations, a white-haired grandma right down to a months-old baby in his mother's arms. Most share oar guy's imperious eyebrows. Their bodies are slack with misery and hardship, and their faces are taut with fear. Of me specifically, but of their current situation in general.

My friend with the oar eases his grip on it somewhat. "Where do you come from? A ship? Is there a ship nearby?"

I shake my head. "Small island. Way off that way." I wave toward the southeast. "What about you?"

I can tell he has a million other questions, not the least of which is, *Then how are you still alive*, but instead he answers mine. "Addis Ababa, originally. On the Libyan coast, we give the man the euros we've scrimped and saved for months—years!—expecting him to take us, but no, he gives us a chart and this piece of garbage"—he kicks the bridge cabin with one foot—"points north, and says, 'Go with God.' For the first few days, we did all right for ourselves, but then on Friday, this massive storm comes through, and a giant wave flips us over, then a second wave flips us over again. We all survived by the grace of heaven and the edges of our fingernails, but all the instruments—the engine?" He draws his fingers across his throat. "Kkkkt! We've been praying for days for a ship to come by, or for that land to get closer. But neither's happened. You know anything about machines?"

I blink. "You could say that," I say.

"Ah! Then perhaps I spoke too soon. Some of our prayers have been answered." He reaches a hand out. "Yonas. In Hebrew, Jonah. My brother-in-law told me people named Yonas should avoid sea voyages. I should have listened."

It's my turn to hesitate. "Ray," I finally say when I take his hand.

TWENTY-THREE

Whispering to each other behind cupped hands and shushing each other with giggles, the kids on board crowd around the open doorway to the cramped engine room when Yonas and I climb into the lower deck. The engine looks old, crusty, and dead.

"I tried to clean it out, but it seemed dry," Yonas is saying, "but when I turned it on, it went boom! And salt water blew all over the wires."

He's holding up a small flashlight so I can see when I open the thing up. "Yeah," I say, "looks pretty corroded."

"I am a schoolteacher, what do I know from engines?"

"You don't teach shop, I take it."

"What is 'shop'?"

"A class for woodworking, a little bit of mechanics. Practical stuff."

"Algebra is very practical. Just slightly less so when dying of thirst on the open water."

"I see what you mean. Hold that light up, will you?"

The engine is a brick, not even registering as a machine to my nanites. But I can tell, just by looking at it, that it is a simple matter of swapping a few wires to get it operational again. We cobble enough dry ones together from the hot plate in the tiny galley and the guts of

Grandma's handheld radio, which she parted with only when we convinced her it was a matter of life and death.

When I yell up for Yonas's wife, Nyala, to try the ignition, the engine roars to life. Yonas and I high-five, and the jubilant family members take turns hugging me. I feel like I'm ten feet tall. I don't need their boat to get to shore; I could swim the rest of the way myself. Now that their engine is fixed, I can just jump back into the water and go on my way like a happy merman.

But I stay. What I need is for a human being not to look at me as a tool or a terror, just as another person. That's what Yonas and his group are giving me. By saving them, I'm really saving myself.

I take the wheel at Yonas's request so he can concentrate on the map. We sail to a buoy marker on the map where he's supposed to contact people on the mainland. He's learned just enough Greek to follow these instructions. The voice on the other end of the radio tells us to wait until nightfall and go to a bit of coast already marked on the chart. Yonas's interlocutor claims they've timed the coast guard patrols so we can just slip on by in the fog.

This turns out to be mostly true. I putt-putt my way as slow as I can. Lights from houses along the coast burn through the mist. Yonas tells me to kill the engine when he thinks we've reached the point marked on the map. When the fog parts, I see a large white van waiting atop a tiny cove of sand. It doesn't take long for two Greeks in a rubber Zodiac raft to start heading in our direction.

I am not surprised they are surprised to see me. They let me help load the kids and Grandma into the raft. Yonas says they have to hurry because the next coast guard patrol will be by soon.

They load that first round of human cargo into the van, then come back for the adults. When Yonas hops down into the raft and I am the last one left on the tug, one of the Greeks doesn't reach up to help me down as he did with the others. Not that I need his help, but it's not very friendly.

"The deal was for twelve passengers, but you are thirteen," he says to me in pretty good English. "Where's my thousand euros?"

"They just picked me up out of the water about eight hours ago. Helped them with their engine trouble, then thought I'd stick around."

"I was going to say, you don't look very Ethiopian." He takes a long drag on a hand-rolled cigarette. "Actually, I don't know what the hell you do look like."

I spread my hands. "Aren't we all unique individuals?"

He doesn't laugh. "You, my friend, are a stowaway. Which is not allowed. For eight hours of passage, you owe me a couple hundred, at least. Cash."

"I lost my wallet. At the bottom of the sea."

The guy curses in Greek and holds his hand out for me. "We'll figure this out on shore. Christos has to get his boat back to the marina where its papers say it belongs."

Christos and I exchange places. He roars off into the darkness in the tug while I take a seat on the raft with Yonas and the other adults. Should I tell them I'm actually six?

Once we reach shore, two more Greeks get out of the cab of the van. A third stands guard by the open back and grabs one of the kids when she tries to leap out to rush to her parents. He tosses her back into the van. I don't see any weapons in the dark, but I have to believe they're there.

"All right, everyone in the van, where the eyes of law can't see," the leader says as he quickly drags the Zodiac onto the beach. "Stowaway, we'll decide how you work off your debt when we get there."

Everyone but me starts walking up the beach to the white van.

"Yonas," I call out. He stops and looks at me. "Don't go with these guys. They're not going to take you anywhere you want to go."

That's all it takes for guns to appear in all the smugglers' hands. The leader pulls a snub-nose Smith & Wesson Model 36 from his waistband and presses it to my temple.

"Yet you still have to go there," he says. "Walk."

I jerk my head back faster than he can pull the trigger, but he nearly takes my nose off, not that that would have slowed me down much. I grab his wrist and his neck and swing him around so he's got his revolver pointing at his own temple now. Everybody screams. The two guys on the sand level their own snub-noses at me. The leader bellows out to them in Greek. He thrashes in my grip, but I've got him fast.

"Listen! Hey! Listen up!" I shake my captive to get his attention. "You chuckleheads aren't used to messing with anyone who knows how to fight back. Tell your stooges to toss their weapons into the sea, and we all get to walk away. I mean . . . you'll be walking away. We'll be taking that van."

The fourth guy by the van pulls one of the little girls out and puts a gun to her head. It's Nyala and Yonas's youngest. They both try to run toward her, but the other two gun thugs on the beach restrain them and point Smith & Wessons at them.

The leader in my hands laughs. "Who's in charge now, freak, huh? Not you! You let me go, or you spend all night burying bodies!"

"Idiots," I mutter. "I really was going to let you go."

I push the leader away from me, hard enough that he goes sprawling on his face in the sand. The other three, seeing me without protection, point their weapons at me and fire. I already have my revolver up, though, and take off the top of the head of the guy on my left. His shot goes wild. The others have shockingly good aim, hitting me twice in the torso and once in the left arm. The hits stagger me back, but not enough to make me miss. One guy gets it on the nose; the other up on the road takes it in the neck. They both drop.

The leader is staggering away, kicking up great gouts of sand as he scrambles toward the tree line. I whirl and am about ready to shoot him in the back when Yonas stands in between me and him. He fixes me with dark, mournful eyebrows.

"That's enough," he says.

Anger burns through me at Yonas denying me the kill. It takes me a second or two to lower the revolver. By then the leader has already disappeared into the early-morning gloom.

I look at the faces of the rest of Yonas's family. His daughter has buried her face in Nyala's side, but one fearful eye remains trained at me. Nyala points at me and cries something out to Yonas.

I look down and see what she sees: The wounds and blood already disappearing, being absorbed into the blank whiteness of my skin like water down a drain. The nanomachines even take the lead of the bullet and turn it into flesh, skin, viscera. Life made out of death.

The shame hits me all at once. Killing's become all too easy for me. Second nature. These regular civilians don't know what to think. They see a monster, even if it's one on their side.

"You have somewhere to go?" I ask Yonas.

"My cousin has a restaurant in Athens. She's offered to let us stay with her in exchange for working at her place."

"Does he know that?" I nod at where the leader disappeared.

Yonas shakes his head. "I don't think so."

"You'd better hope not." *Because if he knows, since we left him alive, he might come looking for you there*, I don't say out loud. I have a feeling the human traffickers were never going to take Yonas's people to his cousin's restaurant; they had some other grim servitude in mind for them.

Most of the migrants climb into the back of the van. Yonas gets into the cab. The smugglers left the keys in the ignition. So he starts it up. I'm not sure where I stand with the family, so I stay on the beach looking at him.

Yonas drives the van around in a circle, then stops, idling, and opens the passenger-side door. "Ray, what are you waiting for? We have to get out of here."

I can't help but grin. "No argument here." I climb next to him and slam the door shut, and he motors off into the night.

The drive to Athens involves first going over ridged mountains dotted with small trees, then, finally, driving through the mountains in mostly deserted tunnels. No sounds but the roll of the wheels echo off dimly lit walls.

When the van comes out on the other side of the last tunnel, it's raining, the drops startling us as they suddenly scatter across the windshield. It's coming down hard, and the road is glistening and slick, so Yonas slows to a crawl as he maneuvers the van down a long, serpentine road.

We turn a bend, and the city is there, modern buildings studded with satellite dishes and ancient temples straddling green hills, graffiti and streetlights, extending out to the harbor. The underlit Parthenon looms over all from the massive lump of the Acropolis. No matter where we go in the narrow streets, filled with angrily honking cab drivers, I can feel the temple watching us, even if I can't see it over the red-tiled roofs at the moment.

I'm happy to be in a big metropolis because I can feel its crisscrossing field of wireless communications—cellular, satellite, Wi-Fi, and so on—comforting me like a cherished childhood blanket. Out in the middle of the ocean, I couldn't tap into my machine-ally abilities without sending up a "here I am" flare for PRS. In the telecom stew of a big city, though, I'm just another stray morsel. My initial signal is extremely obscured, and I bounce it off multiple node stations around the world and in low Earth orbit until my actual location is nearly impossible for Rising Spirit cyberspies to trace backward. They'll get lost chasing their own tail in a Bitcoin server array in a Bangkok suburb or inside a secondhand desktop plugged into a troll farm in St. Petersburg.

I'm now free to do complex computing in relative anonymity, like accessing translation services that let me read and speak rudimentary Greek. The faded street signs unscramble before my eyes into words I can understand. Yonas pulls the van up on the curb of a plaza labeled Monastiraki Square. The rain has driven everyone away this late at night, and only the arched subway station seems to be open.

Yonas takes a sealed Ziploc baggie out of his pocket and removes a hand-drawn map. He leads us down the wide row of a sleeping flea market, shutters drawn across stalls hawking Parthenon T-shirts and Spartan figures with round shields and long spears. He makes a bunch of abrupt turns down various narrow lanes, and if I hadn't been following our progress with satellites, I would have been completely lost.

He comes to the back of a building down a wide cobblestoned alley and, underneath a tree, knocks on a door once, twice. It doesn't take long for an Ethiopian woman to answer the door. She's a few years older than Yonas and looks neither happy nor surprised to see us. Behind her a young girl about thirteen years old is sliding trays into an oven. The sharp, vinegary smell of what I first take to be baking sourdough wafts out the door and awakens my hunger like a startled guard dog, barking loudly.

Yonas and his cousin, whose name I gather to be Liya, bicker a bit in a language the network quickly identifies as Amharic, the main tongue of Ethiopia. I set my autotranslator in motion, and by the time she waves a dismissive hand in my direction, I've got the top few thousand verbs and nouns down pat.

"What about him?" Liya nods at me. "You say you bring me workers, Yonas, but this one is hardly front-of-the-house material."

"Do you need a dishwasher?" I ask in Amharic with what must be a really weird accent, judging from the expression on Yonas's and Liya's faces. "I'm strong, I'm fast, and I only need to sleep about once a week."

Liya blinks dubiously at me. "He's not crazy, is he?" she asks Yonas while keeping me in view. "Because I can't deal with that, I just can't, I have too much else to do—"

"Liya, Liya, don't worry, he's not crazy, he just, ah, has a rare skin condition," Yonas pleads with her, palms pressed together. "He's saved all our lives. Twice! We owe him."

"You owe him. I don't owe him." Still, she throws up her hands. "Fine! But he has to find his own place to spend the night. With all of you staying, I've run out of beds."

"Not a problem," I say. I don't plan on sleeping anyway, particularly now that dawn is starting to glow around the edges of the market buildings. I manage to beg the kitchen girl for some finished crepes—injera, not sourdough, I am told—that are so deliciously spongy and heavy at the same time, rolled up like fancy napkins.

After staving off my hunger, I find a convenience store on the corner advertising disposable phones. I sit on the curb and wait for the owner to arrive and open up. It takes a couple hours, and the city wakes up around me. Those incredible morning sensations: car exhaust mixing with crisp morning air, pigeons discovering stale bread dumped onto the sidewalk the night before, trucks roaring, metal shutters clattering open.

I dug a couple hundred euros in cash out of the pockets of the smugglers lying on the beach and spend twenty of them to buy a burner phone. I rip it out of its package but then stare at it for longer than I should, wondering if it's smart to use it.

Back when I was floating on the Mediterranean, going through my various selves, I tried to empty my thoughts completely and see if the core of me would speak to me, if whatever residual memories I might have could bubble to the surface and, like a fisherman without a rod, I could grab on to them with both hands.

I did catch something, a number, which depressed me. What else would a machine have as a core belief but a number? It was ten digits, which implied a phone number.

My nanites are able to pinpoint the current location of the number, and given the difference in time zones, it should be just past midnight there. I walk back to Monastiraki Square, already filling up with tourists and vendors and panhandlers. I shift my skin color to look slightly healthier in the glaring early-morning light. And I dial the number.

It rings way too many times for me to be comfortable. My heart is pounding.

I am just about to hang up when the ringing stops with a click. The sound of fumbling. Then, a high voice.

"Hey, who is this?" Still sleepy, I must have just woken her up.

"Sorry to bother you," I say, realizing that, like an idiot, I had no idea what to say if another person actually answered, "but, uh, could you tell me who you are first?"

A short pause.

"Bloodshot?" His voice cracks. I'm talking to a young boy, not a girl.

"Yes . . ." I can barely stand. People keep walking past me in the square, but I am on another planet. "Please, sorry, who am I talking to? I may not remember you."

"Oh, yeah. That makes sense. But I remember you. It's Clark."

Jeez.

How old *is* this kid?

TWENTY-FOUR

Clark says he has a lot to tell me, but I don't want to be up on regular telecom for that long. He comes up with a plan to get around that, one that only a twelve-year-old would, but I'm not exactly in the position to second-guess my allies.

Yonas's son Taye is about Clark's age. When I go out on my break to the alley behind the kitchen, where he supervises his siblings and cousins playing, and ask him if he has ever heard of a video game called *Armorines*, he looks like he's going to explode with happiness.

The next morning, before the restaurant opens for lunch, I take Taye to a twenty-four-hour internet café I found down the street from the Archeological Museum, where a crow sits on the armored head of the war god Ares on the roof and caws out for tribute. Green-and-red ceiling lights alternate over a series of cubicles with massive monitors and headsets. Midtwenties dudes in bad need of shaves inhabit the booths, hacking and slashing and shooting and detonating each other for a euro an hour. Taye swears he used to play *Armorines* all the time with people all over the world at his friend's house in Addis Ababa.

I stand over him while he sits in the big ergonomic office chair in the cubicle and slips the headphones over his ears and the game controller into his hands. I have a surplus army jacket on, lapels up, and a cap pulled low over my forehead so I don't stand out too much.

The Armorines Fighter Selection screen appears, and Taye cycles through various armored badasses with varying weaponry and color schemes before he chooses the same big Gold guy he says he always does.

"Gold is the tank of the group," Taye says. "That means he's really good at absorbing damage."

"I'm familiar with the concept."

"He has more confirmed kills than any other Armorine, but really he's a big softie who loves animals."

"Good for him. Listen, the less I need to know this lore or whatever, the better, okay? I just told my contact I'd be on the north side of the, uh, Filchner Ice Shelf Hive. You know what that is in the game?"

Taye nods, waving at me to be quiet. He's already absorbed in the monitor before him. Gold materializes out of thin air into, well, thin air—a cloud-filled sky that quickly disappears as he drops earthward to a snow-swept Antarctic landscape. Immediately he is swarmed by spider-aliens, some flying, some loping toward him across the glaciers on all eights, some erupting from the ground and spraying acid out of their slavering maws. Taye stays calm and maneuvers Gold through the ensuing insectoid carnage with the cool confidence of an Indy 500 driver, slowing only slightly to train his gauntlet Miniguns on his enemies and pulverize them into puddles of ichor and chitin.

"I have to clear this area or they won't open the blast doors," Taye says.

"I still don't care," I say.

Once Gold is the only thing moving in the smoking courtyard of the Antarctic base, massive bulkhead doors rumble open in the wall, revealing a sprawling scrum of multichromatic Armorines locked in apocalyptic combat across a cracked and crumbling ice shelf. The Armorines have little names and numbers above their helmets, indicating the corresponding players' handles and character levels.

"What's your friend's handle again?" Taye asks.

"Waste_Anderstun." I spell it for him in Amharic.

Taye has his father's eyebrows. They lower dramatically. "Is that supposed to mean something?"

"You're asking me?"

Taye blasts off on Gold's boot jets and flies over the battlefield, blowing flittering, dive-bombing winged spider-aliens out of the sky as he goes. Looming over the horizon between the water and the ice is what looks to me like (sorry) a giant turd, maybe fifty feet high, covered in blinking lights and glowing blue veins and antennae-like feelers.

"The Ice Shelf Hive," Taye says. "Your friend is pretty smart to tell you to meet here. Nobody comes to this side because they're too busy blowing away spider-aliens as they come out of the birthing hole."

Indeed, spider-alien after spider-alien tromps, flits, or burrows out of the unpleasant aperture at the base of the hive. Gold blasts on his boot jets above that and around to a calm patch of ice and snow on the hive's blind side. Waiting there is a pixelated Waste_Anderstun, or so the name over his red-armored head says. (His level: seventy-one.)

"Oh, cool, he's Gunner," Taye says. "That's my second favorite Armorine."

When Gold arrives, Waste_Anderstun is the only other figure visible behind the hive. He waves at us and Taye blinks, handing me the headset. "He's asking me stuff in English really fast."

Taye and I switch places. He stands while I sit down in the chair. I put the headset on, and Clark is in the middle of telling me something as Waste_Anderstun. "Hold on, hold on," I interrupt. "Start over. It's me."

"Last I saw you, you and Kalea, my sister, went off to attack the Nursery but I didn't go with you but not because I was scared, no, I was really worried about my mom but Kalea's not back and now Mom cries every day, way more than when Dad left, and—"

"Hey, hey, kid. Back up. I've had my memory wiped. Maybe let's just start at the beginning with detail, okay?"

"Okay, well, one morning Kalea and I were filming one of my movies—Wes Anderson has always been my favorite director, and my handle is like an affectionate parody of his name, you know?—and we found you, unconscious, in a field of blown-up trees. We woke you up and called you an ambulance but it turns out the ambulance people were bad guys and you blew them all away. Next they tried to grab us from our house but Kalea used her psiot brain magic to zap them but you popped out from under their car—she has the power to network people's minds together—and were all like, 'I'm here to save you,' and Kalea was like, 'It's the thought that counts,' and we went to have breakfast at McDonald's and I've never seen anybody eat so much at once! You were like, 'I have no memories, can you help me figure out who I am and why these guys keep trying to kill me,' and we were like—"

"I take it back. You're giving me too much detail. Speed it up."

"Oh? Sorry. Anyway, Kalea hooked you up with Generation Zero and you became friends and you figured out where the Nursery is and you took Cronus and the other superpowered kids to attack it and you left me behind with Kalea's phone, which at first kind of hurt my feelings, but seeing how everything turned out I guess it was pretty smart, huh?"

I'm starting to get a headache, so I can't really agree. I allied *with* Generation Zero against Project Rising Spirit? No wonder my Fresh Kills handlers were so freaked out about this last op. This is what the previous Bloodshot, the Bloodshot I want to be, was up to—before, I guess, Dad and Nina got me back and erased my brain-chalkboard once again.

But we attacked—the Nursery? Why would I do that? The Nursery is a minor adjunct facility in the middle of nowhere in Idaho. Sure, that's where the psiots I capture all eventually end up—I think—but it's tactically insignificant. As far as I know, it's superkid juvie. If the other Bloodshot's objective was to take out PRS's ability to recapture psiots after busting them out, well . . . he'd have to hit Fresh Kills.

"Last I saw you guys, you were off to, you know, storm the castle, but that's all I know. You clearly made it out, but, uh, you don't have any memories again, or so you say, so I guess . . . you don't know anything about my sister, huh? You'd tell me where Kalea was if you knew, right?"

"I would. But I don't." The real mystery is, given how readily Dodge took off Twyst's head, is Kalea still alive? Is any of Generation Zero?

"So, what's the plan, man?" Gunner/Waste_Anderstun is wildly gesticulating and doing some kind of breakdance for some reason. "Put me in, Coach, I'm ready to play! Let's go get Kalea back and maybe even that stuck-up Cronus to boot!"

I stroke my chin, lost in thought. "Let me sleep on it. I'll be in touch. There's got to be a messaging feature in this game, right? I'll contact Waste_Anderstun using this handle—"

All of a sudden, the controller jolts in my hand, and virtual blood cascades across the screen, covering it. When it clears, I'm looking at Gold twitching his life out on the ground, blood seeping out of a shattered headplate onto the pure, white snow. "GAME OVER," the screen proclaims in Greek.

"What the hell?" Taye cries out, looking at the other cubicles. "Who did that?"

"Oh yeah, perfect headshot," yells one of the stubble-covered Greeks in a cube across the aisle. He stands up and shoots both fists in the air. "Triple XP. Ebony and Ivory, why don't you take the act down the street. You can do a little dance for coins at the museum. My friend wants that spot."

I am out of my chair and grabbing him by the throat before he or I know what I'm doing. The players near him scatter, and though there are a few chuckles when I first strike, the room falls silent except for the sounds of virtual tires screeching and distant enemy gunfire when I pick him up by his throat.

"We weren't finished with our session yet," I hiss in his face. I'm not sure he can hear me over his clucking and wheezing.

"C'mon, man, he was just kidding around, he didn't mean anything by it," the gamer next to him says. He's pleading with me, hands in the praying position. "The next hour's on us, huh, what do you say? Just let him go."

The first gamer's eyeballs are just about ready to slide under his eyelids when I let him go. He drops back into his rolling chair, hacking and clutching at his throat.

I look at Taye, and I don't have to say anything. We get out of that café as quickly as possible.

I take a couple days to try to figure out a plan to free me and get Clark's sister and her friends back from PRS. Most of that time I spend washing dishes in Cousin Liya's restaurant. I am surprised at how much I enjoy it. The mission here is simple. The trays and cups and small plates are dirty, and I need to make them not so. A simple mission with simple tools, made easier by the fact that customers eat their food off edible "plates," the spongy, sour-sweet bread called injera. Instead of forks or spoons—though those are available too—you rip rolled-up sheets of injera apart to pick up boiled beets or turmeric-stained goat off the serving tray and pop bites into your mouth, so there aren't very many utensils to wash either. Still, I am extremely good at it and by the end of the second night's dinner rush, Liya starts looking at me with something resembling respect.

Like she said, her small flat in the Pangrati neighborhood, next to a massive marble horseshoe-shaped stadium dating from, like, the first Olympics or something, can barely fit the entire family, so I have to coordinate with my dozen roommates the few hours this week I can get the couch and shut down for a few hours to regroup my mind.

I lie down and close my eyes around 11:00 a.m., and when I wake up six hours later, the small flatscreen TV is on and Taye is sitting against the back of the couch, watching it and laughing. The program he's watching is a Japanese game show, dubbed in English and subtitled in Greek. Attractive Asian twentysomethings in gowns and tuxedos sit in the set of a salaryman's office. After watching for a few seconds, I realize the idea behind the show is that a bunch of the common objects in the room are exactly what they appear to be—coffee mug, pencil sharpener, in/out tray—and some of them are actually cakes expertly crafted to look like common objects. The object of the game is to figure out which things are cake and which things are real.

A round-headed man with glasses and a pageboy haircut gets on his hands and knees before the closed door and wraps his lips around the door handle. He sucks on it a few times before biting into it. He grimaces as his teeth meet the unyielding metal. The door handle is real. The show emcee cries out in delight, and hidden jets in the floor blow a punishment of compressed air into the guy's face for his failure. The studio audience goes nuts.

Next, a woman in pearls and a gold lamé, sleeveless dress picks up the computer mouse off its pad on the desk and turns it over and over in her hands, unsure. Then, all of a sudden, she bites right through the middle of it, and her eyes go wide. She turns the "mouse" toward the camera so we at home can see the cross section: Below its cracked candy exterior are three layers of white sponge cake and vanilla frosting.

Taye erupts in giggles, drowning out even the laugh track on-screen. I must make a noise because he turns around and looks at me.

"Ray," he asks, smile dropping, "why are you crying?"

I say it out loud, even though he can have no idea what I mean: "I'm *cake*."

Days go by, and I have no clearer sense of a way forward than I did when I dove into the Mediterranean. Clark fills up my *Armorines* player-to-player messages with increasingly frantic nagging. My preprogrammed instincts have been pushing me toward doing what I always do when I feel this adrift, and I begin to realize there may be an advantage in doing what PRS expects me to do.

I send Salma an email bounced off an ISP in Tokyo, inspired by the show I just watched. Once we've juggled the time zones correctly, we schedule a video chat. I go to the Municipal Library, a long off-white building with a sloped terra-cotta roof across from a rail yard. They have a small room with a few computers in it, and I pick one facing a blank wall. I close the door so the microphone hopefully can't pick up any staff or patrons speaking Greek in the hallway, and I call my alleged girlfriend.

"Where are you?" Salma asks when we both appear on-screen.

"Alexandria, Egypt." This is where I'm pinging the signal off so anyone listening in on this chat should be fooled. If I had swum south instead of north from Twyst's island, it should be entirely plausible to PRS that I ended up in Egypt instead of Greece.

"Oh, wow! Look at you, jet-setter. Why Alexandria?"

"Dad's at an AI conference. I'm just bored out of my mind in the hotel. My thoughts are getting away from me."

"You do look, uh, a little troubled, Ray. What's wrong?"

"Oh, nothing." I swallow. I used to love confiding in Salma. But now I see that the living room behind her looks one-dimensional, like it's a projected background. She keeps chuckling nervously, like she's on her guard.

"Don't give me that," she says. "I know you better than anybody. Except maybe your dad. I want you to tell me."

"Well, it's just that . . ." Deep sigh. "I don't know, ever since I got released from the hospital, I've felt like—the treatment, right, that cured me, but made me look like this? Am I still me, you know? Or does the fact so much of me has been replaced make me . . . something else? And is who I think I am inside my head just a leftover ghost going through the motions?"

"You ever heard of the Ship of Theseus?" she asks.

I shake my head. "What is that, another koan?"

"Not technically, but I heard it from the same TikTok yoga teacher as the butterfly story."

"Well then, it's got to be solid. Go on."

"Theseus was the hero who went into the labyrinth and killed the minotaur. He rescued all these kids who were going to be fed to the monster and brought them back to their homes in Athens. The people of the city were so thrilled at what he'd done they swore to preserve the ship he came back in forever.

"Except, you know, the ship is made of wood, right? Wood decays. And as planks started rotting and falling off the ship, the Athenians replaced them with new ones. After a while, there was no 'original' part of the ship left. So philosophers started to ask: Is this actually the ship of Theseus, or is it some other thing that just looks like the ship?"

"And what did they come up with?"

Salma laughs, teeth flashing. "C'mon, Ray, they're philosophers. What do you think? Half of them said it was still the ship of Theseus, and the other half said it wasn't. And the two sides never agreed."

"What do you think?"

"I think you just have to pick one side for yourself."

I don't like the sound of that. I don't want to pick; I want to arrive at a logical conclusion based on available evidence. A binary choice: real or fake.

I uneasily realize this is exactly how computers think.

"I'm thinking of coming to Toronto a few days early, like a week before your birthday. Is that all right?"

"Um . . ." The smile wavers for just a second, then returns. "That'd be great. Sure. Do you have a place to stay?"

"Dad will book me someplace online. He's going to have to stay on a little longer here in Egypt to do some consulting work, and he says he doesn't mind if I go back to North America first."

"Awesome! Well, let me know exactly when your flight comes in, and I'll be there to meet you."

"You'd do that? Fantastic! How long has it been since I last saw you in person?"

She hesitates, as if calculating the least obvious lie, but just answers, "Too long."

Right now, Salma is definitely looking like cake.

There's a small, L-shaped Tourist Information Centre in the shadow of the Acropolis, and I stop in before I have to report to the restaurant for my shift and ask the desk clerk where the Ship of Theseus is.

The woman behind the counter just looks at me like I'm nuts, and it can't just be the alien accent that muddies my Greek. Apparently modern-day Athens has no such artifact on display. The ship isn't even a physical copy of a physical copy of a physical original anymore; it's a riddle based on the anecdote of a myth, a myth Tourism Lady has never even heard of before.

I must look totally crestfallen because Tourism Lady takes pity on me and circles on a street map what she thinks is the next best thing. She sends me on a five-minute walk north. On the sidewalk surrounding a fenced-in park is a bronze statue of Theseus himself. He's a good-looking dude, fit but not particularly muscular, naked but for a plumed helmet on his head and sandals, one of which he's bent over as if he's tying it. He's not looking at his feet, though, but off in the distance to one side, as if his future might be creeping up on him.

I stand and stare at the statue for probably too long, out of pure envy. Here's a solid shape of metal that never changes, never has any doubt as to what he really is.

What am I? I'm Theseus! Prove me wrong, Nanite Boy.

I walk back to the restaurant just in time for opening, but the metal gate is still closed over the front, which is weird, so I go in through the back. Yonas and his entire family are in the main dining area, lights off, yelling at each other.

I clear my throat, and they start yelling at me instead.

"They've taken him, they've taken my boy!" Nyala cries, and presses into my hand a piece of paper. These scumbag gangsters must have been feeling witty because they've drawn up a MISSING CHILD poster in Greek with Taye's face on it. His expression is painfully frightened, so they must have taken it just after nabbing him. The background is black and shallow—the back of a van would be my guess.

"We sent him out for buttermilk this morning, but he never came back," Yonas says, eyes white with fear. "Then this was shoved under the gate about an hour ago."

I told you I should have shot that smuggler guy, I somehow manage not to say out loud, but my eyes must say it anyway because Yonas just looks guilty and sick. "It's them, isn't it? The ones from the beach."

"The who from the beach? What have you gotten mixed up in?" demands Cousin Liya, but I raise a hand.

"I'll handle this." There's a phone number on the flyer, next to the cleverly phrased *If you want any information on this child, call.* I dial on my burner phone, but even though I turn my back for privacy, Yonas, Liya, and Nyala all cluster around my shoulders to hear.

The phone rings five times before someone picks up. A low male voice says, "I will only talk to Bloodshot."

Oh, great.

"You're talking to him," I say.

"Acropolis. Eastern end, the overlook facing the Temple of Zeus. Nineteen hundred hours. Come alone and unarmed." He hangs up.

Only Liya knows enough Greek to understand what the guy said to me, and her eyes blaze with fury. "'Bloodshot'? What is 'Bloodshot'? You are Bloodshot, freak? Then you'd better take care of this." She stabs my chest with her finger with each word.

I grab her hand and match her fierce look with one of my own. "Count on it."

TWENTY-FIVE

The so-called dark web, the information underground favored by drug smugglers, thieves, con artists, and child pornographers, among many other scumbags of any stripe, is as accessible to me as its more conventional counterpart. It takes a forty-second image search on my own face to discover that anonymous posters have slapped it on every message board frequented by global bad actors promising a generous, untraceable reward for any information as to my whereabouts, and a king's ransom for my capture.

I swear at myself for being a tool. Had I not been caught up in the throes of my dumb existential crisis, I'd like to think it would have occurred to me on my own to check if Project Rising Spirit had put a public bounty on my head. My hanging around Yonas and his family like a stray puppy who followed them home has put them in serious danger.

I deploy a bot from a weather tower in Alaska to scrub both the light and dark web of my image, and further program it to do so every hour, in case PRS puts it back up again.

I go to the Acropolis half an hour before the meet time, 1900 hours, or seven in the evening for you civilians. This is just an hour before closing time at this time of year, and the sun has already set, so not many tourists are pushing through the turnstile to head up the massive outcropping via the winding concrete trail snaking up and around the towering limestone foundation. Stray cats meow beyond the fence surrounding the grounds, coming close enough to allow tourists to pet or feed them, but not close enough to the bars to be caught. The winding trail up is dotted with spots under-lighting ancient temples and statues on pedestals like runway models. Up, up I go, winding further and further back in history, the city laid out below me like a frozen white sea, the humps of mountains looming even farther in the distance.

It's hard not to think of all the hundreds of thousands of people who have followed this same path, not just tourists to an archeological site but the soldiers and servants and statesmen and philosophers and poets who did the same thing, and now the first sentient nonperson, me. Knowing how history and technology work, I will likely not be the last such nonperson either.

The vertical part of the journey ends at a massive outcropping overlooking the Forum, the ruins of the most ancient part of the city below, mostly white marble foundations and collapsed pillars, except for the mostly intact Temple of Hephaestus. Behind me, every structure astride the bluff is lit up with a golden glow, as if favored by the gods. I pass through the pillared entrance, the propylaeum, and rising out of the scree-covered plain before me is the mighty temple to Athena, the Parthenon itself, no less impressive for being surrounded by metal scaffolding, with a few modern cranes looming out of its center while it undergoes renovations.

I look behind me at the propylaeum, and leaning against the pillars are two guys who look like gangsters. I've got no reason to think they're not. They're the only people looking at me and not at one temple or another. Even with the bill of a ball cap pulled low over my face, my unusual coloration is still earning me some side-eye from my fellow tourists. Still, these guys are the only visitors with their hands inside their bulky jackets. I'd guesstimate I'm surrounded by a hundred, maybe two hundred staff and visitors. Across the exposed red rock, which I'm going to guess dates back to Theseus's time, the blue-and-white-striped Greek flag flutters over an overlook bordered by a waist-high stone wall. I assume that's what the guy on the phone was talking about. As I head over there, my two shadows detach from the propylaeum and follow. They're not even trying to hide their true natures. The bigger, more broad-shouldered gladiator in particular seems pretty sure of himself. Or he's a moron. Of course, the two often go hand in hand.

In a few strides, I see the bearded guy I didn't shoot on the beach, standing with his back to the flagpole, both hands on Taye's shoulders. As soon as I see the kid, a calm washes over me. I am ashamed to admit it, considering the circumstances, but for the first time since the fight with Twyst, I feel calm. Almost . . . content. I have a mission. With clearly defined objectives. And I know how to achieve them. None of this cake-or-not, Ship of Theseus happy crappy.

THIS IS ME, I think in capital letters. THIS IS MORE ME THAN I HAVE EVER BEEN OR EVER WILL BE.

I'd almost thank these douche-nozzles if I thought they were capable of appreciating it.

When I climb the few steps up to the overlook's interior, a young woman with a shaved head and purple lipstick holds up her phone and very deliberately takes a picture of me. She smiles at the guy with Taye. "Got it, Dimitrios."

"'Proof of life,' that's the phrase, isn't it?" Dimitrios says. "For your friends who are looking for you. Send it," he says to the punkette.

Yeah, lady, send it. Send it, I will the punkette, but I needn't have bothered—she immediately transfers the pic to Messages on her phone.

Helena's iPhone is sending this photograph to the following number, Helena's iPhone tells me, and the plan I've been struggling to form for the last few days has all of a sudden revealed itself to me as gloriously as a sunrise.

Dimitrios clears his throat. Oh, yeah. Kidnapped kid.

I hold up what I hope is a calming hand for Taye, who is practically hyperventilating. "It's okay, kid. I'm bringing you back to your folks."

"That he is, Taye," Dimitrios chuckles. "And he's bringing us along with you."

I grunt dismissively. "Why would I do that?"

With a flick of his wrist, Dimitrios has popped a box cutter out of his sleeve and is holding the blade to Taye's jugular. "You tell me."

"C'mon, man. Aren't you already getting paid plenty for that photo you just sent, telling PRS where I am?"

Dimitrios shrugs. "I am a freelancer. First rule of freelancing is get paid whenever and wherever you can. This kid's family never showed to where I was going to be paid to bring them. You snuck them out of the cousin's home and her restaurant is still closed, so you need to show me where they are now. He stays with me until they're in hand, so nobody tries anything stupid. Or more stupid."

"Yeah, sorry, man, that's not gonna happen."

"No, I am sorry, *malaka*, that you are not in charge here. There's only one way off this rock, and that's through those pillars back there, with us." He nods at the guys he doesn't think I already know are behind me. "Make sure he's not packing."

The big bad gladiator dude makes me raise my arms and paws all over me in an exceptionally unpleasant way. "He's clean," the guy declares.

I laugh.

"What's so funny, *malaka*?" Dimitrios is losing his patience with everything.

"He missed one," I say.

"No, I didn't," the big guy says.

"Sure, you did."

"Which one?"

I whirl around and plant my elbow in Gladiator's nose, which breaks with a satisfying crunch. When he doubles over, I stick my hand inside his jacket exactly where he'd been keeping his hand this whole time, and my fingers close around a 9mm SIG Sauer Legion.

"This one," I say, and shoot the slack-jawed Dimitrios in the shoulder. He drops the box cutter with a curse.

"*Hit the ground, Taye!*" I yell in Amharic as I turn and shoot Gladiator's partner in the chest as he tries to fumble his own pistol out of his belt. I see he's wearing a bulletproof vest, but it doesn't do much good against the knockback, which sends him head over heels over the wall of the overlook and screaming down to the ground below.

A middle-aged policewoman is hanging out by the entrance to the overlook—I am going to guess to discourage tourists from jumping. The sound of my shot makes her look in our direction, and the dulcet tones of the falling goon inspire her to trill frantically on the whistle around her neck.

Helena flips a butterfly knife open in her hand, which looks as ridiculous as it sounds. My left boot to her wrist relieves her of the knife; my right bootheel connects with her jaw and relieves her of standing upright. She sprawls across the cobblestones next to her boyfriend, who is screaming "*malaka, malaka*" over and over at me like he can bad-word me to death.

Meaty arms wrap around mine and pin them to my sides. Gladiator lifts me off my feet, which I let him do, only so I can curl my legs up and drop, punching out with my fists. This loosens his grip enough that I can grab his arms and flip him over my head. He hits the white flagpole in the center of the overlook like a giant bald cannonball, and the shaft sways precariously on its rusty bolts.

I glance behind me: a quartet of cops is running toward me, their H&K MP5 submachine guns in their hands, yelling at anyone who will listen to get down on the ground. Confused tourists are caught between running this way or that, so they don't have a clear shot at me yet. If I let the law get its claws into me, I might as well just turn myself over to PRS.

Fortunately, I've figured out there is, in fact, a second way off this rock.

I wait until Gladiator staggers to his feet and starts rumbling toward me for another round; then I take a running start, leap up, and plant both feet right into the wide target of his chest. He flies back and slams into the already-shaky flagpole. With a metallic shriek, the base rips out of the stone, and the pole crashes against the edge of the far wall.

Taye has been lying face down on the ground ever since I told him to, and I scoop him up with one hand and start running up the fallen flagpole just as the cops arrive with their SMGs. "Kill him, kill the *malaka*!" Dimitrios is screaming at them.

I yank the nylon halyard out of its hasp as I run, and just as the cops open fire, I reach the end of the flagpole and leap into thin air. Below me, far away, I see all that remains of a classical temple in the middle of a park, just the tall facade with its high pillars. Taye is screaming like he's going down the first hill of a roller coaster. I probably am too. I can't really tell because of the empty roar of wind in my ears.

I didn't really expect the fallen flagpole to hold my weight once we reached the (literal) end of the rope, and it doesn't. There's a brief jolt, and the nylon of the halyard scalds my palm. I manage to hold on, but it doesn't matter because that's all it takes to rip the flagpole entirely out of the rock above, and I see it pinwheeling above me as we continue to drop. I hope it doesn't hurt anybody too badly wherever it lands.

You can tell how far the rest of my fall is because I have time to think this.

When I hit the red-tile roof of the building one hundred plus meters below me, both my legs shatter instantly. I could try to describe what this feels like, but it's not that I don't have the words; I don't even have the thoughts. Pain lances through my mind, pinning it like a living bug in a display case, legs flailing. Pure instinct makes me pull Taye hard into my chest, and I wrap my body around him to protect him as I roll off the sloped roof and fall through the awning of the café below and into the table where an elderly British couple in anoraks is sipping tea. My abrupt arrival sends them shrieking down the hill.

I roll off the table and land on my back on the ground. Taye gets up and starts calling in broken Greek for an ambulance. I grab onto his sleeve: "It's okay, it's okay." I've already called a car, I tell him. The other patrons and waiters in the café crowd around me, gawking at my twisted legs. Somehow all my bones have stayed inside my skin, despite being in multiple pieces, even though my legs look like misshapen pipe cleaners. I can hear the wail of sirens getting closer.

The car service I ordered halfway through my drop arrives with a screech in front of the café within three minutes, as advertised, and I ask the fitter patrons to help lay me on the back seat. Taye gets in the front passenger seat. I tell him to keep his head down. The driver is also an East African immigrant, and he doesn't ask any questions but is spooked enough by my condition that he slams on the gas and careens the rest of the way down the hill of the Acropolis.

I try not to look at my mangled legs. I can already feel the nanites going to work repairing them, producing an itching sensation that would probably hurt except, you know, I am distracted by the sheer agony of completely shattered legs. Do I need to tie splints around them? Maybe I should. I don't want them to heal in their currently utterly bizarre configuration, like Dodge, but I just have to hope my 2.0 nanomachines are smart enough to remember that human legs are supposed to be straight, not accordion shaped.

We drive past the flagpole, which has lodged itself like a giant spear through an empty Fiat parked at the curb.

I stashed Yonas and his family in an anonymous lime-green motel near the airport. The driver puts his cab in park at the front doors and rushes inside. The front-desk clerk manages to find a dusty wheelchair in a storeroom somewhere and wheels me to the suite I rented. Yonas and Nyala try to crush Taye to death with hugs that they then lavish on me.

Once everyone has cried out their relieved tears and I can finally pierce through the pain to put one thought in front of the other, I clear my throat so everyone looks at me.

"Who wants to go to Canada?" I ask.

Everyone raises their hands.

TWENTY-SIX

Project Rising Spirit may be a fearsome black ops defense contractor full of shady badasses, but they are still a large organization and, therefore, a bureaucracy. There's a chain of command and multiple layers of approvals and authorizations you have to go through to do pretty much anything short of going to the bathroom, and maybe even then.

So when Helena, the smuggler's moll, sent my photo to the number PRS gave her boy toy, it wasn't to an anonymous Gmail account. It was to an actual PRS account on an actual PRS server, and I piggybacked a virtual bot along with it. When my mug arrived there and got attached to emails and shared in internal company Slack chats and so forth, my bot went along with it, every single time that photo was opened. That photo of me on the Acropolis, to use another ancient Greek reference, was my Trojan horse, leaving a trail for me to follow anywhere it went inside the Project Rising Spirit network.

You're watching me? Well, knock-knock, *malakes*. Now I'm watching you.

Literally. I'm up on the security cameras inside Fresh Kills. I'm in the cafeteria. I'm in the nanomachine nutrient bays. I'm in Nina's office as she sneaks a vape hit, hiding behind the cowl of monitors rimming her desk where she thinks the cameras can't see (she's wrong). Dad is smart enough not to have cameras in his office, but I am up on the lens trained on his assistant's desk outside, and I can hear him yelling on the phone to a senator or a member of the Joint Chiefs or some other DC muckety-muck that, no, he doesn't know what the heck happened at the Acropolis, and they should just get all the way off his back about it.

Yes, spying on people is creepy. But the people I'm spying on are actively trying to kill me, so just get all the way off my back about it.

I'm up in a long, featureless hallway, which I am surprised I do not recognize, when I see something I do: a cooler that looks exactly like the one that contained Twyst's severed head. Two workers in PRS jumpsuits are wheeling it on a plastic cart down the hall to a door at the far end. They lean in so their retinas can be scanned; then the door hisses open and they disappear inside with Aaron Twyst's least-used body part.

Enhancing the view, I see the sign above the door says, "CORE Control. Authorized Personnel Only."

CORE Control? What the heck is CORE Control? I thought I had been everywhere there was to go in Fresh Kills. I cycle through the half century of security cameras in the Fresh Kills complex and don't find any other views I don't recognize, so if there are cameras in CORE Control, they're on a separate, isolated network.

Well, that's weird.

I'm also up in the briefing room when they discuss how they're going to get their greedy little paws on yours truly. The place is packed with security, techs, and analysts and led, once again, by Dad onstage.

"Local informants have confirmed that Bloodshot has been in Athens for the last week, hiding with an Ethiopian immigrant family, the Gebres. Yesterday he had a very public shoot-out with the coyotes that brought the Gebres into Greece atop the Acropolis, of all places."

"Lost his subtle touch, our boy," yells some guy out from the darkness, and everybody laughs.

"He has at that." Dad chuckles and then winces and touches the back of his head. Must be still getting those migraines. I can't believe I still worry about him, even after all that's happened. But I do. Some programming is rooted too deep.

"You okay, boss?" Nina asks from the front row. Dad mouths, "I'll be fine," and continues:

"Within six hours of the Acropolis incident, four seats were booked on four different direct flights out of Athens International under four different pseudonyms, staggered across a twelve-hour period, two to Toronto, one to Ottawa, and one to Montreal. The person buying all four tickets has requested curbside wheelchair assistance on every trip, which is a good idea for someone who made the 156-meter jump off the top of the Acropolis—and lived—to do."

The room gasps at the feat. Glad I still have the capacity to impress.

"Someone then remotely booked tickets on Via Rail trains to Toronto from those last two cities. All of these transactions were paid for via untraceable Swiss wireless accounts, just like we trained Bloodshot for improvisational field ops."

"He's going to try and connect with Esther," says Higgins in PsyOps from a middle row.

"Yes, I'd say so," Dad says. "That means I am authorizing the activation of Bloodshot Contingency Plan Epsilon, effective immediately."

Esther. That must be Salma's real name. Even though I am lying in a plane seat pushed all the way back and not moving an inch while I heal, I can't help myself. I let my nanomachines go to town on my legs, every gigabit per second coming out of my brain straining to maintain an undetected presence in the PRS system. I screen-grab Salma's face from my memory files and do an image search on it across all major social networks.

At Fresh Kills, the Greek letter epsilon flashes briefly on the screen behind Dad. "The purpose of this contingency, as I am sure most of you can figure out, is to maximize operational efficiency. The flights to Canada from Greece have already left, not that we would have had time to scramble the resources to intercept him in Europe anyway. Bloodshot, of course, expects us to divide our forces into quarters, staking out all four flights, not knowing which one he's on.

"But, of course, we will not do that. Thanks to the diligence of Higgins and his team in PsyOps"—Higgins clasps both hands together and shakes them in the air in triumph, the jerk—"we do not need to do this. It does not matter in the least *how* Bloodshot gets into Canada because we know exactly where he is going *in* Canada. He is doing what we have repeatedly suggested to his subconscious he should do: He is going to link up with his 'girlfriend.'"

Dad actually uses air quotes when he says "girlfriend." Jeez, man.

I get a hit on the photo on Facebook: Esther Hashemi. Her profile says she is a junior with a major in political science at the University of Toronto. Her relationship status is that she's in one, but with someone named Tamara. The first image in her Photos section is of the two of them smiling, arms around shoulders, atop a ski slope in Banff. I hate myself for the red-hot vein of jealousy that erupts inside me when I see the picture. Our relationship is cake, I tell myself. My feelings aren't real. But my reactions to them are. That's what Higgins and his squad of brainwashers have done to me. Bad enough they plant memories in me of my past, but they can still play my present like a grand piano, even when I know half of what's in my brain is pure cake.

Her profile says her birthday is April 2. She is twenty years old. The other photos of her are at various college parties, at bars, playing field hockey outdoors. She's young and petite enough to look like a high schooler, though. I find a photo of her onstage in a 1940s skirt and fedora, playing the female lead in a musical version of *His Girl Friday*. So she's a part-time thespian too.

I also find Esther Hashemi on LinkedIn. Last summer she interned at a think tank called the Kindt Institute in St. Louis, Missouri, which I know to be yet another PRS front. The whole scam is becoming increasingly clear. Esther gets a swank internship among other perks and bennies in exchange for having Zoom calls with a chalk-faced teenager every few months and pretending to be his Canadian girlfriend. Don't worry if he acts like he doesn't remember your last few conversations; that's actually totally normal. Don't worry if he image-searches you and figures out who you really are. We're just going to mindwipe him every few weeks anyway. You're going to be constantly planning a trip for him to come visit you for your birthday, a trip that will never happen because we keep moving your "birthday" a few months away from whenever you're talking. In two years you're going to leave school, and we're going to have to replace you with a more age-appropriate girl anyway, so it's not like you're committing to this weird side hustle for the rest of your life. Once your creepy faux-girlfriend service has ended, you'll have a cushy entry-level job waiting for you in the defense and/or intelligence field after you graduate.

And if he ever tries to seek you out and meet you in person, well, that's what Contingency Plan Epsilon is for.

The screens behind Dad fill up with photos of an older, postwar, twelve-story apartment building along a tree-lined street and live satellite views of the surrounding block. "We rent for Ms. Hashemi a rather expensive condo on Richmond Street, downtown. Her next-door neighbor is one of ours, her main minder in-country, and we also rent out and keep empty the condo directly above hers as well as the empty döner joint across the street.

"The first flight to Toronto arrives in approximately ten hours. Within eight I need capture teams fully scrambled, with EMP weapons in both apartments above and beneath her, as well as two mobile units at either end of the block on Richmond. We'll be up on CCTV in all relevant train stations and airports. My preference would be to take him right before he walks into the apartment building lobby, so one team inside and the minder will be backup, if necessary. Since we'll be tracking him as soon as he arrives in Toronto, we should have plenty of lead time. Any questions?"

Burke from Tactical raises his hand. "Are we notifying Ms. Hashemi of the situation?"

Dad shakes his head. "Negative. We don't think that's optimal for her safety, or ours."

"Follow-up. What about our friends in CSIS?" The Canadian Security Intelligence Service is their government's primary spook show. "We inviting them to the party, or are my guys going fully off the books on this one?"

"Well, considering I am already thoroughly sick of answering a wide variety of questions from our NATO partners about that fracas in Athens . . . let's just say what our friends at CSIS don't know won't hurt them."

The entire room has a good chuckle at that.

Takahashi from Ops is next. "What about Bloodshot's legs? Do we think he'll be up and moving around by the time he gets to Richmond Street?"

Dad looks to Nina, who's sitting next to Takahashi, crutches lying over her lap. She has graduated from a cast on her foot to one of those big plastic boots. "Our best simulations suggest that, even crammed into economy, it'll take only eight hours for him to repair his legs to ninety percent functionality."

"But let's not give him the chance to run, can we, people?" Dad says to everyone. "Hit 'im with the EMP as soon as he turns his back on you to enter Esther's building. Wrap him up and get him on the next transpo to Fresh Kills before your Tim Horton's gets cold, huh? Let's do this, people!" Dad leads the applause like he's at a pep rally before he has to grab the back of his head with a grimace.

I'm also up on the cameras eight hours later when all the head honchos of the various PRS departments are crammed inside the cube-shaped commander center (not to be confused with CORE Control—I'm still unclear as to what that is), looking up at POVs on their screens of the squad team leaders in the various hiding spots inside and outside the Richmond condo complex. All the planes have arrived by this point.

"Anyone have a visual on Bloodshot? Anyone?" Takahashi asks.

"Don't bother with that," Dad says. "He can change his appearance, his clothes. He could look like anyone. Don't depend on your eyes. It's by his actions that we'll know him."

Nina bolts upright before her terminal. "Just got a hit on the train ticket at the Ottawa train station. It's just been swiped; that's the train he's on."

"See? When does that train arrive? Ten thirty in the a.m.? Make sure we've got eyes on that station when it happens."

They see me on the screen getting off the Express from the capital at 10:34 a.m. I cross the cavernous vault of the interior of Toronto's Union

Station in jeans, a red hoodie, sunglasses. I make sure to change my face on-screen so that the skin color is more natural, but the extreme limp on my right side cannot be disguised.

"He's not fully healed yet," Dad murmurs.

Nina pokes him in the shoulder. "I knew you still cared, you big softie."

"Of course I care. I care about forcing this crap-flavored toothpaste back into its tube."

On the screen, a CCTV in the Union subway platform catches me cramming myself into a 1 train with hundreds of other earbud-bobbing, screen-staring commuters.

"Taking public transportation instead of getting a cab. Good for him and his carbon footprint." Burke leans into the microphone in front of him. "Look alive, people. We have visual on target. All things being equal, we should have showtime in less than thirty minutes. Gunslinger? Proceed with your fireteam into the lobby. Over."

"What are we going to do with him once we get him?" Nina asks Dad.

"Do you really want to know? Look who's the real softie here."

"Do you think . . . I mean, is there hope for him?"

"In the larger scheme of things?" Dad sighs. "Above my pay grade, I'm afraid. But in the short term . . . word came down from on high. The Bloodshot program has run its course. 'Indefinitely suspended' was the terminology used. They think our resources are much better invested concentrating on CORE."

"You know, it'd be nice to know who we actually work for. Then maybe we could question their decisions."

"See why they keep to the shadows? Yes, I've often thought similar thoughts. But don't you worry, my dear. You'll have plenty of new toys to play with."

"And break," Nina says. "And put back together again. And again."

"It is your specialty."

"Look alive," Takahashi says. "He's getting off at Osgoode."

On-screen, I push through the turnstile and wait for the other passengers to leave. There is a ticket seller in a kiosk, and I duck behind a metal support beam where he can't see. And then I shift my face to a new disguise, square-jawed, with an air force buzz cut. Totally unassuming, unless you happened to see someone put that face on like it was a new hat live on CCTV.

"Oh, you think you're going to fool us?" Burke singsongs at the screen. "You don't fool us, we fool you." He enhances my new face, screen-grabs it, and sends it to every in-country squad member. "Listen up, people," he says into his microphone, "this is your new visual on target Bloodshot. Wait for the signal from your fireteam leader to make the grab. Repeat: Wait for your CO's signal."

The new me walks past closed-up bars and clubs along early-morning Queen Street. Nobody in Fresh Kills says anything as screens flicker and change as I pass an underground garage entrance, a Starbucks, a corner where a bunch of kindergartners wait to cross, holding each other's hands in an adorable chain. On the screen, the new me is looking at my phone, head down, avoiding their gaze. But there is no hiding from Big Brother, not in this day, not in this age.

"Two minutes to curtain, ladies and germs," Burke says into his microphone.

The screen shifts, finally, to the view over the entrance to Esther's apartment block.

The camera shows no people on the sidewalk for what seems like forever. Even the squirrels seem to be keeping their distance.

"What . . ." Nina gathers her thoughts. "What does PsyOps think Bloodshot is going to do with Esther if he catches up to her?"

"Higgins made a range of predictions," Dad says. "He thinks there's a sixty percent chance he just wants to talk to her, validate their relationship. There's a twenty-five percent chance he's figured out she's deepfake, and he will attempt to, um, interrogate her for operational details."

He stops talking, so Nina has to say, "And the remaining fifteen percent?"

Dad just looks at her.

"Jesus, Doc," Nina says.

"Calm down. Her next-door neighbor miraculously came into

possession of two day passes for the spa at the Four Seasons he couldn't use. I am told by her shadow that Esther and her girlfriend, Tamara, are currently enjoying a couples hot-rocks massage as we speak."

"Thank God," Nina exhales.

Then I waltz into view, nose still in phone. Just as I turn toward the building entrance, the first capture team, the one in the lobby, moves out. The image warps into static as they hit me with the pulsers, but the CCTV should be far enough outside the cone of fire that it won't be permanently damaged. I don't seem to notice the effect of the pulser, though, except that all of a sudden my phone screen goes blank, so I look up.

I see the capture team moving toward me, then I turn to run, but out of the abandoned döner shop across the street and the abruptly opening side door of a van at the curb come more dudes dressed like ninjas, but with twenty-third-century weaponry.

"Uh, Epsilon Command," the speakers in the command center crackle, "EMPs don't seem to be having predicted effect. Please advise."

"All fireteams, switch to standard Tasers," Burke says.

On-screen, about half the capture squads drop the wand-like pulser weapons and switch to small hand Tasers that fire imperceptible wires. Four of those sparking barbs find their mark, and I convulse, dropping my phone, briefcase, and, ultimately, hat as I collapse to the pavement.

"All right, guys, ask for a doggie bag and get this one to go," Burke says.

A PRS commando whips out a large, well, sack, and the others stuff me headfirst into it. It must have some electrical mesh in it to contain the nanomachines, because only commandos wearing special gloves pick it up and shove it into the side of the van before slamming the door.

"He should have changed," Dad whispers, almost to himself.

"What's that?" Nina looks to Dad. He's as white as a sheet.

"When he lost consciousness, the nanites shouldn't have the independent wherewithal to maintain the disguise. He should have reset to physical baseline."

"He didn't react to the pulsers either. Maybe it's a new part of his evolution?"

Dad grunts.

Takahashi leans into his mic. "Gunslinger, do you see what looks to be a wallet on the ground? Where the target was? Can you check that out, please?"

Gunslinger—a taciturn marine vet I know as Charlie Palmer—picks up the black square on the walkway and goes through it. "Lotta cash . . . credit card . . . Ontario driver's license . . . ID . . . pretty impressive fake. Home address in Ottawa. ID card says this guy's name is Geoffrey Lemiere, and he is deputy director of operations for, uh . . ."

"Spit it out, Gunslinger," Burke growls.

"Says here we have captured the deputy director of operations for the Canadian Security Intelligence Service. Uh. Sir."

Nobody knows what to say to that.

Only the screeching of Toronto police cars on the street breaks the silence. Cops on either end pop out, out of visual, but very much audible: "*Police! Everyone down on the ground!*"

"Gee-zus!" Burke explodes.

"Rules of Engagement specifically prohibit direct confrontations with local law enforcement," Takahashi groans, throwing up his hands.

"*I know the ROE, Bob,*" Burke barks. Into the mic he sighs, "All right. Comply with all local law enforcement. No resistance. Don't tell them squat. We are scrambling Legal."

The PRS commandos reluctantly drop their weapons and lie down on their stomachs with their hands on the backs of their heads while the cops move in, weapons drawn.

"Wait! Wait! That was—that was the ops guy from CSIS? How? How is that possible?" Nina's attention has been transfixed by the screen this whole time, and she just now looks around to realize that Dad is gone.

"*So where is Bloodshot?*" she cries.

And that's when I come crashing through the ceiling.

TWENTY-SEVEN

Fun fact: I never actually went to Canada.

After I booked those four commercial flights, I arranged for a fifth, private one to fly out of the separate charter terminal at Athens International. This flight, however, was headed for New York.

Yonas's entire family was with me, Liya included, with two big shopping bags full of to-go containers that held the final meals made in her restaurant in Greece, for me alone. It would take almost the entire flight for my legs to be reconstructed, and the rest of me was occupied trying to stay up on PRS's network undetected. The kids played games and the adults watched movies on the iPads I bought them. They stashed me in a corner and covered me with a blanket for the whole ten-hour flight. I stuffed my face with injera, jalapeño-spiced beets, bean-and-okra stew, collard greens, and beef, fuel for nanomachines as they very, very painfully rebuilt my legs. Heaven and hell, all in the same trip.

I must have passed out after the initial team briefing for Contingency Plan Epsilon, and it's the landing gear scraping on the runway as we touch ground that wakes me. I slide open the window shade and see the flat rooftops of Teterboro, a private airstrip in New Jersey. I manage to stand up and walk up and down the aisle under my own power, and with minimal pain. The family applauds me like I've medaled at the Olympics.

I hug and kiss them all goodbye, and Yonas sees me halfway down the gangway.

"Sorry I got you guys mixed up in my insanity," I tell him. I have a hard time looking him in the eye. "Particularly Taye."

"Come now, Ray." Yonas puts one hand on my shoulder. "Since we've known you, I can think of a few times we were almost dead without you. And a couple times where we were almost dead with you. So let's say we're even."

"If you say so." I shake his hand. "For obvious reasons we probably shouldn't see each other again."

"In many ways, that is the worst part."

"I tweaked the Canadian customs system so that your passports should get you into Calgary on a tourist visa. After that, you're on your own."

"We know no one there. But considering how we left Europe, perhaps that is for the best." He shrugs and smiles. "A new adventure."

"Yeah."

He seems to sense I'm not going to be the one to turn away first, so he heads back up to the plane. Right before he ducks inside, he says, "Remember, Ray, that you are loved. And you love in return. There is nothing more real than that."

I somehow manage not to cry before the private jet closes its doors, taxis down the runway, and soars into the air.

I take an Uber over the George Washington Bridge and into Manhattan and get out at an uptown bodega that has had the same sun-faded box of Trix in its window since 1997. The shelves are at best intermittently stocked with a twelve-pack of Pacifico here, a loaf of Wonder Bread there. You'd be justified in wondering how a place like this stays in business if you didn't know as I do that the real merchandise is in the back, behind an empty ice cooler with a handwritten "*Fuera de Servicio*" sign taped to it. The man in the back room behind that secret door has an albino python draped hissing over his shoulders and barely looks up from playing dominoes with three buddies when my shadow falls over their table.

"Guns," I tell him. He makes me wait until the game is over. I have a vague sense of having been in this room before, though without any specific memory of what I did here in any of my previous visits. PRS wipes my memory in the short term but leaves me residual knowledge of things like Where to Get Untraceable Guns in New York City so I have some hope of improvising in the field if need be. Hopefully Snake Guy doesn't spend any time on the dark web and doesn't know about the bounty on me. I don't detect a computer in the room; not even a smartphone.

Snake Guy loses at dominoes with a curse, then sells me two Heckler & Koch MP5 machine pistols out of a duffel bag. I really liked how they looked in the hands of those Athens cops atop the Acropolis. I also get enough extra clips to fill every pocket in my cargo pants. He throws in a Borka double-edged combat knife as a bonus. He wants to be paid in cash, but grudgingly accepts my crypto transmission. He recites from memory the account number I'm to send payment to. This transaction is no more real than any of the others I've been doing; I'm just conjuring money from the digital air. But he'll never find out. Money is like magic: If people believe in its value, abracadabra! It has value.

I take a long Lyft ride out to Staten Island, have the driver drop me at the big-box furniture outlet across the street from the entrance to Fresh Kills. The gate is closed and locked, and Reza is the guard in the little guardhouse. Reza's job is extremely boring, which I know because I follow him on YouTube, where he posts all his reviews of superhero movies from inside his checkpoint. PRS must not be one of his subscribers because they haven't fired him yet. At the moment I can see his phone propped up on the guardhouse window, and he is animatedly talking at it, so he is no doubt in the middle of one of his film talks. From his expression I can't tell if he liked the movie or not. He is not going to pay any attention to me.

I make a leaping somersault jump over the razor wire and land in the tall grass, which I hug for a crawl up the nearest hill. There are cameras hidden all around in the young dogwoods and alders, but I have now been up on the PRS servers long enough that deleting my own image from them requires barely any bandwidth at all. There's nobody off shift or on break wandering the park like I used to. Doubt they have the personnel to spare; it's an all-hands-on-deck situation, particularly since they sent their baddest asses to Toronto on my wild-goose chase.

About that: Once I had Cake-Salma's address, I scanned the building's tenant rolls and was not at all surprised to discover that it was a popular residence for members of the intelligence community, which must be how PRS got a sweet deal on owning places there. I sent an urgent message to Deputy Director Lemiere to summon him to a meeting in Toronto, and then I remotely bought a seat on the same train he took. To swap me out for him in the CCTV footage, as seen on Fresh Kills' screens, wasn't easy, but it worked.

I pop open the covering lid of an air shaft just big enough to squeeze into and drop myself inside. I committed the blueprints of these ducts to memory, and I arrive above the command center in time to hear over the loudspeakers:

"*Police! Everyone down on the ground!*"

"Gee-zus!" Burke explodes.

"Rules of Engagement specifically prohibit direct confrontations with local law enforcement," Takahashi groans, throwing up his hands.

"*I know the ROE, Bob,*" Burke barks. Into the mic he sighs, "All right. Comply with all local law enforcement. No resistance. Don't tell them squat. We are scrambling Legal."

"Wait! Wait!" Nina cries. "That was—that was the ops guy from CSIS? How? How is that possible? *So where is Bloodshot?*"

I wanted to wait and see if Dad would come back, but it's too perfect not to drop down when she says that.

I have an H&K MP5 in each hand. Firing a submachine gun one-handed is a really great way to sprain your wrist from bucking kickback and not hit anything you're aiming at, unless you are made of nanites, which you are not. Do not try this at home.

The two PRS sentries are rushing toward me not long before the vent grate falls on the ground and I land on top of it. But I've known where they are for the last twenty minutes and I'm new to them, so I get my shots off first, one to the left, one to the right of me. They both go down.

I know from experience Burke is packing at least a Glock, and sure enough he tags me in the shoulder from behind. I duck and roll and pop up firing, and he and the monitor behind him both go up in smoke.

Takahashi dives for one of the sentries' XM7 rifles. He gets it off the floor, but by the time he gets it and points it at me, he's already looking down my barrel. He is not looking at it for long.

This all might seem a little harsh. Even *I* have to sometimes remind myself these people have been kidnapping, torturing, and mutilating kids for the better part of four years—at least. Maybe nobody deserves the hammer I'm bringing down on them, but if anybody does deserve it, it's going to be a hidden bunker full of child murderers.

Which brings me to Nina. She shrieked and dove out of the way as I landed and has stayed crouched under the console, hands over her head, ever since. She stands up slowly, using the console edge to steady her bad ankle, the shell casings that have fallen on her during the fight dropping off her and clanging across the floor.

We look each other in the eye. "Remember what I said would happen to you if I caught you here?"

"No, I think I blocked it out." She swallows. "I hope you don't—listen. Bloodshot. I can be useful to you."

"Can you get me into CORE Control?"

On her face I can see she considers lying but wisely picks a different path. "Yes, but not here. From my desk in my office."

There are too many variables at play in this situation. I don't have much of a choice but to trust her. "If you double-cross me . . ." I pop fresh clips into the MP5s.

"I won't." She doesn't move for some reason. "I stayed—look, Ray, I knew that if I didn't do this job, they'd just replace me with someone who would. By staying, I can try to make bad things a little better. You can understand that, can't you?"

"I can understand it without believing it. This is the first time you've got a chance to make things better—all right? Contact me on the usual channel when you're ready to get me into the CORE. Whatever they're doing with Twyst's head is . . . not good."

"You don't know the half of it. Where are you going?"

"After dear old Dad." I can see him in the corner of my mind via the security cameras I still control, meeting an assault rifle–wielding security team in the stairwell and frantically waving them in my direction.

"Ray . . ." She waits until I look her in the eyes. "Be careful of him. The next-gen technology he has at his disposal . . . he's the other reason I didn't quit. The things I know about it . . . well, I don't think he'd let me quit. Not alive."

She's serious. I'm sort of amused. "Are you saying my dad is scarier than me?"

"He always was," Nina whispers. "Now he's more so."

The main door to the command center is opening. I grab her crutches off the floor and hand them over. "I'll cover you. Go now!"

She lopes awkwardly for the side exit and disappears through it just as the door opens and the security team hits me with flash-bang grenades. I'm expecting them, though, and cover my eyes with my arm as everything goes white around me.

The first few of the intercept team come in, their XM7s to their eyes and firing. The first few depleted uranium bullets hurt and kill nanites where they hit me, but I have my feet firmly planted and the slugs don't move me. A bunch just pass right through me and explode the monitors behind me, even better.

The PRS guys have very good training—I've seen it—but the reality of facing a combatant like me isn't something they train for. They're just not used to a target that doesn't flee or look for cover and instead stands there and takes automatic weapons fire when they start shooting at him. Regular warfighting says I should run for it, and they can gun me down from behind.

But I don't run. I stand and let myself get shot, and when they're all in the room firing at me, my targeting computers identify the weak spots between the jaw straps on their helmets and where the plates of their body armor end just above their clavicles, and I fire five shots with one of the MP5s. Five shots, five perfect direct hits on their necks.

I am out through the doorway before the fifth body has hit the floor. I could grab an XM7 off one of them, but I still have plenty of ammo left and I like holding death in both hands. In the camera view, I can see that the remaining eight guards are all hunkered down elsewhere in the complex, guarding huddled masses of civilian workers. Standard live-shooter drill stuff.

All I care about is Dad, but I don't see him anywhere on the camera feed. Could he have beat me to CORE Control while I was distracted? Doesn't seem possible.

I take the stairs three at a time down the central shaft of what used to be a missile silo to the cafeteria. The complex is completely silent, except for the buzz of fluorescent lighting. It's creepy as all get-out.

At first, I don't see anybody when I get down there. "Dad? You down here?" I call.

"Right here, son," I hear behind me. He wasn't there a half second ago. I turn and look, but nobody's there.

"It's time for us to talk."

"I'm not going to talk to you when you're like this, armed," the voice says.

"You don't have a choice."

"Oh, but I do."

Then the hammer gets dropped. On me.

TWENTY-EIGHT

The blows come out of nowhere and everywhere, all at once. They're not all that powerful but land in such rapid succession and in sensitive areas like my kidneys, ribs, and jaw that they smart like heck.

I look around the seemingly empty corridor and fire my weapon literally at the shadows, convinced I am fighting an invisible enemy, but the slugs ricochet harmlessly down the halls.

"Oh, right," a voice chuckles behind me. I whirl and fire, but the speaker is suddenly standing directly to the right of where the voice came from.

It's Dad. "Silly me. I was about to say this fighting style must be familiar to you, but I guess it wouldn't be, would it? You had your dustup with Telic and the rest of Generation Zero before your last mindwipe. She's been accelerated into the timestream so can act a few seconds before everyone else. Wild, isn't it?"

I look around but don't see any Telic. I don't have any idea what that person looks like, but I don't see anyone else at all. "Where is she? Did you turn her against the rest of Generation Zero? Where are you keeping them? I don't want to hurt you, Dad, but I am not leaving here without them."

Dad blinks wonderingly. "You've changed in so many ways, I thought maybe the mindwipe didn't take this time, but . . . hmh."

With difficulty, I point the gun at him. I don't like doing it. I think of us tossing around the football beneath the wheeling gulls.

But then I realize that's the only thing I can remember doing with him. My filial devotion to him, such as it is, is another phantom limb. It's cake. "Don't make me do this."

"I'm not making you do a thing. Not at the moment, at any rate. Nor anymore. Sorry to say, son, this is the end of the road for you. Dodge—Red Cell—wasn't exactly the most popular person around here, I doubt you'll be surprised to hear, and I might have been able to talk the PRS Board into sparing you even after you turned him into a birthday candle, but after this latest stunt . . . I mean, you do know you've wiped out over half the security force here, don't you? Even if that wasn't enough for the board to authorize terminating you, the sheer number of meetings and Google Doc condolence forms I'm going to have to fill out for the next ten days or so makes me want to terminate you."

His eyes gleam, nested in their crow's-feet laugh lines as always, but his voice is so cold. The conclusion I've been avoiding for days now seems unavoidable. My palms are sweating and I have to tighten my grip on the pistol.

"You're not really my father, are you?" I ask, voice cracking.

He just makes this little shrug, damn him. "I'm the closest to one you've got, or will ever have. But the short, simple, truest answer to your question is . . . no."

"Then I am trying to figure out why I shouldn't pull this trigger like I would on any other faceless PRS goon."

"Lifeline, Cronus," he says, and I don't really know what those two words attached to each other are supposed to mean.

At first.

The air ripples and parts visibly between his hand and my chest, and suddenly my shirt and the skin and muscle beneath burn in a way I can't even describe. I know it's the raised hand of Garrison (*don't call him Dad, he's not your dad, not really*) who's doing it, so I roll sideways behind a table. His hand follows me like a spotlight, and all at once it's the table that's now being eaten away into amber embers with an unnatural sizzle.

I look down: My nanites are trying to rebuild the front of my rib cage, but it's much slower going than usual. Somehow, instinctually, I know: It's because I have fewer of them than I had before. The power Dad—Garrison—has just used on me has actually destroyed the nanites that were once there. Panic spikes, and I try to tamp it down. I have a feeling that takes me a second to place because I haven't felt it in a long time:

Fear. Blind, existential fear.

There are powers out there that can kill me.

"Cronus is truly an amazing kid," Da—Garrison is saying, walking slowly around the table to get another shot at me. "He could have really been something, had I allowed him to be. But his power has a much better home with someone who knows how to use it. And that person would be me. He slipped from my grasp once, but you brought him back in the end."

When Garrison blasted the table, he blew one of the seats and the metal arm that attached it to the rest of the unit free, so I grab it and sling it as hard as I can at his head.

"Lifeline! Castle!" he barks, and a translucent force field wraps around his entire body. The plastic seat bounces harmlessly off his eyes.

I manage to get my feet under me. As I rise, he twists his waist and shows me the back of his head. It's shaved in the rear, and I can see a small red bump. "It's all in there. The sports car that makes you look like a horse and buggy, Bloodshot. A neural implant, developed with your nanomachine technology, that can give anyone psiot powers—well, anyone, provided their neurology is compatible with the tech. Whether or not I am is a bit of an open question in that regard, given my migraines, but I'm trying to stay positive. Still, you think I was going to let anyone else get ahold of this power? Son, have I ever told you about Edwin Drake, the man who invented oil drilling? Well, I am not going to end up like—"

I fire three quick rounds at the implant, but the slugs ping futilely off the Castle force field. I tell my nanites to try to latch on to it remotely, but the signal is scrambled. Also . . . distant? I'm not sure what that means.

Garrison brings his head up with a smile. "Ha! That scrunched-up nose on your face means you're trying to remotely control the Hard CORE, doesn't it? Sorry—we engineers love our acronyms. Cybernetic-Organic Retrofitting Engram. This little chip can swap signals from preserved parts of psiot brains in and out of my own. And to do so, it has to use an advanced, constantly shifting nanotech that's simply too complex for your own nanites to push around. Sorry.

"These bugs learn almost as fast as yours. Their processing time has decreased by a factor of twenty since I blasted you with Pulse power in the Nursery back in Idaho. Watch: Lifeline? Animalia."

Switching between powers means he has to drop the shield. I fire, but as he said, the transition is almost instantaneous. A flat, monochrome substance ripples across his body. My bullets embed in that shell with dull cracks, stopped cold. Then the trigger clicks under my finger with no result. Out of ammo.

"Our shrinks concluded the psiot code-named Animalia was scared by a Japanese cartoon her older sister was watching on TV when she was very young. So she wrapped herself in animated forms because it made her feel fearless, by embodying what scared her most.

"But she's a little girl. I'm a man. I have a man's fears. Loneliness scares me. Betrayal is something you always have to look out for. And persistence. A thing that keeps coming back and coming back, no matter how many times you're sure you've killed it."

Garrison's voice growls in a familiar, respirator-assisted rasp as he expands into muscly veins and grotesque teeth, bulbous eyes, a chest full of tentacles. It's Red Cell—back from the dead but now ten feet tall and bulletproof.

With a hollow bark, this grotesque copy of Dodge swats the pistol out of my right hand with one veiny claw and then launches me across the room with the other. I slam into the metal shutter sealing off the kitchen from the rest of the cafeteria. It buckles and collapses, and I am bouncing across the tiles, finally stopping against the metal prep islands in the center.

This is not going very well for me.

Garrison/Red Cell is still talking. Why do people always want to rant at me while they're beating me up? I've got to start fighting ninjas. They're deadly but silent.

"I know you're going to find this hard to believe right now, kid, but I really am a sentimental old fart at heart. Part of me wants to just subdue you, and wipe your memory again, and try and give you a fresh start, but I suspect flushing your short-term has fallen victim to diminishing returns. Turning you over to the Gen Zero kids corrupted you, made you all gooey with sentiment. An insidious impulse toward mercy has been hard-wired into your behavior now. We're not going to be able to just point you at a psiot and say 'Fetch!' anymore."

He kicks the door in with one monstrous foot and splinters and cracks the lintel as he shoves his massive bulk through the doorway.

I holster my one remaining gun and grab one corner of the giant twelve-burner oven against the wall and pull it into the aisle as far as I can, putting it between me and him and slowing his advance down. The gas pipes rupture with popping hisses. Red Cell strides toward me, grinning. He has me caught. Still, I pull cast-iron skillets and steel pots hanging from hooks on the ceiling and hurl them at him. He bats most of them away with a growl, but a few find their mark, cracking his Extreme-Dodge shell and, more importantly, mussing up that smug facade of his.

"I thank you, then, for convincing me," he breathes, "to shove you headfirst into a cyclotron and tear you apart atom by atom."

He leaps up onto the oven with a roar, and that's when I grab a Scripto wand lighter off the counter, click its flame, and toss it at the exposed, hissing gas pipes. There is a solid wall of sound and heat like I've never felt. The fireball blows him one way and me another, through the double doors at the far end of the kitchen.

With a whine and a stuttering spritz, the bunker's fire-control system turns on above me, and in addition to all the other things I have going for me, I quickly become drenched from the sprinklers overhead. The hiss of foam comes from the kitchen, as well as the extremely satisfying sound of Red Cell screaming in agony, which ratchets up gradually into Garrison's actual higher-pitched timbre.

Every inch of me is begging to lie down and not get up again, but I ignore the urge and pull myself up by the drinking fountain mounted on the wall. I'm not literally on fire anymore, so that's a positive development. Blackened bits of skin and flesh fall off the surface of me as I move.

Also, Dr. Motormouth may be annoying as all get-out, but amid all his verbal vomit, there were a few chunks I can actually use. All that talk may have been to try to conceal the fact that the Hard CORE has one obvious weakness I can exploit.

Now all I need to do is find it.

TWENTY-NINE

Static lances through my mind and I wince.

"Bloodshot? Do you copy me?" It's Nina's voice, distant, sounding like she has a mouthful of cereal.

"Barely. Took you long enough."

"Yo, dickhead, you're the one who broke my ankle in the first place. So I'm crutching my ass around the middle of a war zone and you don't get to complain."

"Okay, okay, sorry, I don't—"

"Remember, yeah, I know that tune. Listen, I had to take my laptop into the Faraday cage to keep Ray Sr. from tracking my thoughts. Can't get a remote signal out so I'm talking to you on a security guard's walkie-talkie tuned to your lowest frequency."

"I can pick up radio signals?"

"Sure. You didn't know that? That should have been in your baseline. Oh, well. Get down to the CORE Central entrance. You know where it is?"

I can see it in the camera view. I can also see the remaining guards, who went to ground to safeguard the civilian staff and are now sprinting out of their rooms. Incredibly, the civilians do the same. I can hear the crash of their footsteps on the metal steps as they run their way toward me. I look down the catwalk and see them streaming up the silo, crawling over each other like ants to get at me. Their eyes have the same dilated pupils I have seen in a unified mob once before.

"Jeez, you guys already uploaded Twyst's powers into CORE? The head was barely cold."

"Oh, believe me, Ray Sr. has been praying for nothing more than to get his hands on some straight-up, no-doubt mind-control juju for some time now. He had lab techs start in on surgically prepping Twyst's cerebellum for transfer on the flight back from the island. I should be okay inside the Faraday cage, but everyone else? Forget it. He's already practiced on everybody. He knows their minds inside and out. He has a whole slew of meetings set up for Washington next week, where he's going to basically wrap the entire Senate Appropriations Subcommittee on Defense around his little finger. Then he's going to debrief the Project Rising Spirit Board of Directors in person, make them his sock puppets too. By the end of the year, using Twyst's power, he could become the most powerful man in America. Maybe the world."

"Wonderful. Guess I've got to make sure he doesn't leave this bunker then."

I wait until the first mad-dog scientist puts his foot on my level before I elbow the glass of the fire-hose cabinet on the wall behind me, shattering it. I wrap the nozzle around my wrist and jump off the railing down into the center of the silo as the whole crowd literally falls over themselves trying to grab me.

This drop is nothing compared to the Acropolis. The hose snaps taut when I'm ten feet or so from the bottom level. I let go and fall the rest of the way to my feet. Some of the mindless mob jump off after me and land with sickening crunches. I could try to catch some of them, but I don't have time. The rest turn around and start slavering and half-falling their way back down the stairs.

I dash to the CORE Control door. "Nina, can you even unlock the door inside your cage?"

"Yeah. The system is on an insulated network, so you can't connect remotely. Fortunately, I've got my machine landlined into the main trunk. Gimme a second . . ."

"Hurry," I say. The mob has already reached my level. I spin-kick the lead guard unconscious. He falls across the others, tripping them up a bit, but it's a temporary slowdown at best.

I back up against the door. The masses surge over the fallen guard, their feet stomping him bloody. A hundred fingers reach out for me. "*Nina . . . !*"

"Got it!" The door slides open, and I almost fall through. She slams the door shut just as quick. From the yelp on the other side, it sounds like somebody's fingers got pinched. Can't say I'm too sorry about that.

I look around. This section looks unfinished, as opposed to the rest of the bunker, with smooth concrete walls and metal pipes crisscrossing everywhere. I get the sense the chamber is much bigger than I can see. Most of it is taken up with cryo tubes that have kids inside them. Through small windows, I can see their faces. Some of them look sicklier than others.

"These aren't just heads?" I ask Nina. "Dodge said Garrison prefers to keep them alive if they can."

"That's right. We just extract a few cells from the base of the skull and clone their cerebellums using the same nanotech that heals your tissue. We still don't know enough about how psiots' brains interact with the rest of the nervous system and body to produce power effects. And we haven't learned all we can through live testing."

"Listen to yourself. These are kids you're talking about. You ought to be ashamed."

"You see them as kids. I see them as weapons of mass destruction with zits and hormonal spikes of irrational behavior. We can argue about the best way to handle them later, but it's inarguable that they are fundamentally dangerous, Bloodshot."

I let that one go unanswered. My attention is drawn to a platform raised slightly up from the center of the room. Innumerable wires snake down from the ceiling and go into plastic nodes bristling across the shaved scalp of a teenage girl. She lies in a padded chair, like you'd see at a dentist's office, surrounded by monitors and life-support equipment. Her cheeks are sallow. An IV bag on a stand drips nutrients into her arm via a tube. Her eyes are closed, but her fingers hover over tablet screens that are hooked into two massive glowing servers set into the floor. Thin wires spiral out from under her fingernails. Her hands tremble over the screens, like a pianist preparing to play. She's just waiting for her cue.

"What's this chick's deal?"

"Her code name is Cloud," Nina says.

In fact, in the crook of her right arm, I see her cradling a small plushy cloud with cartoon eyes. Uh, what?

"Is this Clark's sister?"

"Who's Clark?"

"Cloud's brother." I hop over the railing and look down on Cyberpunk Sleeping Beauty. She's wearing an oxygen mask over her mouth. Her chest rises and falls in equal, drawn-out measures. "What the heck have they done to her?"

"Garrison is using her as his Lifeline. Her power is to network minds together. He tells her which power he needs, and she switches the engram almost at the speed of thought. He had a staff member doing it before—okay, me—but Cloud is much faster. And as you can see, he has her on call twenty-four seven."

I draw the one MP5 I still have holstered. "So if I take her out, he has no way to switch powers?"

Nina pauses before answering. "Correct," she says.

I point the pistol at Cloud's sleeping face. I don't like the idea of explaining this to Clark. I promised him I'd save his sister.

As I look at her, another image pops in my head. This face, this face before me, but with wispy blonde hair swept over the left side of her head past her ear, right side shaved. Green eyes, long lashes. Small nose stud, left nostril. She's leaning on the railing of a balcony overlooking a glittering cityscape. She's looking back toward me, smiling.

I pull the gun back, and I hear Nina let out a relieved breath in my ear.

A dull thud rings out from the ceiling above. I look up and see a manhole-sized circle start to burn itself into nothing, the bonds between the molecules breaking down and vanishing before my very eyes. Ray

Garrison drops down through it. The entire upper half of the tailored suit he was wearing is burnt away, along with his hair and the cartilage of an ear, leaving only a small hole on one side of his head. He does not look happy.

"Get away from her!" he shrieks.

"Make me," I say, a great comeback, I know, and train my MP5 on him instead, but before the muzzle gets there he barks, "Lifeline! Headspace!"

I hear Kalea's nails tap once, twice on the tablet screen, and suddenly Ray Sr. is a Doppler afterimage rushing toward me, then gone.

His arms are around my neck before I know it, lifting me off the ground. I try to reach back with the gun but can't extend my arm far enough to get off a shot.

"Lifeline! Pulse!"

I can guess what's coming, and it's not going to be good. I kick straight up and over Garrison's head, breaking his hold on me and dropping off the Lifeline dais just as the air crackles with ozone. A corona of blue sparks envelops him, and he blasts out with an incoherent growl, arcing electricity just past Kalea's still form, barely missing her.

I let the MP5 in my hand rip in his direction. Garrison turns toward me just as I unload, and with a flick of the wrist, he's created a wall of static in front of him that captures the slugs in midair. He drops the field, and the bullets drop like metal rain to the ground.

"It didn't have to be . . ." Garrison's saying, mouth twisting as if the words were in some alien language. He's slurring some too. "Liiiiiiike thiiiiiiis," he adds, and blasts me with an open palm right in the chest with a lightning eruption, and for a minute there, everything goes

---

blank

---

but then I snap back to consciousness, though on my back, and it takes me a minute to go, *Where am I, what am I doing?* Like walking into a room and forgetting what you went in there for, except in this room there's also a psychotic stepdad with an encyclopedia of superpowers at his fingertips trying to kill you.

"Bloodshot . . . he's . . . levels spiking . . . don't have much time." Nina is mostly static at this point.

Garrison tries blasting me with his left hand, but I roll out of the way and the crackling tines of electricity dissipate harmlessly on the tiles. He takes a step forward, readying another blast, but then he makes a high-pitched scream and grabs at the back of his head. He may be stupidly powerful, but he doesn't have any real combat experience that I know of. He's taxing the Hard CORE harder than it's ever had to be taxed before. When he lowers his head, I can see the implant glowing red hot at the base of his skull. It's hurting him, disorienting him. I won't get a better chance.

I fire the machine pistols at him, but the triggers click empty. I throw them at him, screwing up his aim when he has to bat them away. I follow the guns, running toward him and casting a 360-degree spinning kick at his head.

I don't see what happens, but it feels like somehow I missed completely. When I drop back down on both feet and nearly fall over, I see that the foot I tried to hit Garrison with is gone. The nanites are dissolving in a dusty cloud away from that knee.

The shock lingers because Garrison, literally drooling incoherently at this point, blasts me with both hands, and I go flying back and slam into a cryo tube with some blonde-haired older boy in it. I try to reach out behind me with a hand, but there's no hand. I try to bring it to my face to look at it, but it's already gone. My forearm vanishes before my eyes, dissolving away into a dirty cloud. I fear how far the rot will creep, but it stops at my elbow, leaving a completely white, completely flat stump behind. The static Pulse power can destroy the bonds between me and my nanites, apparently wiping their memory so they "forget" to keep my form. This must be how he got me the last couple times, in the woods, in the Nursery.

I try to get up, but all the electricity now leaps out of his body and envelops me, breaking me down and keeping me in one place at the same time. I am fading away, starting from the tips of my remaining fingers and the crown of my head, disassembling into my component grains of computerized sand, slipping away like sand through an hourglass, as relentless and irreversible as time.

It's happening. The mindwipe. It's happening again but much slower this time, and I'm awake for it. I see each memory as it gets flushed away, pages torn from a book and thrown in a fire.

Helping Cousin Liya make injera in her restaurant kitchen, pouring the gray batter onto the griddle and watching the bubbles inside pucker and grow while it cooks.

Floating on my back in the Mediterranean, marveling at the glittering mess of the Milky Way reflected on the dark waters all around me.

The seagulls wheeling annoyed above me, and Dad throwing the ball around in the main meadow at Fresh Kills.

I realize that I have a past now. A past of my own, not one that was handed to me like a play script I'm supposed to memorize. One that's a part of me, that can't be so easily erased. They told me lies so I would serve them, but now, with my own self, I am my own master. And I will fight to the last individual nanomachine to keep that from being taken away from me again.

I see Kalea in her chair behind Garrison, and I remember—I remember now!—sitting next to her on a picnic table in a park somewhere, and she's telling me a story, a story about how she accidentally networked all these minds together in a movie theater and the disaster that caused.

"Lifeline!" I cry out, in Garrison's own voice, thanks to a quick rearrangement of my larynx with my remaining nanites. I am basically nothing but a mouth at this point, as most of the rest of me has faded away to dust. I have no lungs, but I can scream.

"*Cloud!*" I yell just before my eyes start to fade away. I am basically a face resting on an unswept floor at this point. Kalea's finger taps across her interface and switches Garrison's powers to her own. His electrical field abruptly snaps off, and I can already feel the disparate units of my nanite body again.

Garrison screams and claws at the implant on the back of his neck. Even from where I'm lying on the floor, I can see the eyes of psiots inside the cryo tubes all around me snap open. Clark told me Kalea's power was to network other minds together. From the looks of it, she has networked him to every Generation Zero kid in here.

The kids he hunted. The kids he made live in fear.

The kids he tortured. The kids whose special abilities he stole.

The kids he imprisoned. Cut into. Cloned without their permission.

They can see inside his mind too. And see his raw hunger for power.

So they give him all their power. All at once.

For just a second, the pain leaves Garrison's face. He blinks, as if awakening from a dream. He looks lucidly at me.

"The future is now," he says.

His head explodes. I try to flinch my head away, but I don't have a neck. Bits and pieces of hair and skull and blood geyser outward like a water balloon hitting the sidewalk after a twenty-story fall. His legs teeter in the first full second, post–head explosion, but then they get the message and he falls over with a thump onto the floor.

For a few seconds there's quiet, glorious quiet, except for the mindless hum of machinery all around me.

"I tried to explain to Ray Sr. that his neurology was incompatible with the implant; it's why he got such terrible migraines from it," Nina says in my ear, static-free. "But he was just too paranoid to entrust the tech to anyone else."

"Can't talk," I whisper at her. "Re-forming."

It takes a while. Long enough for me to watch Kalea stir in her chair, carefully remove the wires from her fingertips and the cables from her scalp. She swings her feet to the floor and goes over to another console. A computer voice announces she has begun the mass dethawing of the captured kids.

At last she comes over to me, squinting a bit so she doesn't have to look directly at me. Hard to blame her. I must be an alarming sight, like a sand sculpture at the beach half-demolished by encroaching tides.

"Does it . . . hurt?" she asks.

"Only everywhere." I smile through gritted teeth. "Why can't I make nerve endings last, I ask you?"

"Yeah, seems masochistic."

"I think . . . the simulation of the body has to be as close to the real thing as possible, or the simulation of the mind doesn't work."

"Ah." She is finally able to look at me. I now have a fully formed head, neck, and torso. The rest of me is filling in at a satisfactory rate. "Do you have any idea who I am at all?"

"Only from my dreams."

Kalea smiles. "That's a start."

THIRTY

The Washington, DC, area has the largest Ethiopian diaspora community in the United States, so the options for great Ethiopian restaurants are everywhere. The one I'm walking into, Awash, is, according to Google, one of the best, just down the street from the Watergate Hotel, off a wide cherry tree–lined avenue.

The sharp, sour smell of bubbling injera hits me as soon as I push through the door, an odor that I associate with calm, refuge, safety. He chose the venue of this meeting, and he's already trying to manipulate me, even before I lay eyes on him.

The hostess looks up from her stand and smiles at me. She tries to hand me a menu, but I hold up a hand. "I'm here to meet a, uh, someone. Thanks, though."

I almost said "a friend," but that's not right at all.

I don't see him on the ground level of the restaurant, but a spiral staircase connects this floor to the lower one. He's down there, of course, away from all the windows, where there are only four or so tables with patrons at them. The devices they have are all connected with each other, so they all clearly work for him. Their comms are also connected with smartphones at the kitchen entrance and the side exit into the alley outside, by the restrooms. They have me completely surrounded.

Or so they think.

He's sitting in a corner booth with nothing but a glass of sparkling water on the table. He is wearing a navy-blue suit with a darker blue vest and gold cuff links in the shape of doves. His goatee is so neatly trimmed it's only noticeable when I'm two steps from the table.

I don't sense a communication device on him. But then, he *is* a communication device.

"Have a seat," Toyo Harada, allegedly the most powerful psiot in the world, says to me. "I almost don't recognize you when you're not covered in bullet wounds."

"I clean up okay." I slide into the booth across from him. For this meeting I chose a gunmetal-gray polo and black yoga pants. "You don't want to check me for weapons?"

"I already have."

Great. Every person on this level of the restaurant is probably a Harbinger Foundation psiot. "They can see I'm not packing through my clothes with their Perv Vision?"

Harada allows himself a little smile. "You really are, in many ways, just a child, aren't you?"

"I just turned seven, but I'm big for my age."

"Incredible. Garrison actually came up with the first great technological innovation of the twenty-first century, and all he can think to do is shoot people with it."

"That's cool, you talking about me like I'm a botched science experiment to my face. Really making yourself out to be a true ally, referring to me as an 'it.'"

"An excellent point. Forgive me, I meant no offense. It's rare one meets the Bogeyman for lunch. I'm a bit taken aback."

"Ditto for me and would-be messiahs."

"Is that what you think I am?"

"Isn't that what you think you are?"

The tight little smile again. "I asked you to meet with me, for one, to thank you. Project Rising Spirit tried to frame me and my foundation for a massacre on Mr. Twyst's island, and you put a stop to it. And I wanted to express my gratitude in person."

"You're welcome. Though I'd be lying if I said I did it to help you out. Red Cell and I had been needing to work our bad blood out for a while."

"Be that as it may. There's so little justice in the world that its rare appearance is a cause for celebration, regardless of the motivations behind it. And it led me to believe you might be open to joining our organization."

"Why would I want to do that?"

"You're distrustful of people who want to poke and prod you, trick you into being their cat's-paw. I can appreciate that. But the incident in Greece shows you can think of more than yourself. You helping that migrant family? Yes, we know all about that. I was a refugee myself, once, after the bomb fell and incinerated everything I knew. Such selflessness towards those with nothing is quite admirable."

"Answer the question."

"I am. You freed Generation Zero from Project Rising Spirit, and for that, all psiots the world over should sing your praises. But you left the job half-finished. You just sprung those children into the wild, to fend for themselves."

"A lot of people call that freedom."

"Freedom without security is just the freedom to starve. The freedom to be exploited."

"And security . . . that's what you're offering?"

"What the Harbinger Foundation can guarantee, yes. We can train Generation Zero. House them. Feed them. Give them a higher purpose."

"Destroying your enemies."

"I have no enemies. Only those who oppose me because they fear a new world, or the dysfunction of this current world is to their personal benefit."

"Huh. I bet you actually believe that."

"There's also the practical matter that I'm not going to let you leave this restaurant without your telling me where they are."

"Alive."

"Pardon me?"

"Most people, when they make that threat, they add 'alive,' as in, 'I'm not going to let you leave this restaurant *alive*,' but you're smart enough to know I'm maybe not alive in the usual sense, right? Of course, that doesn't really matter. Not to you. Even if I was totally human, I'm either on your side or I'm in your way, right? That's how you see everything that can think for itself, machine or otherwise."

"I wasn't aware you could read human minds as well as machines."

"I can't. But I know you can't read my mind either. That's the real reason for all the firepower, all the threats, am I right?"

"I've made no threats. The worst I've done is pay for lunch."

"Come on. But I threaten you, don't I? Because my hive mind is inaccessible to you. You can't get inside my head to see where Gen Zero is. That's also why you want them so badly. Because if you don't have them in hand, you don't control them either. You want to live in a cartoon world of good guys and bad guys, and the moral high ground just happens to be wherever you're standing. But not everybody wants to choose a side in your little war. We're capable of living our lives without your all-knowing guidance."

I raise my voice toward the end of that, and now the other psiots seated behind me stop pretending not to listen to our conversation and turn toward the corner booth.

Harada shakes his head. "I had hoped this meeting would go some other way. I knew it was unlikely, but still . . ."

"You asked me here anyway. Now let me tell you why I agreed. I wanted to tell you something. By now it should be pretty obvious, but I'm going to say it out loud anyway: Leave me alone. Leave Generation Zero alone. I get a sniff of you going after them, and I mean just a whiff, I will take a wrecking ball to your organization as hard as I took one to Project Rising Spirit. I know you think you're smarter than them. So prove it by backing off. You can't manipulate me, you can't bribe me, and trying to destroy me is going to waste more time and resources than even you can spare. It's a stalemate. The only way you can avoid losing to me is to not play games."

I raise my voice on purpose this time. The psiots now all stand up and fall in with the tromp of a well-trained phalanx behind me. Light begins to seep out of eyes. Frost forms crackling around hands. One girl's hair literally lights on fire.

A skinny kid who all of a sudden has white eyeballs starts to float toward me until Harada holds up a hand. "Peter, wait." He looks me calmly in my eyes. "Bold talk from an unarmed man."

I stand up and raise both arms. There used to be chairs underneath the table, disguised by the tablecloth. I touched them. My nanites touched them.

And rearranged them into Omen automatic sniper rifles. I point one at Harada, the other at Peter.

"You sure about that?"

The look on Harada's face is priceless.

The psiots all lunge for me at once, except for the boss man himself, who's just sitting there with his mouth open, utterly surprised. Before they get anywhere close to me, I'm whirling and firing at the chandelier overhead. It drops with a sparking crash, and when it explodes onto the table below, it plunges the entire basement level into darkness, thanks to my remotely switching all the other lights off. The Harbinger psiots all start blasting where they think I am with their laser eyes and such, but while looking at the mirror behind Harada, I had the nanites already calculate the best escape route. I roll under a row of tables and pop up behind the scrum of enemies. I dash down the hallway past the restrooms to the fire-door basement exit, just as a big broad-shouldered skinhead teenager is coming through it.

I fire a 40mm grenade at his chest with the underbarrel of the Omen in my left hand, and his body kindly opens the fire door as he crashes through it, making a sizable crater in the concrete wall of the stairwell outside. His jacket and shirt have been blasted away, but his skin and torso are totally unharmed. Creating psychic force fields must be nice. I wish someone could teach me that trick.

I take the side steps up into the alley as the smoke from the grenade blast billows up and past me, obscuring my face. Pedestrians have stopped to gawk in the direction of the noise. I've already told my weapons to go bye-bye, and they dissolve into a cloud of nanites before anyone sees me.

"Call the fire department now!" I yell, throwing in some hacking and coughing for good measure. "Hurry, there are still people down there!"

I run down to the nearest intersection, where Headspace is sitting under the shadow of a cherry tree in his Pacers jersey, bobbing his head to tunes on his retro headphones.

He jumps up as soon as I tap him on the shoulder. "How'd it go?" he asks me when he takes the headphones off.

"Like we thought. Time to motor."

Headspace nods, and reality warps around us.

Next thing I know, I'm being shot at.

"Bang, bang! Bloodshot's dead!"

Just as Headspace and I step out onto Twyst's island, Isiah leaps out from behind a statue of Hermes, with his winged sandals and no head, and he shoots his finger at me. I clutch at my shirt and go down onto the flagstones. Little Castle giggles and jumps on top of me.

"But . . . somehow . . . I'm healing!" I cry. He grabs my arm as I stand up, swinging from my biceps like a monkey bar.

"That's great!" Clark shouts. "Hold it just one second more!" He's shooting us with a digital recorder he found in one of the trailers. The footage is being saved to a hard disk inside the camera, not uploaded to the internet. Kalea and I told Clark he couldn't upload any of that footage without giving away our location, which he wasn't thrilled about, but fortunately he didn't take that much persuading. Just a few hours later, he declared he was no longer interested in big special-effects monster movies—"junk cinema," he sniffed—but was going to make an epic documentary about life on Psiot Island, which he's been editing obsessively on a computer he found in the makeup trailer. He can keep working on this movie as long as he wants, since who knows when it'll be safe enough for us to let him release it?

"And . . . cut," Clark says, and Isiah drops from my arm and runs off to his friends with a laugh and without a care in the world.

"Dude, don't say 'cut' when it's a documentary," Headspace says. "Aren't you supposed to be just a fly on the wall or something?"

Clark rests the camera on his shoulder. "Hey, man, don't tell me how to movie."

Ferrying Generation Zero out of the Fresh Kills base required little more than staggering the arrivals of baffled Uber drivers at the parking lot in the furniture and mattress superstore across the street to carry away four psiots at a time. Getting the deed to Twyst's island took a little more doing, once I created a phony legal entity that could buy it, and arrange in-person go-betweens so the sale couldn't be traced back to me. My logic was, this is the last place PRS or Harada would look for us, someplace they thought had already been cleared. Cronus, Kalea, and I run daily evacuation drills just in case I end up being wrong about that, but for now, they splash in and out of the two pools, chase each other through the sculpture gardens, and have plenty of beds in the sprawling villa to sleep in—best summer camp ever.

More kids than usual are screaming and cannonballing into the pool under the summer Mediterranean sun. Cronus supervises them from a beach chair, but when he sees me, he hops to his feet and comes over.

"Can I add something to the list for your next supply run?" Thanks to my shapeshifting ability, Headspace and I handle going to the mainland for groceries and any other stuff we may need. "Chlorine for the pool? I found a YouTube video on how to clean it, and I can tell you exactly what to look for. I can't get kids to stop peeing in it."

"Yuck. ASAP. Anything else?"

"More calculators? Like ten, at least. Kalea's got to teach these little rascals long division at some point."

Their parents don't know where we are, but we arrange for visits back whenever we can. That may come back to bite us later, but PRS can't watch every family all the time, all at once. At least, I hope they can't.

A twelve-foot-tall purple gorilla suddenly steps off the villa balcony, scooping kids out of the pool and dropping them squealing with delight on her shoulder. I can hear the dinner bell ringing inside the villa.

"Animalia's gathering everybody for supper," Cronus says. "You coming?"

I spy Kalea sitting on the wall surrounding the infinity pool, staring out at the sea. "In a minute."

I go over and sit on the wall next to her. "Hey."

"Hey," she says without looking at me.

"What are you thinking about?"

"Tomorrow's lessons." Kalea volunteered to homeschool the younger kids for the few hours a day we can get them to sit still in one place. "I want to do more reading, but I don't think we have enough tablets to go around."

"I can grab more on my next trip into civilization if you want, but things got a little hairy in DC. I should lay low for a few days."

"Sure, whenever you can get to it."

"Okay, then."

The situation with Kalea has been, well, bizarre. I feel like something happened between us, before I got mindwiped for the last time; not something bad, necessarily, but something I can't talk about since I can't remember what it was. Something she won't talk about because she doesn't know where to start with someone who didn't experience it. So our conversations have mostly been in single syllables and searching looks.

The sun's setting now, and the marbled brush-crickets have started strumming in the underbrush.

"Hey, you want to see something cool?" I ask her.

"Why not."

"Count the number of cricket chirps you can hear in fourteen seconds. Start now, okay?"

She's giving me a funny look. "Got it."

When the crickets stop their strings, I say, "Now add that to forty, and what do you get?"

"Thirty-two, so . . . that's seventy-two."

"It's seventy-two degrees Fahrenheit right now. And that works to tell the temperature every time."

"Uh-huh. That is pretty cool. Who taught you that?"

I think about it. "I don't remember. Someone important, I bet?"

All of a sudden, Kalea starts to cry.

"Oh my God. Did I say something wrong?"

"No, no." She smiles through her tears. To my surprise, she wraps both arms around me and puts her head on my shoulder. "You're gonna be all right, Ray. I think we're all gonna be."

Ray. She called me Ray.

The waves crash, the seagulls call, the crickets chirp, and I recall something I was told about loving and being loved. I know I am real, I know I am a person, and I am the only person who needs to.

Everything is going to be okay.

EPILOGUE

Adele Poole sits and fidgets in the chair. The brick-red jumpsuit they gave her doesn't entirely fit, bulging and tight in all the wrong places. The concrete room is featureless except for the benches and the buzzing fluorescent lights. When the air vent rumbles to life and starts blowing, she jumps.

It's hard to wait. So close, you'd think she could muster patience, but it turns out, the closer you are to something you've wanted this badly for as long as you can remember, it's more agonizing than not having any hope of attaining it at all.

Patience, *she tells herself.* You've waited for years. A few more minutes isn't going to kill you.

There's another person in the room with her, a boy her age, with floppy hair and the tan of a lifeguard, sitting on the bench by the opposite wall. He's in a similar brick-red jumpsuit. "Miller" is the name stitched over the yellow triangle logo on his breast.

She needs to take her mind off the waiting somehow, and this guy is cute, at least. "What's your first name?"

He looks at her like he's surprised she can speak. "Sorry?"

"I see Miller's your last name. What's your first? Mine's Adele. Poole." She points to the name tag over the triangle-with-the-heartbeat-line logo on her left breast.

"Mason," he says. He leans awkwardly off the bench and across the floor to shake her hand.

"When'd you get the word? I mean, that you were eligible for the surgery?"

"A couple days ago. My mom found the listing online, we took the test from AccuChieve, and the word came back, like, fast. Less than a week. She's always said I'm special. She's always looking for opportunities, and as soon as this one popped up, she signed me up in seconds."

"You . . . thought you were latent before? A psiot, I mean?"

"For a little bit. Sophomore year. I was kind of dating this girl who was a full-on psiot, but then we went to the movies one time, and . . ." He blushes and looks at his feet. "It's not important."

"Yeah, I thought I was, like, 'sensitive' since, I'd say, the seventh grade? I mean, those kids online, even if half those videos were faked . . . I just wanted to be like them, you know? I even got into this reality show that was training would-be psiots how to use their powers. Got flown out to this resort island in Greece and everything, but the guy who was running the show, he turned out to be a real skeeve."

That memory, the night everyone at the Power Party *shoot got released from Twyst's mental control, is less than pleasant, so Adele is actually grateful when the orange alarm starts spinning in one high corner of the room, along with a startling Klaxon. One entire concrete wall of the room slides upward, revealing a much bigger chamber beyond.*

Adele looks at Mason Miller. Mason Miller looks at her.

"Here goes everything," she says.

Adele is the first out the door, into a large room that looks like an obstacle course, with gymnastic horses and mats all over the floor and rings sticking out of the ceiling big enough to fly through if people could fly. She can see other walls sliding open all around the circular perimeter of the training area and boy-girl pairs emerging from their own small waiting areas, as blinking and confused as she must look.

In the center of the room is an old dude in the same brick-red jumpsuit everyone else is wearing, standing up on a little podium with his hands clasped behind his back. He reminds her of her last gym teacher.

"All right," the old guy says, "line up in front of me, two rows, let's go."

Everyone moves slowly, hesitantly, and he has to yell, "Move, I said!" to get a spring in their step. Adele makes sure to stand in the front row and can see the name "Palmer" stitched over the old guy's heart.

"I hope you are all fully recovered from receiving your implants because from this point on, the amount of mercy I will be showing you will be precisely zero," Palmer yells. A full day removed from the implant surgery, Adele has finally stopped touching the red bump at the base of her skull where the tiny engram device was inserted, and doesn't want to start again now. The lump itches a bit when Palmer mentions it, though.

"Just because you were determined to have brain patterns compatible with the engram does not mean you are automatically on my team. That is what the next few days will determine. I will be your drill instructor and field commander. When, and only when, I decide you are ready, you will be sent into the field to combat hostile psiots and . . . other more-than-human individuals. You will likely be facing down mundane opponents with more conventional firearms as well. Regardless of who you face, the desired outcome of any hostile encounter will always be the same. Survival."

He takes his hand from behind his back, and now Adele sees he has a shotgun in it. He pumps it with a hand. Then he points it and fires it at her.

The boom is deafening, and the other trainees scatter, but Adele isn't there anymore. She saw the shotgun and moved to one side. She feels a slight sting on the side of her hip as a few stray pellets tear at her uniform, but she doesn't think about that. She's moving forward, cutting through the air with a hiss, like she's a human whip, cracking.

Adele snatches the shotgun away from Palmer with her right hand and instinctually lashes out with her left. She hits him harder than anyone she's ever hit before, and the translucent force field that surrounds his body the instant she connects is the only thing that keeps his ribs intact—of this she is certain.

Still, he flies back off the dais and skids, bouncing on his ass, across the floor. Adele nearly cries out in joy. She's super. She always knew *she was super! But she now actually did a super thing! It feels amazing.*

But then she gasps. What has she done? She just knocked the teacher on his butt in the first seconds of her first day of class. Is she in trouble? Is she going to get kicked out? To finally have achieved powers after so long, after wanting them as hard as she's ever wanted anything, including oxygen, would just be the cruelest punch line to a short life she's already seen as a bad joke.

When Palmer picks himself up, though, he's grinning wide. "What's your name, trainee?"

"A-Adele, sir," she says. "Poole."

"Adele Poole." He shakes her hand after taking the shotgun out of it. "Excellent response time, Miss Poole. Welcome to the Harbinger Active Resistance Division. We call it HARD Corps."